The Loophole

Arunendra Nath Verma

Vitasta

Let Knowledge Spread

Published by
Renu Kaul Verma
Vitasta Publishing Pvt Ltd
2/15, Ansari Road, Daryaganj
New Delhi - 110 002
info@vitastapublishing.com

ISBN 978-93-82711-59-9

All characters in this book are fictitious. The story, however, is so close to real life that many people may find the images of people known to them or of themselves in the characters of this book. All such resemblance is coincidental.

Typeset and Cover Design by Vits Press
Printed by Vikas Computer and Printers

Dedication

This book is dedicated to those tormented souls who in a sudden surge of desperate anger or grief extinguish their own lives without pausing to think of the utter devastation their singularly rash act will bring in the lives of those who loved them. In life one may act in a hurry to repent at leisure.

Death permits no repentance. It only leaves in its wake pain, suffering and irreparable loss. May God grant a moment to such tormented souls in which they may pause and reconcile before they take that irreversible leap.

Foreword

The scourge of dowry has been a blemish on the face of our country for a long time. The lawmakers have tried to tackle the evil by framing very strict laws for Dowry Prohibition. Unfortunately, the remedy has not been very effective and at times has turned out to be worse than the malady. As the highest court in the country and many High Courts have pointed out from time to time, there is indeed a pressing need to curb the misuse of the Dowry laws by unscrupulous elements by removing its obvious inadequacies and some of its very overbearing sections.

The Loophole gives an in depth account of the harrowing experience a family has to go through after the suicide of a young daughter-in-law. The background created is compelling. The characters and the situations are very real. Inspite of the grim subject matter, Arunendra Verma has sprinkled it with plenty of satire, drama and humour to make it an imminently readable book. What is more, it makes the reader think too.

—Justice K N Singh
Former Chief Justice of India

Author's Note

Our lawmakers began with the most laudable intention of obliterating the scourge of dowry from our society. They decided to deal with the sinners ruthlessly. But in their excessive zeal they have created a Frankenstein who has managed to send thousands of innocent victims to languish in jails. Extortion and blackmail adorn the flip side of the draconian measures called Sections 498 and 304 (B) of Indian Penal Code; an anomaly in our jurisprudence in which an accused is considered guilty till he proves himself innocent.

The Loophole is a novel based on the travails of an innocent victim of this overzealous law. It aims at touching the hearts of thousands of people who may have watched the law's hapless victims suffer under its insensitive provisions.

It is not intended here to hurt the sentiments of any person or class of persons or to tarnish anyone's image. There is but one purpose behind narrating this fictitious story—to focus the lawmakers' attention on the draconian nature of the Dowry Laws which have unfortunately overshot their intended terrain to venture into the realm of legal tyranny and blackmail.

Yet, this tale is not a tearjerker. The greed and extortion practiced by the blackmailers, by all segments of the legal fraternity, police and prison authorities and even the media provide ample scope for amusing caricatures. It is a lifelike story told in a frontal manner without overbearing literary pretensions. If it keeps you engrossed, if the insensitivity of the law provokes you and if the twist in the tale takes you by surprise I shall be utterly satisfied. What else could a debutante novelist aspire for?

One

I rarely get a chance to admire the beauty of a full moon on a pleasant November evening. Basically, I am a fowl, rather than an owl. The lush green fairways of the Golf Club with pearly drops of dew on the grass, resplendent in the blushing rays of the rising sun enchant me. The opportunity to spend these tranquil moments in idyllic ambience beckons me to the golf course even on very cold winter mornings. But finding time to enjoy the bliss of a moonlight washed evening is a rare privilege. With the office hours extending usually till about eight in the evening, I would rather pamper my tired limbs by leisurely watching my favourite TV programme and comparing notes about the day's activities with my wife Ratna and our children. Yet, sometimes, standing out in the lawn and indulging in a peek-a-boo with a full moon can be even more soothing.

ᢀ2ᢁ

That day, when forced to wait for my family before going out with them to attend a social function, I decided to do so in the small lawn in front of our house. I was dazzled by the brilliance of the full moon as I came out on the lawn. I remembered that it was the birth anniversary of Guru Nanak (Guru Parab) on that full moon night. Not being very religiously inclined, I would not have associated the full moon with the religious festival but my younger daughter-in-law Simran, who was a practicing Sikh, had told me in the morning that she was going to the Gurudwara (the Sikh temple) along with my son to seek the blessings of Guru Nanak. Now I was getting quite annoyed with the delay, but my annoyance evaporated with the cool touch of the gentle breeze and velvety rays of the moon. Peaceful and sublime images of Guru Nanak floated softly in my mind as the beauty of the silvery evening slowly soaked in like a tranquilliser.

But the bliss was suddenly shattered by a piercing cry, 'M a a, P… a… pa… a!' The loud wailing was very unnerving. It was my younger son Unmesh. His cry was a strange combination of utter shock, deep pain and total helplessness. The anguish in the voice of my son almost froze me but I quickly regained composure and started running towards the source of the shrill cry.

Ours is a double-storied house. On the ground floor, my wife Ratna and I occupy one bedroom, while my elder son Harish and daughter-in-law Veena occupy the other one. A third room serves as a guest room. The first floor has a suite with an attached terrace and balcony. My younger son Unmesh and his wife Simran occupy this floor. A passage leads from the main entrance to the family lounge on the ground floor. At the outer end of the passage begins a staircase leading to the first floor. When shut, the doors of the passage leading into the ground floor lounge provide complete privacy. This door was left ajar when I had come out on the lawn as I was expecting my two sons, both daughters-in-law and wife to join me soon for going to my friend's house.

As I heard Unmesh's shrieks, I ran towards the entrance but my elder son had already rushed out from the lounge of the ground floor. He was leaping up the stairs three-four steps at a time. Immediately behind him came my wife Ratna, running as if in a daze, looking very incongruous as she was bedecked in her best jewellery and a gorgeous sari. Our eyes met. She cried anxiously, 'What happened?' Before I could answer, Harish had already reached the first floor and entered Unmesh and Simran's room. Even before I could react to Ratna's anxious query, we heard a shrill and loud cry from Harish, who was shouting at the top of his voice, 'Papa–Maa, come here at once!' And then we heard a second, heart rending cry from Unmesh. 'M-u-m-m-y.' No words followed this soul-shattering cry. I almost collided against Ratna on the staircase. I overtook her and started running upstairs, taking two steps at a time. Even though handicapped by her heavy sari, Ratna was close at my heals. I reached the landing leading to Unmesh's room. The door was wide open. There was nobody in the bedroom. The door leading into the bathroom was also ajar. As I rushed in and looked into the bathroom, I found

Harish hugging Unmesh, who was sobbing in uncontrolled grief.

Just next to them, on the bathroom floor was lying my daughter-in-law, Simran, apparently quite dead.

Ratna followed me closely as I entered the bathroom. We saw Harish too sobbing uncontrollably. Ratna cast a glance at Simran's body lying on the floor, and then her shriek echoed loudly in the small space of the bathroom. I was totally shaken by Ratna's hysteric shrieks and by Harish and Unmesh's sobbing. I just froze on the spot. But a slight movement of something above her body made me look up towards the ceiling.

Just above Simran's body was the ceiling fan from which a turquoise-coloured rope, actually cloth, was hanging down, gently swaying above us. The loosely hanging cloth had been cut with some instrument. Its other end was wrapped around Simran's neck as she lay face up on the floor. She was dressed in a salwar suit of bluish colour, matching the turquoise colour of the cloth wound around her neck. Obviously, the cloth hanging from the fan with a part wrapped around her neck was her chunni. Just next to her body was lying a pair of scissors, broken into three pieces. Near her feet was the washing machine tilted at a grotesque angle against the bathroom wall.

I went down on the floor with the intention of loosening the chunni around Simran's neck, but found that it had already been loosened. I tried to feel her pulse by touching her wrist, but I was too tense. I couldn't decide whether any trace of life was left in her. The body was cold to the touch. I guessed immediate medical aid might, with a lot of luck, still save her life.

Since I did not remember the phone number of the nursing home right behind my house, I decided to dispatch my domestic help Raju to fetch a doctor from there. I walked towards the staircase landing to call Raju but found him already standing at the entrance to the room. He was trying to absorb the scene but looked petrified. I asked him to run to Doctor Narula's nursing home and fetch a doctor immediately.

I then picked up the phone on the teapoy in Unmesh's bedroom and dialed 100. The call was attended instantly. An alert voice came on the phone, 'Noida Police Control Room, Shrimanjiee. How can I help you?'

I said, 'I am calling from E Block in Sector 90. My house number is 308. A member of my family has committed suicide in my house.'

The pleasantness in the voice immediately disappeared. The tenor of the voice became quite sharp. 'What is your name? Who is the person who has committed suicide?'

'I am a retired Air Force Officer, my name is Wing Commander Vinod Asthana. The person who has committed suicide is my daughter-in-law', I said. It has been my experience that even after retirement, mentioning my Air Force rank has helped in my very rare brush with government officers. This time, however, I found that the mention of my Air Force rank didn't bring about the desired impact. In fact, his voice was, by now, pretty curt. 'Is she already dead or any life is left in her', he asked.

'I have called for a doctor and only he can say for sure, but I think she is dead.'

'Alright, please stay there and make sure nobody leaves the house. I am informing the mobile squad. It should reach your house in a few minutes.'

I then dialled another number. This was the residential phone of Simran's father, who also lived in Noida, just a few kilometers away. The phone kept ringing for a minute or so before I remembered that he had planned to go to Jalandhar to spend a few days with his wife, who had been recently transferred there from Noida as the Head Mistress of a school. He did not have a mobile phone but his son, Anand, who was younger to Simran, had one. I did not remember his number, so I asked Unmesh. But he seemed to be in a daze. Gripping his shoulder rather violently, I repeated loudly, 'What is Anand's phone number?' This time, Unmesh mumbled out the number which I dialed. After the initial burr...burr...burr.... a voice intimated, 'The mobile phone which you are trying to reach has been switched off.' I was getting desperate now. I asked Unmesh if he remembered his uncle-in-law's phone number. I knew that Simran was the favorite niece. Unmesh whispered, 'Please check up in the address book next to the phone', and sat down with a thud on the floor next to the body of his wife. He took her hand in his hands and started wailing, 'Why did you do this Simran, why did you do this to me?' His body shuddered and his head drooped to his chest. I could see the drooping of his shoulders and the trembling of his whole body. By now Harish and Ratna were sitting next to Unmesh. Ratna's hand was on his back. Harish too had one hand on his back while with his other hand, he tried to hold his mother. But he was looking too shaken himself to be able to console either of them. I picked up the address book lying on the bedside table and checked out Simran's uncle's phone number.

While I was going though the address book, Veena entered the room. She had been dressing up in her ground floor suite for going to the function along with us. With everybody rushing to the first floor, she had an inkling of a major mishap. She now stood at the entrance to the bedroom. She asked me, in excited short breaths as she had apparently run up the stairs, 'What's happened Papa?' Before I could answer, I had found Simran's uncle's phone number. I punched the number on the instrument. The phone was received by her uncle, Colonel Suri, just after one ring, 'Colonel Suri here', he said.

'Suri Saheb, this is Simran's father-in-law Asthana. I have been trying to contact Simran's father but....'

'Oh! He just left for Jalandhar yesterday to be with Jaspreet, his wife', he interrupted me and continued, 'Anand usually comes back late from his college, so probably, there is nobody at their house right now. Anyway… what's the matter?' he said in his congenial voice.

I had enjoyed very good relationship with Colonel Satbeer Suri. He was the elder brother of Simran's father, Manbeer Suri. While Manbeer was still serving in the Army as a colonel, Satbeer had retired from active service. I had always liked Col Satbeer for being a very polished and suave person. I braced myself to break the shocking news. 'Suri Saheb, I am extremely sorry to tell you, in fact I don't quite know how to break this news to you, but Simran is no more', I said.

'What? What are you saying? I don't believe you! Has she met with an accident? Was Unmesh with her? Were they driving or something?'

His questions flew in a torrent. At the same moment, Veena heard me breaking the news to Satbeer. She shrieked and ran into the bathroom. I gulped. My mouth was dry. I was having a tingling sensation in my temple due to the rush of blood. I somehow composed myself and swallowed a bit of dry air. There was no saliva in my mouth. I then remembered I was talking to Simran's uncle and mumbled, 'I don't know how to say this, but there has been no driving accident or anything. She seems to have killed herself.'

'When did this happen? Have you informed Manbeer or Jaspreet (Simran's mother)?'

'We discovered it only a few minutes back. The first thing that I have done is to send for medical help and try to contact Simran's parents and brother but have been unable to do it so far', I said.

'Okay, I will inform them. Kindly don't try to talk to them. I am coming over to your place as soon as I can', said Satbeer.

I did not fail to notice how soon Satbeer Suri had regained his composure. He spoke like a man who had suffered a lot of pain and had a capacity to suffer even more with fortitude and patience. I thanked my stars that the first person from Simran's family to whom I had broken the news was this man. I was quite sure that the reaction of her parents would be quite different and very stormy. How could I blame them for the intensity of their emotions? I was myself shaken to the core. But this was hardly the time to worry about emotions—theirs or ours.

The realisation that the police patrol van will soon be reaching my house forced me back to the ground reality. I thought I must inform as many of my neighbours, friends and relatives as I could. I had a premonition that once the police arrived, there would be a lot of complications and legal formalities. I quickly went down to my room on the ground floor to fetch my telephone diary. Raju, who had been sent to call the doctor, had not yet come back. I looked impatiently at my watch and realised that, in fact, only about ten minutes had elapsed since I had rushed upstairs and seen the still body of Simran lying on the floor. I quickly picked up the address book and went up the stairs, back to Unmesh's room.

As I was climbing the stairs, Raju came up behind me with the doctor's bag in his hand. The doctor followed him. I turned to the doctor and explained to him that a body was lying in the bathroom. He rushed into the room and then into the bathroom. The very young doctor plugged his stethoscope into his ears and placed its disc on Simran's chest. He held her wrist in one hand but didn't bother to hold it for very long. He shook his head incredulously, his face as ashen as that of my wife and probably my own. It was obvious that just like all of us, it was his first brush too with a human body with a noose around its neck. He snatched his bag from Raju's hand, but did not open it.

'Any chance of reviving her?' I enquired.

'No', he said gravely. 'She has been dead at least for the last few hours. Have you informed the police?' he asked.

I nodded and said, 'They will be here very soon.' My reply seemed to have hit him like an electric shock. He almost ran towards the door.

'Will you give me a death certificate?' I asked, taking out my wallet at the same time. He did not wait for me to take out the money for his fees from my wallet, nor did he stop even for a moment to answer my question. While rushing down the landing, he said, 'My director does not like to get entangled in police cases. In any case, there will be a post-mortem, so there is no need for a death certificate from us.' Then he disappeared down the staircase.

I shook my head in disbelief and then dialed the number of the secretary of our Residents' Welfare Association. As he responded, I hesitantly informed him that my daughter-in-law had committed suicide. I then dialed the number of my wife's sister who was a senior officer of the Government of India and then my elder daughter-in-law's father, who was also serving in the Indian Administrative Service. There were lots of other relatives to be informed yet. But the panicky behavior of the young doctor, who had only attended a call of duty and yet had very strict instruction from his boss in the nursing home to avoid getting entangled with the police, reminded me that I too must now brace up for my first encounter with the law.

It was time to seek more details from Unmesh who was sitting by the dead body lying on the floor. He was flanked by my wife and my elder daughter-in-law Veena, who were totally dazed. Unmesh and Harish were sobbing. Unmesh appeared to be incapable of answering my questions, so I asked Harish, 'How come the body is lying on the floor?' He said, 'When I reached upstairs after hearing Unmesh's shrieks, I found he had broken the bathroom door, which was latched from inside and taking the scissors from near the washbasin, had cut the chunni to bring down Simran's body which was hanging from the ceiling fan. I helped him by holding the body and laying it down on the floor.'

I said, 'Harish, you shouldn't have brought the body down on the floor. It was best to leave the scene undisturbed. After all, she has been dead for some time.'

Harish was annoyed. He angrily retorted, 'It was only natural for Unmesh to cut down the chunni while I tried to support the weight of the body. Even I felt that she might be revived by the doctor if she hadn't been hanging for very long.'

I saw the logic in his statement but my gut feeling was that it would have been prudent to leave the body untouched as there were bound to be many questions about this aspect alone. In fact, I was dreading the moment when Simran's parents and brother would arrive. I was quite sure we would have to face a barrage of questions and regardless of what we said, they would ultimately hold us responsible for her death. That is why the two relatives I decided to call first were both senior government officers in preference to my elder brother and sister. Having informed these two on the phone, I was going to ring up the others when I heard the loud wail of the siren on the police van. Its wailing reached a crescendo before the van halted in front of my house and then the siren was abruptly cut off. Suddenly there was total silence in the room, broken only by the loud ticking of the wall clock and the sobs of Ratna, Harish, Unmesh and Veena who had huddled around the dead body.

Three uniformed policemen, escorted by Raju, burst into the room. The trio comprised an Assistant Sub-Inspector and two constables. The ASI, sporting one star on each shoulder, came straight to me and asked, 'Did you ring up the Control Room?' I nodded in confirmation. 'So you are Wing Commander Asthana Saheb.' It was a statement rather than a question. I kept quiet. He took a few steps forward, stopped at the frame of the bathroom door and made a mental note of the scene of the tragedy. My eyes followed his searching eyes. For the first time, I also took a look at the area surrounding the body and the four grieving persons who were still bending over the body in a fitful daze. Both, the ASI and I, noticed the crack on the bathroom door at about a meter's height from our floor. The door opened inside the bathroom and now rested along the wall on the hinged side. The longer portion of its sliding latch was bent. The screws holding it to the door had come out from their grooves. The smaller portion of the latch, which secured it to the door frame, had come unstuck and was now lying in a corner of the bathroom floor. A pair of scissors was lying near the washing machine. Of the two round grips at the lower end of the scissors, one had broken and a semicircular piece of metal was lying two feet away from the broken scissors on the ground. There was no other sign of any disturbance in the bathroom. A couple of bath towels were hanging from the towel stand pegged on the wall.

The policemen had a careful look at all these, then the ASI asked me, 'Who are these people around the body?'

'They are my wife, my elder son, his wife and our younger son, whose wife the deceased is.'

'Please ask them to come out of the bathroom. Leave the body alone. Don't touch anything else there. You all may remain in this room. Just don't go out anywhere. We shall wait for the CO Sahib, who is on his way.'

'CO?' I asked.

'Circle Officer; he is the Deputy Superintendent of Police, in charge of your sector', he said.

He took out a packet of cigarettes from his pocket, extracted a cigarette, tapped it on the packet and moved to the entrance to the room to light it. He took a puff and exhaled some acrid smoke. The smoke suddenly reminded me that I had not smoked a cigarette since I had reached home from office. All of a sudden I had a very strong urge to smoke. I did not have a cigarette with me and wanted to fetch one from my room on the ground floor.

꧁14꧂

I started moving towards the staircase to go down and get some cigarettes. But the policemen stopped me. The ASI said, 'You had better remain here right now. When CO Sahib comes, you may take his permission to leave this room.' It was obvious that there would be a lot of new situations which were bound to be unpleasant. Right now there was only one thing to do—wait for the Circle Officer to arrive, wait for Simran's parents, brother and other relatives to arrive, wait for my own close relatives to arrive. With each arrival, there would be a fresh deluge of questions on how, when, why did it happen. I was clueless! The events since that morning flashed in my mind.

Two

Suresh Chandra had been a bosom pal of mine for the last four decades. His younger son Vishesh was to get married on 20 November and on the 19th, a big function called Ladies' Sangeet was to be held at their residence. We were looking forward to actively participating in the fanfare. In fact, Harish had been practicing for the last two or three days some typically racy film songs to suit the occasion. A common friend of ours and the Chandras, Air Commodore Savinder and his wife Jyoti, were coming from Chandigarh to attend the marriage. They had planned to stay with us and had arrived at our house the previous evening. We had spent a wonderful evening together talking about the good old days. On the 19th morning, Savinder and Jyoti were ready by 8 o'clock to visit Gurudwara Rakabganj on the occasion of Guru Parab. We were to meet at Suresh Chandra's house in the evening for the sangeet function. As they came out of our guest room, they were greeted by Unmesh and Simran who were also ready and dressed to go out. Savinder was rather surprised to see them ready and spruced up so early in the morning. They explained that they were also planning to go to the Gurudwara to offer their prayers on the occasion of Guru Parab. Savinder was glad that we had a Sikh girl as a daughter-in-law in our family and were giving her full freedom to practice her religion. Unmesh and Simran were going to the Gurudwara in Noida itself while Savinder wanted to visit one in Delhi. Unmesh and Simran took leave and went away in their car. After they left, we had breakfast and then I took Savinder and Jyoti to my factory. After I had finished showing them around in about thirty minutes, a cab was called to take them to Delhi.

Before leaving the factory, I had shown Savinder and Jyoti the office on the ground floor in my factory used by Unmesh and Simran. The office was empty as they had not yet come back, though they had planned to come straight from the Gurudwara to the factory. It was about 11 o'clock in the morning when Savinder and Jyoti left. I walked to my office on the first floor of the factory. The moment I sat down in my chair, I got totally submerged in the routine work. Once I got busy with my tight schedule, I could only get some respite at lunchtime which was in fact the best part of the day. That is when Harish used to come over to my factory from his unit while Veena was away in her office at the *Times of India* where she worked. Unmesh and Simran, who had their offices on the ground floor just below mine, would also come over to my office on the first floor. Ratna used to join us for lunch before proceeding to our third unit, where she held charge of the production.

But lunch hour that day had been different. Usually, we had a light breakfast at home as each one of us had different morning hours. But that day, we all had a very heavy breakfast along with our houseguests, Savinder and Jyoti, and had decided to skip lunch. So at lunchtime I did not meet Unmesh, Harish, Simran and Ratna at all. At about 5 o'clock in the evening, Ratna reminded me on the phone to come home early as we had to reach Suresh Chandra's house by 7.30 pm. I left my office at about six in the evening, good two hours earlier than the usual. On my way out, I just peeped into Unmesh's office and found him busy with some visitors. Simran was not there. I presumed she must have left the office a bit early to visit her beautician and to dress up for the party that evening.

After reaching home I spent a little time trying to absorb my daily dose of the *Times of India*, which I had not had the time to read properly in the morning. While I was reading the paper, Ratna said, 'Just tell Unmesh and Simran also to come home early. Let us not be too late for the function. Suresh and Kamal have planned it with a lot of enthusiasm. They will be quite annoyed if we reach very late.' I could not help smiling as it was always Ratna who was religiously unpunctual on every occasion. Anyway, I decided not to tease her on this point. I just rang up Unmesh in his office and said, 'Unmesh, I hope you remember we have to reach Suresh's place by 7.30 pm and have told Simran also to come early and get ready in time.'

He replied, 'Yeah, I will come over as soon as possible but right now I am sitting with some customers and I might have to rush later on. You please tell Simran also, as she must be at home.' I asked him, 'What time did she leave the factory?'

'Oh! She had left in the afternoon itself', he said as I put down the phone. I then tried to call Simran on the intercom but there was no response.

I turned towards Ratna to convey this but she had overheard me. 'She must have gone to her beautician to get a facial and hairdo. I hope she comes back soon. I have been telling Unmesh to give her a new mobile phone, but he keeps forgetting. Now, I can't even contact her if she is alone. How irritating!' grumbled Ratna. I considered it prudent to quietly slip off to the washroom to have a shower instead of staying put and listening to Ratna's cribbing.

When I came out of the shower I found my suit hanging from the curtain rod and a fresh set of undergarments, a shirt and a tie placed on the bed. I started changing and kept talking to Ratna, who was busy with her makeup sitting by the dressing table. 'I hope Simran has come by now', I said.

'Not yet', she replied, 'I tried calling her again on the intercom but there was no response. I thought there could be a snag in the intercom, so I had sent Raju upstairs to tell her that Unmesh will be coming late. But their room was locked. There was no response to the knocking on the door.' I understood that knocking on the door was essential to check whether someone was inside the room or not, because it had an inbuilt lock on the door rather than a padlock fastened to a bolt on the door.

'Unmesh should contact her on the beautician's phone and ask her to hurry up. Let me ask him to do so', I said and dialled Unmesh's number in the factory. He picked up the phone and I started cajoling him. 'Unmesh, you are still sitting in the factory and Simran has not yet come back from wherever she went. Just check if Simran is with her beautician. You had better pick her up from there fast. I shall prefer if we all go together as a family for the function rather than drop in one-by-one.'

'Papa, actually I am also getting a bit worried. When I rang her up there was no response from Simran on the landline in our room. She had left office in the afternoon itself. I also presumed that she must have gone for her facial or something but she hasn't gone to Mrs Kapoor's saloon where she normally goes. I just checked.'

'But Unmesh, you had said just a little while back that she had left the factory in the afternoon. Why didn't you check earlier? Did she leave after a tiff with you?' There was a few moments' silence on the phone. If Simran had some argument or a misunderstanding with Unmesh, it would not have been for the first time. Of course, they didn't have frequent fights but like in all marriages, they too had their differences once in a while inspite of theirs being a 'love marriage'. What was worrisome was that Simran was definitely a strong-willed person with strong reactions at times. Worse, Unmesh was not any less headstrong. But had it been otherwise, their marriage would not have taken place at all.

My mind had just started wandering when Unmesh's voice broke the silence on the phone. He said, 'Actually Papa, we had some argument in the factory after which she left in a huff. But then, she normally cools down very soon. I thought she would realise her mistake in hindsight, but when she didn't ring me up, I decided to take the initiative in patching up. I tried to ring up on the landline a little while ago. But the phone was not attended. I thought she was still angry and was avoiding me. But not to worry, you know, once earlier too she had quarreled with me and had gone to her Mom and I had to go and appease her and bring her back. This might be a repeat performance. Right now, since her parents are also not around, she might have gone to her Uncle's place. Anyway, you don't worry. I am coming home. I will change and then go and pick her up from her Uncle's home. I suggest you all proceed to Uncle Suresh's house and I will come later in my car and bring her along for the function. This way at least, all of you will not get delayed.'

Unmesh's answer put me off. He had married Simran for love and yet, within the last two years since they had married, there was at least one occasion on which I had to intervene and patch up their differences. I had excellent relationship with my two sons, whom I treated like friends ever since they were in their teens.

Even with both my daughters-in-law, I had enjoyed an excellent relationship. Ratna and I had always wanted to have a daughter but we had been blessed only with two sons. After the marriages of Harish and Unmesh, this void had also been filled. A very good relationship had evolved between our elder daughter-in-law Veena and Ratna but in case of Simran, though she did admire many facets of her personality, Ratna found Simran a bit immature at times. I enjoyed pampering them as I would have done my daughter, yet, I also knew that Simran was a bit immature and when she became annoyed she tended to lose control over herself. Most of the time though, she had a very pleasant personality with an ever smiling face, which broke into a wide grin and loud guffaws at the slightest provocation. I realised that telling Ratna that Unmesh did not know where Simran was would not serve any purpose.

'The best thing would be not to wait any longer for them. Let them come on their own later. I am ready to go, just call Harish and Veena as soon as you are ready to move', I had said. I had then gone outside to the lawn and was enjoying the brilliance of the full moon when I had heard his shriek after Unmesh had gone upstairs to his room.

The moment I thought of his heart-rending shrieks, I was jolted back to the grim situation at hand. Unmesh was continuing to sob. I sat down on the ground along with him and held him in a sideways embrace.

Three

The noise of two or three pairs of boots climbing up the staircase a few minutes after a motor vehicle stopped in front of my house heralded the arrival of more policemen. I looked up and saw a burly police officer entering the room, followed by two more policemen. This officer had three stars on his shoulders. The name plate on his khaki uniform read Santosh Singh. As he came up to me, I stood up from the floor where I had been sitting on my knees holding Unmesh in a loose embrace. I stood up and approached him. He introduced himself. 'I am the Circle Officer here. Are you Wing Commander Asthana Saheb?' I found his way of addressing me soothing. I nodded in assent. 'Tell me what happened. But before that, just tell me if any member of your family has left your house after this tragedy was discovered?'

I told him that all the members of my family were present in the room itself. Pointing out Ratna, Harish, Veena and Unmesh to him, I introduced each one to him. Then I indicated my domestic help.

'Have you found any suicide note?' he asked.

'We haven't noticed any note near the dead body or in any prominent place, but we have not looked for it inside the drawers etc. There has been no time to do anything except to inform the police control room and to call a doctor. Let us see if we can find one now.'

'No, you don't worry about it. Now my men shall look for it but you will have to allow them to go through all the cupboards and drawers of the table. When did the deceased come up to her room from downstairs? Is there any chance of her leaving a letter or a suicide note in any of the rooms on the ground floor? She must have visited the ground floor also.'

'I don't think so. We don't really know what time she came up to her room but according to my son, she had left her office at about lunchtime and probably came home directly. But she was not noticed by anybody on the ground floor as the staircase goes up from outside the ground floor and the entrance on the ground floor is normally kept closed. My two sons and I had left home for our offices in the morning and have just come back a little while ago. My elder daughter-in-law works in Delhi. She also left in the morning itself and has just come back. My wife left at about midday, along with a couple who were our houseguests. She too came back just now. We don't really know what time she came home. She had the duplicate key to her room while one key remained with her husband, Unmesh. The door has a built in lock. So from outside, one cannot make out whether somebody is inside the room or not', I replied.

CO Santosh Singh twirled his moustaches and addressed Unmesh and Harish, 'Did you two find any suicide note?'

Unmesh just shook his head from side to side but Harish said, 'Didn't Papa just tell you that no suicide note has been found?'

'Young man! Don't give me a chance to teach you how to talk', barked Santosh Singh. 'I know you are dressed up like a hero but better don't get the idea that you actually are one. You will forget your suit, boot and *akad* (arrogance) in no time, once I take you along with me to the police station for further questioning.'

With the sudden change in his tone his personality seemed to have undergone a total transformation. His left hand went back to his moustache and he started twirling it. His right hand started tapping his thighs with the brass-headed baton which he had been holding. I was amazed at the dramatic change in his way of talking. He had been quite courteous with me so far, but his voice assumed an altogether different tone now. He looked towards me and commented, 'Commander Saheb, all of you seem to have dressed up for a party. Were you celebrating something?'

I was not too sure whether he was being just sarcastic or it was a genuine question but I suddenly became very conscious of the fact that we were all actually dressed up for a party. Both Ratna and Veena were dressed up in their best party wear and wore a good amount of jewellery. 'Actually, we were all about to leave for a ladies sangeet function at a friend's house', I said. I realised my voice sounded rather apologetic.

Singh did not miss my discomfort and decided to increase the pressure. 'Oh, I see. But the deceased does not appear to be dressed up for a party like the rest of you all. Apparently, nobody was interested in taking the younger daughter-in-law along. Nobody seems to know when she came home and now she is lying dead in her normal day-to-day wear. Was she at all supposed to accompany you?'

His questions were making me feel hot under the collar. So I gave him a lengthy answer about the day's events. Before he could ask anything further, about five to six people could be heard climbing the stairs. Presently they rushed into the room. It was Col Satbeer Suri—my daughter-in-law's elder uncle with Anand, Simran's brother. They were accompanied by five more people, three of whom I recognised as relatives of Col Suri and the remaining two were unfamiliar faces. Suddenly, loud wailing from the three relatives filled the air. Col Suri was obviously very sad and silent tears were streaming down his eyes, which were red. The other two men had grim expressions on their faces but they kept quiet. They could see from where they were standing, the dead body lying on the bathroom floor. They moved towards the door. Anand rushed towards Simran's body. He stooped down and held her head in his hand and broke into bitter crying. Col Satbeer and the others also followed Anand inside the bathroom and stood near the body where Unmesh was already sitting. Anand sat down next to him.

'Who are these people?' asked the CO.

I told him about Simran's relatives. Singh moved up and said, 'Kindly don't touch anything here. I would request you gentlemen to please come out of the toilet and stand here'. Anand and Unmesh took no notice of what he said but the others came out.

A few more people had come up the stairs in the meantime. Amongst them were my sister and brother-in-law and a few neighbours of mine. They were all stopped at the landing by a police constable as there was already quite a crowd inside the room. I came out of the room along with Ratna and my sister took her in an embrace. I drew near my brother-in-law, who held me by my shoulders, with a sad and curious expression on his face. My sister's face was wet with tears.

I came back to Col Suri and said, 'Satbeer, I am really shocked and don't know what to say. Have you informed your brother and sister-in-law (Simran's parents)?'

'Yes, they were in Jalandhar. I have told them that Simran has met with a serious accident because I didn't want to give them such a shock. I would like to break the news gently. They are taking a cab and should be able to make it by about 3 am. I have informed my other relatives.'

While he was saying this I could hear more people coming up the stairs. This was a loud lot. There were two men escorting three ladies who were wailing and shrieking at the top of their voices. As they came up, I recognised them as Simran's relatives whom I had met in her marriage two years ago but had not seen them since. Apparently, they were not very close to the Suri family but I noticed that their shrieks and wails were the loudest.

In fact, I could arrange the people present now in order of their closeness to the Suri family by the loudness of their crying. The quietest person was Simran's brother Anand, whose eyes were red with tears and who could be seen sobbing. Col Satbeer Suri was very grave. Suddenly, two ladies amongst the relatives whom I had not recognised shrieked loudly, '*Hai-hai. Maar dala na inna ne. Main te pehla hi kahendi si ke in Baniya de naal byaa naa kar. Jaspreet ne meri ik na suni. Maar dala na.*' (They have killed her. Didn't I tell her not to marry her daughter in this Baniya family—but Jaspreet never listened to me. Now look, they have killed her.) These words were like molten lead poured into my ears. There had been strong opposition to the alliance of Unmesh and Simran from her parents but they had slowly come around and acquiesced to their marriage. But there had been utmost opposition from Simran's aunt (elder sister of Simran's mother) who would just not accept the idea of her niece marrying a non-Sikh boy. I had never met this particular aunt of Simran, as she and her husband had boycotted the marriage and never once met Simran and Unmesh after their marriage. The lady making the cruel remarks now and cursing us at the top of her voice resembled Simran's mother. 'This has to be the aunt who was the staunchest critic of their alliance and had boycotted the marriage', I thought. I went back a couple of years down the memory lane when Unmesh had first told me that he wanted to marry Simran.

Four

'Papa, how about a walk in the park with me?' asked Unmesh.

It was a summer evening two years ago. The weather was not very inviting for a walk in the park. The day's hot loo winds had still not cooled. But I said, 'Alright, let's go!' I knew it was a habit with Unmesh since his adolescence to join me in my walks and coax me to allow him to do something, which he had been restrained from doing. He had always been a very persuasive youngster. I knew what I was in for and had a clear inkling of the subject he would take up. He would try his very best once again to persuade me to agree to his marriage with Simran. Actually, the first time he had expressed his desire to marry Simran I had burst into laughter and he had become too embarrassed to coerce me into agreement. I had found it silly that my just twenty-year old son, who was preparing for his MBA entrance examination after graduation, wanted to get married at such a tender age. He was at least three years away from being financially independent. He was still a child full of pranks and a zest for adventure. He still liked to show off to his elder brother his control over a fast driven motorbike. He still had a very innocent look on his face. Now this young boy, who had barely crossed his teens, wanted to get married!

Who was this young girl whom Unmesh wanted to marry? We knew her very well. It had all started with Unmesh finishing his graduation. He wanted to acquire a Masters in management from some well-reputed business school. The entrance exams for admissions to the MBA course were conducted in the month of December and the session commenced in July. Unmesh had completed his graduation in May, so he still had six months to prepare for his entrance exam. He could work in my small-scale industry during the intervening period. The work experience would help in getting admission in a good business school. Thus it was that Unmesh had started working in our family business. I had entrusted him with the marketing of our products. It suited his extrovert personality and his good communication and persuasive skills. But I asked him to devote only a few hours every day to the job and spend most of his time on his preparation for MBA.

As was his wont, Unmesh had jumped into the activities and responsibilities with great gusto from day one. We had a small team of three sales executives to promote and secure orders for the items that we manufactured. They were asked to interact with

Unmesh. Unmesh wanted them to contact individually all major potential institutional customers. It was planned that our three sales executives visit each and every major institutional user of the product. But after a month of sustained activity along with his team, Unmesh did not report much success. He found that our marketing executives were being turned back on their cold calls. They were being advised to call only after fixing an appointment with the purchase manager, but the appointments were hard to get. When they tried to get an appointment on phone they were told that the concerned person was not available or was busy in a meeting and they should try later. They kept trying repeatedly and met the same wall of resistance again and again. Unmesh had a suggestion for this. He said, 'We must employ girls to make telecalls and seek an appointment for our marketing executives with the purchase manager of the potential customer.' I was not very enthused and said, 'Unmesh, aren't you sick of all the telemarketing by these credit card, auto loan, home loan and personal loan companies. At least I am fed up of such calls and feel like banging my phone down when they disturb me.'

'Oh, Papa you wouldn't know. All purchase managers aren't old men like you', he chuckled.'You should just see how much the young people enjoy talking to these girls.'

'I don't know about other young people but you obviously very much enjoy these chats', I returned his smile and he burst into laughter.

'Of course I do!' he said mischievously.

ꙮ31ꙮ

And so it was that I, who hates promotion calls on my own mobile phone so much, got persuaded by Unmesh to hire girls for making tele-marketing calls to fix up appointments for our sales executives. 'For doing just this much, the only qualifications required are fluency in English and Hindi and a sweet voice', Unmesh said.

'She should also be young and good looking. Isn't it, you crook?' I said a bit cynically.

'Why not? Do you have any specific objection to that?' he teased me.

'Yeah, only one. I wanted you to devote only a few hours to your job and the rest of the time to your MBA entrance preparation. With this sort of assistance available to you in your office, I think your marketing target may or may not be achieved but your MBA entrance exam could certainly go for a toss.'

It is indeed difficult to dissuade Unmesh from doing something once has made up his mind. I knew I would have to acquiesce. Without wasting any time, operation tele-marketing was launched next day itself. The first step was to select a suitable candidate for the job. Advertisements were placed in two newspapers. We had decided to initially hire only one girl and to take one more later, if the results were encouraging. Unmesh was assigned the job of scrutinising the applications to select the best three candidates for an interview with me.

Thus it was that I got to interview a smart, very presentable, young girl who introduced herself as Simran. She was an Arts graduate and had some training on computers. Being an Army officer's daughter, she had had her education in various places in good English medium schools. Her marksheet showed a consistent average performance. No exceptional achievements in academics but she had been an active participant in extra-curricular activities. She had been a good swimmer, done a bit of horse riding and enjoyed driving cars. I found her very cheerful and ready to burst into spontaneous laughter at the slightest pretext. She was a vivacious extrovert, quite at ease with herself during her interview. We would have liked to employ a girl who lived not too far from our factory, as commuting is a big hassle in our fast developing industrial city. On this score too she was a preferred candidate as she lived with her parents in an Army officers' colony just fifteen minutes drive from our factory. She mentioned that her father, Colonel Manbeer Suri, was a serving officer in the Indian Army. He was posted at Chandigarh but the family comprising his wife, a son and a daughter, preferred to stay in Noida, where they owned a flat. The interview with Simran stretched well beyond the ten-fifteen minutes that I had planned to spend with each candidate. The reason was not far to look. As an Ex-Air Force officer, I had a natural affinity to another service officer's child. But this was indeed not the only reason. I have already mentioned that she was quite a charming young girl, quite self-confident and at ease in a new environment. She spoke fluent English and had a very pleasant voice. There was really not much beyond all these that we were looking for in our ideal candidate.

There was no need to test her knowledge in any academic field. So, the last question from my side was about the salary she expected. She said, 'The salary really doesn't matter. I got a couple of good offers from other companies too, but I do not wish to commute to Delhi for more than an hour each way every day. This office is very close to my house; my parents will feel quite comfortable if I join somewhere close by'.

'So you are treated like a kid even now?' I teased her.

'Of course Sir, they do think I am a kid. In fact, my Mom decided to chaperon me even for this interview', she said with her smile turning into laughter once again. By this time I had made up my mind that this was the girl who could charm even an iceberg of a purchase manager on telephone. There was no need to look any further.

'Is your mother waiting outside at the reception?' I asked. She nodded and I said, 'Why don't you call her in. I think the image of a jungle inside the factory will be erased from her mind when she finds that I am also an Ex-service officer.'

'Oh, Sir I would love it. I have actually never served anywhere. My parents are quite apprehensive about my taking up a job at this stage, that too in a factory. I am sure my mother will feel quite comfortable about my job if she meets you.'

I asked my secretary to send Mrs Suri in. She turned out to be quite a polished lady. Unlike Simran, who was dressed in trendy blue jeans and a white cotton top, she was dressed in a salwar suit. Both mother and daughter were quite short and very fair complexioned. Mrs Suri had put on a bit of weight, quite normal for her age, which was around fifty. But she was not plump. Her accent clearly showed her good schooling. It is now difficult to pinpoint what exactly it was that made me think that she was very obviously a school teacher.

'Are you also working somewhere Mrs Suri', I asked her.

'Yes, I am teaching in Saint Mary's school', she said. The school she had mentioned was a well-reputed school in Noida.

'Which subjects are you teaching?' I asked.

'I am teaching in the Primary Section. We have to teach all subjects to the kids.'

By the time we finished a cup of tea, Mrs Suri was happy with the idea of Simran joining an Ex-Air force officer's company though she didn't hesitate in telling me that in her view the best job for a girl was as a teacher or as a computer professional. She was quite straight forward, at times blunt, as I would discover later. I told them that they would hear from us very shortly and bade them good bye. When Simran bid good-bye to me, she had a lustrous shine in her eyes and a broad smile on her lips. There was no doubt in her mind that I had selected her for the job, although I had avoided making a firm commitment. It did occur to me that if I had liked so much the charming face and the pleasant manners of the young candidate, young Unmesh will be totally knocked out by her. But we had always been a very broad-minded family. Both Harish and Unmesh had been quite friendly with a number of girls and their friendships had been quite healthy. Simran was selected to join our company, which she did the very next day. After she came, Unmesh went ahead with his tele-marketing campaign with a lot of gusto.

It didn't come as a surprise to me that what did show an immediate upswing was not the sales figure but the time Unmesh was spending on personally supervising Simran at work. She could have easily been given a list of potential customers and their phone numbers and left to herself to contact them, but Unmesh, I soon found out, was spending a lot of time at her office table. I could smell the budding romance. Initially this didn't actually disturb me in the least but I soon started feeling uncomfortable about his friendship with a girl who was an employee in our factory. I knew for sure that this will invite sly and lewd comments from the employees in our company. Ratna is very traditional in her views on such matters. So I thought it would be best not to mention to her Unmesh's leanings towards Simran. It was a question of only a few months and like all seasonal romances of immature age, this budding romance would also die a natural death once Unmesh moved away to his college campus. Moreover, the tele-marketing concept itself had been visualised as a temporary measure. Little did I realise that this was not to be a story of adolescent infatuation; it would develop into a serious love story.

With the advantage of hindsight, I now realise that I myself had become quite fond of Simran. In the very first week, I had found her to be quite a charming young girl. Her perpetual smile was indeed captivating but the real reason for my fondness for her lay somewhere else. Both Ratna and I had always wanted to have a daughter but after our second son also arrived after a Caesarian section, we had been advised not to go for a third child. Thus, in spite of being blessed with two perfectly lovable sons, our secret hankering for a daughter had not been extinguished. After all, Simran was also from a services family background like ours and was in no way unsuited to be Unmesh's bride. But my main concern was their tender age. After all Unmesh was barely twenty years old. We didn't visualise his marriage in less than five to six years at least. For all we knew, it could well be a case of puppy love. So it was that I neither dissuaded Unmesh strongly from being chummy with Simran, nor did I encourage him in the least.

As anticipated, Unmesh did qualify for admission in two reputed B-Schools. One of these two was located in Mumbai, a thousand km away from our hometown Noida. The other one was only twenty-five km away in Ghaziabad. The one located at Mumbai enjoyed a slightly better reputation and had an edge over the Ghaziabad one. I had no hesitation in sending Unmesh to the distant one, but he came up with many arguments as to why he should prefer the one nearer home. While he was strongly advocating his case for the business school closer to home, Harish and Veena kept smiling. At the end of Unmesh's declamation, Harish burst out laughing. I also could not help smiling as both of us could guess why Unmesh preferred to stay close to home. Ratna was not very much amused but in her heart of hearts she was equally keen that he join the B-school at Ghaziabad rather than move to Mumbai. The decision was thus taken unanimously by all of us. One fine day Ratna, Harish and I went along with Unmesh to Ghaziabad to drop him at the hostel of his B-School. We came back with mixed feelings of pride and happiness on the one hand and sadness on the other, due to the imminent two-year separation from our son. 'These two years will pass just like that', I snapped my fingers to emphasise my point to Ratna and we came back home after dropping him.

After Unmesh left for his higher studies, my enthusiasm for the sales campaign initiated by him dwindled. After the initial rise, our sales figures had reached a plateau. There seemed to be no point in continuing with the tele-marketing effort but I was finding it difficult to tell Simran that her services were no longer required. But she stole my thunder just a week after Unmesh moved to his college. She came to me and informed me that she wanted to quit her job. It was good news for me as it alleviated the need for me to take the initiative in the matter. I asked her which company she intended joining now. 'I haven't yet got an offer but I think after the useful experience in this company I should easily be able to get a similar job in some other organisation', she replied with a smile.

'Then, what is the big hurry? You may stay here till you have your next job lined-up.'

'No sir, actually Unmesh sir used to give me a lot of guidance. Now that he is gone, the other marketing executives feel that I am no longer very useful for them.'

38

From the very next day Simran vanished from our lives as suddenly as she had come. I didn't know then that she would come in our lives once again, apparently to be with us forever. Of course, it was impossible to imagine that the next time she would disappear from our lives, it would give us an unbearable jolt.

Unmesh went through the usual ragging in his hostel but unlike most of his other batchmates, he seemed to enjoy it. Apparently, he had easily assimilated in the college fraternity. He used to visit us on weekends and regale us with lots of very funny stories about his college. He seemed to be enjoying all the curricular and extra-curricular activities there. I knew he had a tremendous capacity for hardwork and a burning desire to excel and stand out in a crowd. So, when his weekend visits home gradually became infrequent, I assumed that the pressure of studies was holding him back from visiting us. Ratna was not very happy with the situation. One day, when she was cribbing at home as to how her 'poor child' was being made to work so hard on Sundays too, Harish heard her and burst out laughing. He said, 'Oh Mama how gullible you are? You think studies are stopping him from visiting us on weekends, eh?'

'What do you think he is busy doing', she asked irritably.

'Apparently he enjoys Simran's company more than yours', said Harish with a broad smile.

'Are you trying to say that he comes here on weekends and goes to Simran's house instead of coming home?'

'He doesn't have to do this, when she is herself willing to go all the way to his institute.'

'How can she go to the institute, a good 30 km away from her house? Do you think her mother, who is a Head Mistress, and her father who is a Colonel in the Army and her young brother will all allow her to loaf around like this?'

'How does distance matter? She has her own scooty on which she used to come for work to our factory. On Saturdays her mother is in her school and her brother is in his college. Her father is posted in another city from where he visits only on one or two weekends in a month. So where is the problem in going from her house to Unmesh's Institute? Besides, she doesn't have to go there every time. Unmesh alternates the visits to her house.'

It was my turn to butt in, 'Does that Colonel father of hers entertain him at his house?'

'Do they have to meet at her house? They go and see movies together or go to parks and old monuments like thousands of other young couples are forced to do in this godforsaken country of ours!' said Harish with a mischievous smile.

'How do you know? You accompany them or what?' I asked.

'Why should I be the dog in the manger? I just heard from a friend of mine that he had seen Unmesh taking a girl on his motorbike. I asked Unmesh next day if he had a new girl friend. First he tried to confuse me, but then confirmed that he was going around with Simran.'

'How stupid of him. He has no time to visit us and he is spending all his time with that girl', said the jealous mother.

'Why? What's wrong with that? Come on Ma. Its time he spent his weekends with his girlfriend rather than with his foggy parents', retorted Harish.

'Who is a foggy parent, you Joker?' I chipped in jokingly.

'Stop joking about it', commanded Ratna. 'Twenty is no age to get involved in a serious relationship with a particular girl. He is too young to be able to choose a life partner dispassionately.'

'Oh, come on Mom, I just mentioned that he spends a few weekends with Simran and you are already talking about his getting married to her. If a young boy has to marry every girl that he goes to movie with, we shall all end up with big harems', said Harish cheekily.

'The way you are handling his brief, it seems you are also going steady with some girl. In his case at least we know who it is that he is moving around with. Looks like you will turn out to be the *chhupa rustam*', I said

'Na baba (Oh no), I don't like to get involved in a serious relationship at all. In any case, don't you worry Mom, whenever I decide to marry I will prefer to depend upon yours and Papa's judgement. I know if I want to marry a really good girl, I will have to do well in my business. Of course my MBA and the St Stephen's tag, our three industrial units and all will be a great help. But what's the harm if I have a good time in the meanwhile', said Harish, a little seriously this time.

'You are talking a lot of sense my dear, but your Mom is actually all tensed up for Unmesh who is too young and, therefore, more emotional. All we want is for him to concentrate on his studies till he completes his education', it was time for me to chip in.

'Yeah, I know and after that till he settles down in business or in the corporate sector job and then wait till I get married, because being younger he must also marry after I do. What a short script you have written down for the poor guy. Please, Papa, why don't you relax and let the poor chap lead his own life?' I winked at Ratna. There was no point in arguing with Harish. It was obvious there won't be any point in raking up the issue with Unmesh either.

Days turned into weeks and weeks turned into months. Unmesh's MBA course involved exams in a few papers every trimester and studies kept him very busy. So whenever we met, and of course we talked a lot on telephones too, one thing that we strictly avoided was any mention of Simran. He had understood our viewpoint; probably most of it was conveyed to him by Harish. But we continued to get news from various people that he was always seen in the company of one particular girl whose description always fitted Simran. Another thing that we had to get used to when Unmesh came home for a weeklong break at the end of the second trimester was blank telephone calls. Our residential phone would often ring and when I or Ratna picked it up, we would only hear a click as soon as we said, 'Hello.'

Five

When Unmesh told me that he wanted me to join him for a walk in the park on that summer evening, I knew very well what the agenda would be. He was home for a month-long summer vacation after completing the first year of his MBA course. He had got a summer job in a very reputed multinational company. I would have much preferred if Unmesh had devoted all his energy and attention to his summer job, but obviously it was Simran who topped his priorities. I consoled myself with the thought that he had managed to do fairly well in his first year studies inspite of all the attention he was giving to his friendship with Simran. Ratna and I had repeatedly discussed his love for Simran but always reached the same conclusion that though she was a pretty good girl, it was too early for Unmesh to select a life partner. Unmesh never broached the subject with us. We only gave gentle and indirect hints to him from time to time about our views, without overtly mentioning Simran's name. On the other hand, Harish had lengthy arguments with us, taking up cudgels on behalf of Unmesh. Harish's arguments were not in favour of this particular girl. He only championed the cause of individual freedom. His refrain was that when and whom Unmesh married was entirely his choice; we had no business in interfering and dictating terms. While Ratna strongly opposed Harish and called him sentimental and impractical, I remained caught in a cleft. My mind wavered and I found myself agreeing with Harish when I was not listening and agreeing with Ratna. Was this conflict only idological? Was it due to my greater exposure to Simran's pleasant personality which Ratna didn't get during her few months employment in our company?I wasn't sure.

By inviting me for the walk, Unmesh had pushed my back against the wall. I knew he would try and seek my approval for his liaison. Before venturing out I wanted to be sure myself about what my answer would be. The only conclusion I could reach was that if he wants to marry her, why not? But our blessings would be conditional. He would first finish his MBA, commence his career in the corporate sector and in the meantime, we shall persuade Harish to get married first, though he was in no hurry to do so. And after that, Unmesh could get married to the girl of his choice, who we knew was Simran. Harish was already on his side. Once I gave in, he would persuade me to lobby for Simran with Ratna and Unmesh's battle would be won.

I braced myself and said, 'Yeah, Unmesh, let me see what you want. I am sure, you aren't taking me for a walk to improve my health.'

We entered the park. The lawns were not very green but not exactly brown either. A gardener was trying to water the lawns by laying down a hose pipe from the tap to the brown patch. A few children were kicking a football around. Two, three stray dogs were lazing near the Raat-ki-Rani bush.The summer breeze was still warm and not many people were around. Unmesh had indeed chosen the right place and time for his serious lobbying. We started walking on the jogging track along the periphery of the park. But Unmesh remained quiet. Very uncharacteristic of him! I thought. We remained silent for a few minutes, but the suspense became too much for me. I broke the ice, 'Yeah, go right ahead. What do you want to discuss?'

'Papa, you know very well what I want to say. Why are you unnecessarily teasing me?' He was very serious. Usually he is very playful and our conversations are full of friendly banters. I could sense the tension in his mind. There was an unusual expression in his eyes—distant, dreamy, unhappy or worried, I couldn't be sure. I couldn't bear to keep him on tenterhooks for very long. 'It is about Simran and you, isn't it?' He nodded his head.

'But beta, you know very well our stand in the matter. Look, your Mom and I have got nothing against your marrying a girl of your choice. We have nothing against Simran in particular. It is only the timing that worries us. There are sound arguments why you should wait for a few years before marrying, be it to anybody. So why don't you just wait for a little while?'

'Papa, I agree with you. I understand your reasons. But her parents are not willing to wait. They want her to get married now. At the most, they can wait up to my final exams. But they want a formal engagement to be announced straightway', he replied.

'Oh! The matter has already reached this stage! Have you already met her parents and asked for her hand?', I asked a bit incredulously.

'No, I haven't asked them formally. Simran has done all the talking. I was no stranger for them. I met her father when he came to our factory to pick her up once or twice when her own scooty was unserviceable and he was here on leave.'

'Well! If they all approve of you so much and are keen that she marries you, it shouldn't be so difficult for you to convince them that they should wait for, say two years.'

'No, it hasn't been that simple. They were totally opposed to her marrying me. In fact, not only her parents but almost all her extended family is dead set against the idea.'

'And why so?' I asked. It must have hurt my ego that they could be opposed to marrying my son, an MBA student at a good business school, coming from a well-educated and financially well-off family.

'They were opposed to a whole lot of things. Theirs is a family with a military background. Her father, uncles, grandfather are all serving or retired Army officers. They want her to marry an Army officer of their choice. Then there is the hurdle of my being a non-Sikh. Although one or two of her cousins trim their beards, they are very particular about her marrying a Sikh boy only. Some of her close relatives like her mother's sister and her husband are devout Sikhs. They have stoutly opposed the idea of her marrying a non-Sikh. Her maternal grandparents are also very perturbed about the proposal and they are held in great regard by her parents.'

'Then what made them change their stance? You say they are now agreeable but only want an immediate marriage. How come such a turn around?'

'Papa, it hasn't been easy for Simran to persuade them. She had to fight a long-drawn battle against her parents and other relatives. Poor girl! She has reached a point of utter exhaustion by now. She has been struggling for the last one year to convince them.'

'But that doesn't answer my question. I am curious to know what made them concede finally.'

'Let it be, if they have finally given their consent, it is good enough for us. It really doesn't matter how she convinced them.'

Unmesh has a habit of avoiding inconvenient questions. The moment he avoids answering direct questions, I can make out he is uncomfortable with the answer. 'Well, it does matter. I am curious to find out how come this change of heart was achieved. Beta, a marriage, as we in India understand, is not only a coming together of two individuals, it also means coming together of two families. If her parents are so opposed to her marriage with you,

you will never be at ease with that family.'

'Forget it Papa, they have consented and that is what matters.'

My curiosity was now fully aroused. I know my son very well. He was very obviously hiding something from me and it provoked me. I saw no reason why Unmesh must marry into a family which was so opposed to their daughter's liaison with him. It hurt my ego. I blurted out, 'Alright! They might have agreed, but now I oppose this marriage. You are young and have a great future ahead. There is no dearth of good girls. Just be patient and we shall find for you a girl much better than Simran. I don't like the idea of your gatecrashing into a closely knit family.'

Unmesh was taken aback. He wore a shocked expression on his face. 'Papa, can't you understand that I love her and she loves me and this alone should be sufficient?'

'You are too immature. What you call love is nothing but infatuation. You are seeing too many romantic Hindi movies, that's all.' I decided to make the atmosphere lighter by trying to sound funny.

It cut no ice with Unmesh. He became very grave. Then in almost a whisper he said, 'If I don't marry her, she will commit suicide.'

This time my laughter was spontaneous. 'Don't be silly. All this suicide drama happens only in bollywood movies. No girl actually commits suicide if the boy she loves doesn't marry her.'

Now Unmesh's facial expression changed from serious to morose. His whisper was hoarse now, 'She has already made two attempts to commit suicide. That's how her parents have surrendered to her. Now, if there is a 'No' from our side, she will definitely commit suicide. And she won't fail this time.'

It was my turn to suffer a severe shock. 'How do you know? Did she invite you when she tried to commit suicide? This is only what she told you, isn't it?' I blurted.

'I know for sure Papa. I am telling you a fact. The first time she tried to commit suicide was by cutting her veins. She slashed her left wrist with a blade. She did it in her room and her mother happened to enter the room by sheer coincidence and her good luck. She was rushed to the hospital and saved.'

'But this is what she told you.'

'Yes she told me, but she also showed me the deep scar on the inner side of her left wrist when she met me in my institute a month later. I was complaining that she did not come on the previous two weekends to meet me. Then she showed me the scar and told me the reason for not coming on the previous weekends.'

'My God! But you say she tried to commit suicide twice', I asked.

'Yes, her parents initially adopted a softer approach after her first attempt. But then, after a month or two, they again refused to listen to her. That is when she made a second attempt by consuming rat poison.'

'Was it in your presence this time?'

'No. This time she rang me up on a Monday and told me that she had consumed rat poison. Her father had come over from Chandigarh to spend the weekend here. She spent the whole weekend trying to persuade them, but they did not concede. Finally, on Monday morning, after her father had gone back to Chandigarh, her mother was at school and her brother had gone to college, she consumed rat poison. She rang me up to bid good bye. I rushed to her home immediately and enroute to her house went to her mother's school and brought her along. We reached her house to find her lying unconscious on her bed. A bottle of rat poison was lying by her side. We rushed her to a nursing home near her house. There, the doctors applied a stomach pump. She was admitted and saline drip was administered besides some antidotes.'

'Didn't the nursing home people say that it was a medico-legal case and the police ought to be informed?' I asked incredulously.

'Yes, they did. But Simran's Mom personally knew a senior doctor in the nursing home. She begged him to keep the matter under a wrap. He reluctantly agreed when he saw that Simran was responding to the treatment and was regaining consciousness. Then it was entered in their books as a case of food poisoning. By evening she had become much better and was brought back by both of us to her house.'

'Didn't her Mom inform her father and brother?' I was curious.

'No, she didn't. By the time Anand came home in the evening, she was much better and he was told that she had suffered a severe attack of gastroenteritis. Her mother thought it prudent not to inform her father at all. Simran once told me that he has a fiery temper. Her mother thought that he would have a bout of severe rage and would only blame her for not taking adequate precautions and leaving a bottle of rat poison within Simran's reach. It would be best if the whole thing remained a secret shared only by the mother and daughter. Her brother too need not suffer a shock.'

'But Unmesh, how could you be a part of all this? I mean, keeping such a secret from her brother and father. Is that the type of family you would like to marry in?'

'Papa, as far as they were concerned they did not even know that I had come from my institute to help her mother in this crisis. In fact, the whole episode only helped me. Her mother felt deeply obliged to me for the timely help. She has become convinced of my devotion to Simran. What is better is that her attitude towards me has totally changed. She was the one who surrendered first to Simran's desire to marry me and finally, she has been able to persuade her father too.'

If I had been shocked by Unmesh's revelation of her first suicide attempt, I was now speechless. I felt as if I had stumbled into the house of horror and was now falling deeper and deeper into its abysmal depths. I swallowed hard and remained speechless for a while. When my voice returned I heard myself literally whining. I said, 'Unmesh, pl-e-a-se my son! I was not very happy with your intention of marrying at this stage in life but I am now aghast. I strongly implore you not to marry a girl who has actually attempted suicide. That too not once but twice! My opposition is not to Simran but to anyone who has attempted to commit suicide.'

☙51❧

'I think you are overreacting. She tried to commit suicide because she was desperate. Now that she has achieved her objective and her parents are convinced, you are unnecessarily balking. After all it is not her hobby to attempt suicide.'

'Unmesh, you better discuss this with a psychiatrist. I am not qualified to speak with authority on the subject, so you may question my wisdom. But I have read enough and seen some cases to know that usually there are serious psychological problems with people who develop a tendency to commit suicide. It is evident in this case too. She failed in her first attempt and she tried again. There is no guarantee that she won't try it the third time or the fourth time or that she will always fail in her attempts', I countered.

'Oh Papa, your imagination is running wild. She attempted suicide because she was desperate. She thought she wouldn't be able to live without me. That is the depth of her love for me. I can't believe that one can inculcate suicide as a habit.' Unmesh waited for a moment and then said with deep emotion, 'Besides, how cruel it will be on my part to reject her love because she tried to commit suicide for marrying me?'

I was exasperated. 'I can see that it is futile to try and drill any sense in your head. I don't approve of this marriage and that's final. You are grown-up and can do what you want to do. Why do you need my consent?' I hissed.

My strong words brought forth an even stronger reaction from Unmesh but he attacked me from a totally unexpected angle. 'Alright, don't agree, but stop putting on a garb of secular outlook on your basic reasoning. First, it was her people who were unable to breach the religious divide and now it is you. Why don't you just admit that you too are basically opposed to my marrying a Sikh girl?' he asked.

If any remark could have made me lose my temper completely, it was this one. His hurtful remark showed an utter disregard for my well-known secular outlook. I could not take it lying down.

'You have gone completely crazy. I do not consider Sikhs any different from Hindus. You have to read the *Granth Saheb* and listen to the Gurbani to realise that fundamentally their teaching is no different from what most Hindu religious texts say. In fact, Sikhism gave a militant outlook and military type attire to its warriors, basically to defend the Hindu religion against the onslaught of Islam. Some of my closest friends are devout Sikhs and then there are Uncle Aftaab Hussain and Uncle Anderson. So my dear son, you accuse me of religious bigotry because you are unable to comprehend my worries due to her suicidal tendency. In fact, you are refusing to even understand that there is something called a suicidal tendency. Well, I have said enough to dissuade you. My answer is still n-o NO. Do what you are bent upon doing. It is your funeral', I said. That my last words will turn out to be almost prophetic, I did not know then.

There was no scope left for a dialogue. I was worried and angry. I did not care to round off the discussion in a positive manner and walked off indignantly from the park. Unmesh remained there, probably ruminating over our unpleasant and acrimonious discussion and came home much later in the evening.

On reaching home, I related to Ratna all that had transpired between me and Unmesh. She was equally upset. We slept fitfully that night. We were unanimous in thinking that Unmesh was hellbent upon taking a wrong decision. We were both familiar with his stubbornness. Once he made a decision he would go to any length to execute it. And if Simran could go to the extent of committing suicide rather than accept defeat in love, he too will not change his mind easily.

Ratna toyed with the idea of our talking to Simran directly. She suggested that I call her to my office on some pretext. I should then discuss her affair with Unmesh and explain to her that getting involved in a serious relationship or marriage at this stage, when he had yet to complete the second half of MBA course would be ruinous for his studies and career. She should be requested to wait for at least one year before reaching any firm decision. But even as we discussed it, the hollowness of the plan became quite obvious. We had no control over Simran. When even Unmesh, who was financially dependent on us and had much stronger emotional bonds with us, was not willing to listen to us, how could she?

It was a night of agony for Ratna and me. The thought that Unmesh could have just cooked up the story of Simran's suicide attempts also kept disturbing us. Our relationship with both our sons had been built up on a foundation of complete trust and faith from their infancy. We did not claim to be ideal parents, but we had been honest with our children and they had also reciprocated with the same confidence. Yet, Ratna and I had a nagging suspicion that he could have invented the stories of her suicide attempts to pressurise us emotionally into submission. But it wasn't a pleasant thought for us. If it turned out to be a fib, it would hurt us even more. If not, it was a matter of great concern.

We tried to sleep but sleep wouldn't come. It was about three o'clock in the morning when we reached the conclusion that we should seek advice from our elders in the matter. Ratna's parents and my elder brother seemed to be ideal for this purpose. The decision gave us some respite. My brother was a thousand miles away in Hyderabad and my in-laws were at Lucknow–also none too close. We could not disturb them at that unearthly hour and would have to wait until morning to contact them on phone. This decision soothed my taut nerves and after a little while probably Ratna was still twisting and turning in the bed when I finally dozed off into a light sleep.

Next morning we rang up Ratna's parents. I spoke to my father-in-law and Ratna had a long discussion with her mother. They were also upset to learn the real cause for our worry. My father-in-law did not give a hasty reply. He sought some time to ponder over the matter and said he will call me back a little later. My brother was quick in offering his advice. He said, 'Look Vinod, this generation does not like the idea of the elders taking over the reins of their lives. They are a smart lot and can take their decisions. Unmesh is a man now. He has every right to live his life at his own terms. You have done your duty of warning him of the pitfalls. Now why don't you leave it to him to choose his own path?'

'But Bhai Saheb, I too was quite willing to let him marry his sweetheart. It is the news of this girl having attempted suicide which we are finding so very disturbing', I said.

'What if he married another girl of your choice and you all discovered after the marriage that she too had tried to commit suicide earlier, after being jilted in love by some other man? Is there any concrete scientific evidence based on a systematic study that if a person fails at a suicide attempt, he will necessarily commit suicide later on? I know it is not a very appetising thought that our future daughter-in-law has attempted suicide in the past. But all things considered, you are not left with much of a choice', said my brother quite convincingly.

I felt that there was a lot of sense in what my brother had said. Later in the day, my father-in-law rang up from Lucknow. He came up with some difficult questions. 'Unmesh is twenty-one years old. Ratna says the girl is also the same age. He is doing MBA from a good institution. The girl can very well get an employment elsewhere if she is not already having one. What exactly is there to stop them from marrying, even if you do not give your consent to their marriage?' he asked.

'I agree with you Papa, but should we encourage him to get married to this girl?'

'It is not a question of your encouragement. You have tried to dissuade him and he is in no mood to accept your advice.

Evidently, the girl too is very stubborn. Your role only appears to be ceremonial at this stage; you might as well give your concurrence now or be prepared to receive an invitation to bless the couple after they have undergone a civil marriage at the court. Vinod, none of us is very happy with his choice but I think we must accept the fait accompli graciously.'

'You are right. I agree we have only the Hobson's choice in the matter. But we shall remain worried that Umesh's wife is an emotionally unstable girl. Later on in life, whenever they meet a stressful situation, she might be a drag on Unmesh rather than a pillar of strength as an emotionally healthy and strong life partner on whom he could lean.'

'Don't worry on that account. Unmesh is a strong young man. He has had a happy childhood and has always had a very supporting family standing by him. He would be able to tackle all stressful situations in life on his own steam. Besides, time heals all wounds. She too will gain emotional strength and stability once she gets married to the boy she loves with such intensity.'

'Alright Papa. We shall abide by your advice. I will try and persuade them to wait for a little while till he completes his MBA. Also, I would like Harish to get married in the meanwhile. After all, he is four years elder to Unmesh. Let's see what their response to this suggestion is, once we give our concurrence for his marriage with Simran', I said and breathed a deep sigh of relief.

Ratna did not need much persuasion. She normally doesn't need much cajoling to agree with what her parents suggest in any situation in which my views are divergent. And in this case, everybody including me, seemed to have reached a consensus. Conveying our decision to Unmesh could have been a very pleasant duty to perform but we were not sure how he would react to our suggestion that he should get officially engaged to Simran but marry only after about one year to gain time to complete his MBA course and to let Harish get married in the meantime.

Umesh slept on till much later than his usual time that day. He too must have spent a sleepless might. But I wanted to give him the good news before I left for office. Ratna and I woke him up and told him what we had decided. He leapt up from his bed and danced a jig. Then he hugged his mother while I waited enviously for my turn. He was ecstatic with joy. Our suggestion that we carry out the engagement ceremony immediately and wait for the marriage to be performed a few months later was well-taken. He mentioned that Simran's parents had agreed for her marriage with him, only on the condition that it should be performed without further delay. But he was confident that he would be able to persuade them to wait a while for the marriage once Simran gets officially engaged to him. He was also confident that he would be able to persuade our elder son Harish to get married soon, although he had always been reluctant to get married in a hurry.

'And how will you do that?' I asked.

'I will just tell him to get some training in babysitting and be ready to play with a nephew as the bachelor Tauji (elder uncle)', he said and burst into laughter.

Six

The loud wailing and cursing of the lady, who must have been Simran's aunt most opposed to her marriage with Unmesh, was getting louder by the minute. It brought me back to the present from that morning when we had succumbed to Unmesh's pleading and agreed to give our blessings to his marriage with Simran. Here I was, sitting like a caged bird in my own home after just having informed the police that my daughter-in-law had committed suicide. A suicide that I had foreseen three years ago like writing on the wall! Colonel Satbir was lost in thought, maintaining a stoic silence. Anand looked dazed and kept sobbing. Unmesh sat next to him, quite shell shocked. The other two men who had come with the aunt were steadily increasing the tempo of their loud cursing. These three now focused their attention on Ratna and Veena who had tears in their puffed up red eyes but were not crying loudly. The angry aunt now started pouring venom on Ratna and Veena. 'Hai-Hai, look at the mother-in-law and the sister-in-law of our darling daughter. They have already started the preparations for their lal's (darling son's) second marriage. Hai-hai ni, look at the ornaments she is putting on. They have killed her for the sake of these ornaments, and now they just cannot wait to deck themselves up with her jewellery. And look at the heavy saris they are putting on. Their daughter-in-law's dead body is lying, waiting for the funeral and these besharams (shameless creatures) are all set to party and celebrate. *Hai-mar dala re-meri kudi nu* (they have killed our poor daughter)'. The aunt then switched over completely to Punjabi, which she apparently found a more forceful medium to convey her anguish.

While Unmesh remained oblivious to all the cacophony around us, Harish who had been standing quietly in a corner of the room, came to me and whispered, 'Can't you ask the bitch to shut up? There should be a limit to this indecency.' I held him by the shoulders and whispered back, 'Please Harish, control yourself. They are shocked and deeply aggrieved. Sometimes people do cross limits when they are badly hurt. Please try to understand. They have lost their girl in our house and it is natural that prima facie they hold us responsible. Just keep quiet and avoid paying any attention to what she is saying.' The young blood flowing in Harish's veins was boiling with rage but good sense prevailed. He did not say anything further, moved away to the balcony and stood there gazing at the silent moonlight outside.

And yes, our family was indeed dressed up for a party which we were supposed to go to. But how will they know? This business of our being too nattily dressed was turning out to be a major embarrassment. I removed my coat and tie and so did Harish. We looked less formal in our shirt, trousers and pullover. Ratna and Veena needed to go to the ground floor in order to change into their daily wear and remove their jewellery. I considered it prudent to seek CO Santosh Singh's permission for this. He appeared to be pleased with my humility. He said, 'Yes, the ladies can go downstairs and change. Let them rest there but none of your family members should leave the house. I am also going back. My men will remain here. I will come back when the parents of the deceased arrive.'

After the police officer left, Ratna and Veena went to their bedrooms on the ground floor. Harish and I remained upstairs along with Unmesh. My neighbours also went back one by one and that left about ten of us in the room and the adjoining balcony and terrace. The wailing of Simran's grieving relatives had subsided. We were quietly waiting for dawn to break so that arrangements could be made for the funeral. The clock was ticking away. I was surprised to note that it was already 3 am.

The grim silence was broken at about 4 am when a few cars came and stopped in front of my house. Eight to ten people came out from the vehicles, wailing loudly. Apparently Simran's parents had arrived along with many other relatives and friends.

As if on a cue, the 'Wailing Aunt' who was taking a breather after apparently having exhausted herself, came back to life and with what gusto! She, along with the other men who had accompanied her, started the torrent of abuses this time with renewed vigour. As Ratna's parents came up on the landing, 'Wailing Aunt' rushed out and embraced Simran's mother Jaspreet and then started her breast beating again. But her grouse this time took a different tack as she cried, *'Hai-hai-ni, maar dala kudi noo. Hun araam nal neeche ja ke bete de byah di tayyariyan kar rae ne.* (Oh, they have killed our daughter. And now they are relaxing downstairs and making preparations for the son's second marriage.)'

More shocking for me than the abuses hurled by this Wailing Aunt was Simran's mother's aggressiveness. She too started crying loudly and plunged at Unmesh, who was sitting near Simran's body. I winced but tightly held Harish's hands with both my hands. I was worried sick that this aggressiveness could get the better of his self control. Unmesh, luckily, did not react. He just started crying uncontrollably. Col Manbeer Suri, Simran's father, displayed a lot of tact. He held his wife's hands and pulled her away from Unmesh. Mrs Suri snatched her hands away and fell over Simran's body and held her in a tight embrace. Col Manbeer also sat down near her and patted the cheeks and temple of their deceased daughter.

Ratna had heard the renewed commotion and guessed correctly that Simran's parents had arrived. She came upstairs alone. Veena had stayed back. She was dressed in a plain white sari and had removed all her jewellery except the inseparable mangal sutra. The moment she entered the room, the Wailing Aunt shrieked at the top of her voice, *'Hai-hai-ni, maar daala kudi nu. Hun var-var fashion parade kar rai ae.* (Oh she has killed the girl and is now conducting a fashion parade.)' Oblivious of the venomous remarks, Ratna came to Simran's mother and tried to hold her hands but was vigorously rebuffed. Jaspreet jerked her hands off and turned her face away from Ratna. She started crying loudly but fortunately refrained from pouring any venom against Ratna. She kept on invoking the name of God and complaining to Babaji (Guru Nanak) that he had taken away the most precious gift he had bestowed on her on his birthday—the Guru Parab.

Ratna was totally confused and at a loss to understand why she was being targeted by the Wailing Aunt. But she got a breather when the Wailing Aunt noticed that Veena had not returned from the ground floor and directed the fire towards her by crying, 'Hai-hai the darling daughter-in-law has pushed off to sleep in her comfortable bed while our poor little girl is lying dead on thc bathroom floor.'

The Wailing Aunt repeated her complaints about Veena being away on the ground floor and I whispered to Ratna, 'If Veena has changed why don't you call her upstairs?' Ratna retorted, 'Certainly not. She is already in a state of shock. I don't want the poor thing to come here and face the volley of abuses. For that matter, I myself have had enough of this cursing and abusing. I am going downstairs. Call me only if it is unavoidable.' Harish also butted in and whispered, 'Yes, Mummy, you go downstairs and stay with Veena. She has never seen death so closely and is shocked.'

The Wailing Aunt was not going to miss this opportunity when four of us could be targeted together. This time her refrain was, *'Hai-hai-ni!* Look at them whispering and conspiring. God only knows whom are they are trying to get rid of next.' Ratna just turned her face away and walked out of the room and then climbed down the staircase. Wailing Aunt had achieved a solid victory. One enemy had already deserted the battlefield. She got encouraged. So far her targets had been only Ratna and Veena. Now was the time to go for big game. She finally focussed her crosswire on me, 'Hai-hai-ni! Look at this man standing alone like a thief. He thinks his murderous family can avoid the gallows by just slipping downstairs one by one.'

My biggest worry was that Harish would not be able to take all this for very long and would react. I had been holding him by the hand, gaining some solace myself from the physical touch while restraining him from reacting violently. But things could get out of hand very soon at this rate. I whispered to him, 'Harish, you also go downstairs and take care of Veena and your Ma. They are under severe strain. And for Heaven's sake try to keep your cool.' Harish took my advice and also followed Ratna down the staircase. The Wailing Aunt fired her fiercest volley to raze the last rampart of the fort, 'Hai-hai ni, look at them running away one by one. What more proof is required of their being murderers.' I had kept reminding myself that I was the head of our small family, the Captain of the ship which had to be navigated through a deadly storm and I shall have to remain composed. I had to lead the family by example. But suddenly, after this outburst, the reservoir of my patience cracked and burst open. My throat choked, my eyes brimmed with tears and I found myself crying. And I cried till Unmesh, who had been sitting through all the commotion like a statue, got up from near Simran's body, came to me, held me in a tight embrace and started crying too, audibly this time.

How long we cried and sobbed in each other's arms I cannot say, but I was brought back to a state of more self-control by my brother-in-law. He whispered in my ear, 'Please control yourself. Just see what these guys are doing in the bathroom.' I looked up and found three men along with Simran's father and uncle examining the toilet floor, washing machine and the ceiling fan above quite closely. There were two policemen standing along with them. My brother-in-law went and said to one policeman, 'Don't you think we should not allow anybody to disturb anything here. It will be best if everybody remains out of the toilet.' These comments were heard by the men trying to ape Sherlock Holmes. They reacted by walking out of the toilet. As they were coming out, we found CO Santosh Singh entering the room from the landing. These people went to him and started talking animatedly but in very low volume. I could not hear what exactly they were saying. Santosh Singh listened to them patiently and asked them to wait outside on the landing. Then he said to me.

'A panchayatnama (an inquest) will have to be carried out in the presence of a Magistrate. The body will have to be sent for a post-mortem. All this will be done after about 8 am. A recently married woman's death due to unnatural causes is a cognisable offence. The girl's people want to lodge an FIR (First Information Report) for which they are going to the police station. I am also going back now. My men will remain here', and then he walked off. He was followed by Simran's father, uncle, three other relatives and the other two men who did not appear to be their relatives.

The moment they left, all the loud crying and wailing came to a sudden halt. Wailing Aunt obviously cared to perform only before a selected audience. I looked at my wristwatch. It was 5.30 am.

Seven

There was now complete silence inside the room as well as outside my house which is in a quiet residential suburb. The moonlight on the street was still as brilliant as it was in the evening. It would still be an hour before the street sweepers and newspaper vendors arrived. Even the Wailing Aunt appeared to need a breather after her powerful performance. The few male relatives left behind, went down to the lawn. Their conversations in hushed tones could be heard as a faint murmur in the room upstairs. Other female relatives were apparently quite tired. At about 7.30 in the morning, there was an influx of a large number of people. My parents-in-law, Ratna's sisters and their husbands, and Veena's parents, all turned up. They had all traveled overnight from distant Lucknow. Many of my neighbours who had gone away at night also came back. And then came a jeep carrying a magistrate accompanied by a couple of police constables. CO Santosh Singh also turned up at the same time, to my surprise accompanied by Simran's father, uncle and other relatives.

An inquest was carried out in the presence of the magistrate. Five men, all of them relatives of Col Suri, went and examined the body of the deceased and again carried out a detailed examination of the toilet. A photographer took several photographs of Simran lying in the bed and quite a few more of the toilet and bedroom from various angles. He photographed the ceiling fan, the tilted washing machine, the broken bolt on the toilet door, the broken scissors and the broken portion of the door latch still lying on the toilet floor. He then came and informed Veena's father that for the time being he had taken all the photographs but will come back when the body is taken for the post-mortem which he thought will only be after a few hours. I was intrigued by his reporting to Saxena (Veena's father), who had just arrived from Lucknow. Saxena saw the curious expression on my face and said, 'I asked one of your neighbours to arrange a photographer to come and take these photographs. So he has been directed to report to me.' Saxena had been a magistrate himself and was familiar with the intricacies of court procedures. I just nodded and kept quiet.

The inquest was prepared by the magistrate in his own handwriting at the end of which he took the signatures of five witnesses. I was surprised to see that not even one of the five signatories on the panchayatnama was a neighbour, friend or even an acquaintance of mine. They had all come along with Simran's parents, who had obviously not driven straight from Jallandhar to my house and had picked up these people before coming to my house. The magistrate pushed off in his jeep after the inquest formalities were over. A police official informed me that the body would have to be carried to the police mortuary in Ghaziabad for a post-mortem by government doctors. All this would take time, probably a few hours.

Unmesh, Harish, Veena, Ratna and I had not slept a wink throughout the night. The evening tea had been the last meal for all of us. We were too tired and drained but there were questions and more questions to be answered for the benefit of all our anxious relatives who had come after travelling overnight from Bareilly, Lucknow and other places. We hardly had any information to give except the fact that we had all came home from work and were about to leave in the evening to attend a function when we had discovered Simran hanging from the ceiling fan in the toilet. Unmesh could have given us some background information about her. After all, something must have happened; some extreme emotional shock must have triggered this impulsive act. But there had been no opportunity for us to catch a few moments alone with Unmesh, to find out what had transpired between Simran and him since they left home in the morning.

Simran's relatives had left and all my neighbours had gone back. Now was the time to find out more from Unmesh, even if he was looking dazed and stupefied. I knew it would be downright cruel to subject him to our grilling at that moment, but we had little time to indulge in considerate behaviour. We had to ask so many questions that only he could answer. So it was that we huddled together and Unmesh faced a question mark writ large on everyone's face. There was total silence for a few moments till I broke it. 'What exactly happened Unmesh? Can you just tell me what all did you two do since you left home in the morning for going to the Gurudwara, till you came home alone in the evening.'

'Yes Papa, I will tell you. We had a quarrel in the morning in the Gurudwara itself', said Unmesh in a choked voice and then the dam burst. He started sobbing bitterly. Tears had stopped flowing from his eyes, but he was shivering though it wasn't very cold. Between sobs and shivering he described how a minor difference of opinion with Simran had blown into a fight.

'As we entered the Gurudwara, Simran told me that she wanted to make an offering of Rs 5001 at the holy Granth Sahib. I suggested that she make it Rs 1001 and she became very irritated. She said, "I am sure you had made a much bigger offering at the Krishna temple on the Janmashtami day, that's why you didn't even show me what amount you had put in the offerings box." I was surprised and hurt at the wrong accusation. I told her that on that occasion too, I had made an offering of Rs 1001, but she refused to believe me. I was so annoyed that when she sarcastically said that she won't make any offering at all if that pleased me, I told her I couldn't care less as to what she did but she should refrain from making false accusations. The result of this unsavory argument was that she actually refused to make any offerings at the *Granth Sahib* or in the donation box of the Gurudwara. After bowing our heads at the holy book we just came out from the congregation hall. Simran took the *kadaa prasad* in her hands with bowed head and then came to me. She pulled out one hand of mine and thrust the *kadaa prasad* in my hand with her other hand. She hissed at me with gritted teeth, "Here! Take this free prasad. You don't have to spend a single paisa for this." I wasn't quite prepared for this, and the prasad slipped from my hands and fell on the floor. Now she went almost berserk and said loudly, "You have not just insulted me but the holy offering of Baba on his birthday." I was struck speechless with this baseless accusation. By this time, other devotees at the Gurudwara had started staring at us and muttering amongst themselves. Simran bent down on her knees to gather the *kadaa prasad* lying on the floor. I did not join her and walked out of the Gurudwara. She followed me after a minute or so but instead of coming to the car she went to an auto-rikshaw standing by the roadside. I went to her and requested her not to make a scene. Somehow, good sense prevailed and she came and sat down in the car. She didn't talk to me during the drive as we came to the factory, nor did I make any effort to start any conversation.

'Even after reaching the factory she remained very tense. When we reached our office, the phone on Simran's table was ringing. She picked it up and said, "Yes Aunty, I have reached my office". Then she heard the voice on the other side for a minute or so and banged the phone down very angrily. I have a feeling it was someone she had met in the Gurudwara and who was now trying to add fuel to the fire. She once again lost her cool and started shouting at me. While she was screaming loudly, our designer entered the office and saw the unpleasant scene. He became very embarrassed and immediately turned back on his heels. His dropping in on this scene and witnessing the humiliation being heaped upon me infuriated me. I became extremely annoyed and shouted back at Simran.'

I could see how utterly self-conscious and ashamed he was to describe the unfortunate situation in front of our relatives who were listening to this horror story, without displaying any reaction or emotion. There was a pause in the narrative. Unmesh was looking down shamefacedly. My heart sank. I really did not want him to continue narrating this sordid story in front of my close relatives. But we had to know the whole truth and the sequence of events. I swallowed to wet my parched throat and asked, 'What happened then?' Unmesh kept gazing at the ground silently. I had to coax him to continue. After a few moments of silence he whispered in a choked voice, 'Papa, there was a limit to what I could take. I also shouted and said, "Get out of this office. I don't need you here." She suddenly stopped shrieking and said, "Alright, I am going out of this office—and also out of your life." And she went out of the office.'

'What happened then? Didn't she take the car keys to leave the factory?' I asked.

'No, she didn't take the car keys. I was so angry that I just sat in my office for some time. After about fifteen minutes, I came out and enquired about her and was told by the chowkidar that she had hired a cycle-rickshaw and had left at about 12:30 without saying a word to him.'

'What did you do then?' I asked.

'I got busy with some paper work. I had a business appointment at an Export unit in Noida. I was there from 1.30 till 3.30 pm, and then I came back to my office. After some time when my anger had subsided, I rang home but there was no response. I presumed she might have gone to the beautician as planned in the morning to get ready for the evening's function. Then I got busy once again in a meeting with some clients in my office. That is when you rang up to enquire about Simran. I found out from her beautician that she had not visited her. I presumed she had gone to her uncle's place and I came home.'

'But then, why didn't you check if she was with her uncle?' I asked.

This time he just mumbled. 'You know the reason. I didn't want to tell him about our quarrel.'

Yes I did know the reason! It was many months ago when Unmesh and Simran had had a bout of a serious nature. He was hinting at that now.

That day, my wife had told me in the evening that Simran had gone to her parents' house without informing her. This wasn't exactly earthshaking news. After all her parents lived in Noida itself, only few kilometers away from our house. But Simran had gone to her parents place only very ceremonially on the fourth day after her marriage, that too escorted by her brother Anand, who had come to fetch her. She had stayed there for a week and had come back to our place. Thereafter, she had never expressed any desire to stay with her parents even overnight. Her suddenly going to her parents' place, therefore, was quite unusual. Even stranger was the fact that she had made no mention of it that morning. Unmesh did not volunteer any information except that they had planned to see a movie in the evening, but she had changed her mind and decided to go and stay overnight with her parents. The whole story sounded fishy when my further probe revealed that she had gone alone, unescorted by Unmesh and had not carried any overnight kit.

I did not need any prodding to ring up Col Suri to enquire about her. I wanted to talk to Simran. We were very fond of both our daughters-in-law. Simran was the younger one and very childlike. She had a very open and informal nature. And then she had worked in my factory for many months before marriage. She was therefore quite uninhibited and frank with me unlike my elder daughter-in-law Veena, who treated me with greater traditional respect. Simran, on the other hand, was a typical Punjabi girl from a Services background. She never hesitated in laughing loudest at my jokes when Veena only smiled or in humming her favorite songs loudly even in my presence which Veena never did. When I rang up Col Suri, I was shocked to hear from him in a rather curt tone that she wasn't well and did not want to talk to me. I did not need to be told more plainly that something was seriously amiss. I informed my wife about my conversation with Col Suri and told her that Unmesh and I were going to pick up Simran.

Col Manbeer Suri gave us a rather cold welcome. His elder brother Col Satbeer was also present at his house. While Manbeer maintained a sullen silence, Col Satbeer gave me the shocking news that Unmesh and Simran had a bitter argument and Unmesh had crossed all limits by slapping her. I was stunned. It was unimaginable that a boy from our family would hit his wife. All I could think of was to summon Simran and check up if the allegation was true. When she did so between her sobs, I became petrified. I did not go into the reasons. I was sure in my mind that whatever the provocation—WHATEVER—Unmesh had no business hitting her. My immediate reaction was to ask Unmesh to seek their forgiveness. I did so myself by saying that I was ashamed that my son had descended to such a level. I assured them that it would be my personal responsibility that such an event never took place again in my house. But having said this, I said to Simran, 'Beta, I am sorry to see that your quarrel became so bitter. Yet, quarrels between husband and wife do take place. One has to learn to solve the problems with one's spouse. Yours was a so-called love marriage against the advice of your elders. Now you have to decide yourself whether you are willing to forgive and forget or you want all this to lead to a divorce?' Simran burst into deep sobs. But she did not need any further cajoling to declare that she still loved Unmesh and wanted to come back to him.

I looked at Unmesh. He was looking humiliated but shook his head in acquiescence. After this, Simran had joined Unmesh and me in coming back home.

On reaching home I had to reveal the evening's happenings to my wife and Harish. Harish became very annoyed. He said, 'Why didn't you ask me or inform me before you rushed to Col Suri's house? I was not at home at that time. I would have advised you not to go there and let Simran come back to her senses.' Harish then narrated what Unmesh had informed him earlier. When Simran and Unmesh were getting ready to go for the movie, they had an argument over a pair of shoes. She was complaining about a new pair of sandals that pinched her feet and yet wanted to wear the same pair. He had laughed and made fun of her. She had become angry and said something rude to Unmesh. This had led to a verbal duel, at the end of which she had become so angry that she had taken out her sandal and thrown it at Unmesh. And Unmesh had become so infuriated that he had given her a slap. After this she had walked out of the house and had gone away to her parents' place.

'Why didn't you tell me immediately when you learnt about it from Unmesh?' I asked Harish.

'Because I wanted you to come back from office and tell you at home instead of ringing you up in the office. When you came back, you were in such a hurry that you immediately rushed to her parents without discussing anything with me.'

'But Unmesh could have told me', I protested.

'He was feeling too humiliated to tell you this sordid story; moreover, I had assured Unmesh that I will break this to you', said Harish. He continued, 'And when you asked Simran at her house if Unmesh had actually hit her, couldn't you at least ask her, why?'

I felt like a fool and could only mumble, 'I was too ashamed to know that my son could beat his wife. I need not ask the reason. Whatever the provocation, he shouldn't have hit her.'

'Whatever the provocation? Even if the wife abuses you and throws a shoe at you? You might be very keen to put on the mantle of Mahatma Gandhi but how did you expect poor Unmesh to do so under such provocation? If you had not rushed in there, she would have realised her mistake and would have returned in the morning. Now you have further humiliated that poor boy in front of her parents.' Harish was very angry. Probably it was the first time that he had talked to me in such a high pitch.

I didn't know how to hide my regret that I had been rash in rushing to act before finding out full details. I concealed my embarrassment by saying, 'Let him suffer. Did he listen to me when I advised him to wait before getting married so young, that too to a girl whose rash and unpredictable temperament was known to him?' and walked out of the discussion.

As if my cup of misery was not already full to the brim, Harish followed me outside the room and said, 'You have no idea how headstrong and difficult she could be. Unmesh knows how fond you had become of her. You would only blame him for all her doings. You don't even know what happened during her Kanpur visit three months ago.'

'What happened? I asked. 'Had they abused and hurled shoes at each other there too?'

Harish was referring to the visit Unmesh and Simran had made to Kanpur about three months ago. They had been invited by my sister-in-law at Kanpur to spend a few days with her family. Unmesh and Simran had gone there over a weekend and when they came back, they had not reported any unusual occurrence.

'No, they didn't', Harish said. 'It was a solo performance by her. They had gone to a multiplex to see a movie. There they had a heated argument over a very trivial matter. She had become so disturbed and excited that she fainted on the roadside.'

I was amazed at what all Unmesh had concealed from me. Harish paused momentarily. 'Then what happened?' I asked.

'Nothing much. They were right in front of a hospital. Unmesh had taken her there to the emergency section. But she had recovered by the time the doctor attended to her. He just prescribed a tranquilizer to sooth her nerves and advised Unmesh to seek a psychiatrist's help later.'

'My God!' I was aghast. 'You knew all this and never told us?' I said accusingly.

Harish's voice was a little uncertain now. 'What was the use? You would have only upbraided Unmesh for being very rash in marrying her against your advice. He had started realising by now that she was very headstrong and never gave up till her every wish was fulfilled. He could understand that her suicide attempts before marriage were manifestations of this aspect of her psyche. But you had already warned him precisely about this. Now, he was too embarrassed to tell you anything about his problems. He had taken a promise from me to keep all this to myself and not burden you or Mummy with this knowledge', said Harish and finally stopped with a deep sigh.

I had been dumbstruck with these revelations. I was struck with deep remorse and guilt. Had I not bowed down before his persistent pleadings in the park and acted like an impenetrable wall rather than a weak, loving father, the situation today wouldn't have arisen. If indeed Simran was suffering from repeated occurrences of uncontrolled rage and its uninhibited display at small provocations, wasn't it incumbent upon us to seek psychiatric help for her? After all, psychiatric problems and psychosomatic diseases were as real as physical ailments. It took me only a moment to grill Harish with my next question. 'You are his elder brother and his confidante. Didn't it occur to you or to Unmesh in the first place to seek psychiatric help for Simran?' I said in exasperation.

'No, I didn't fail in my duty', said Harish. 'In fact, Unmesh had himself thought of this after the Kanpur incident. But Simran had refused to see a psychiatrist. She accused him of unjustly magnifying the issue. When Unmesh mentioned this to me, I confronted her.' I could feel the pain of failure in his voice. He continued speaking, 'I took Veena's help also in persuading her. Both of us told her that there was no harm in seeking help from a psychiatrist. But she kept on asking— "Help for what? Do you think I am mad? What should I get treated for? Everyone gets angry once in a while, so do I. Unmesh sometimes gets fits of laughter even in only slightly funny situations. Shouldn't he also seek psychiatric help?" But we didn't give up and raised the issue with her at least thrice. Finally she had agreed.'

'Oh, did she?' I was very curious.

'Yes', continued Harish. 'Unmesh then did take her to Dr Veena Ohra in the Psychiatry Department of Ram Manohar Lohia Hospital. Over there, she had a half-an-hour long session with the psychiatrist. She had talked to her in the presence of Unmesh and also alone, and had finally recommended some mood elevator tablets and asked him to bring her back after two weeks and to avoid any discussion on contentious issues in the meantime.'

'What happened then?' I asked.

'Oh, she was very sullen on the way back home. On reaching home, when Unmesh asked her what all had the doctor discussed with her, she said that there were many questions about her childhood. The doctor had dwelled long upon those years in which her father had been posted at non-family stations and her mother had taken up a teacher's job in a school to keep herself busy. She used to spend long hours at home with her brother or all by herself when he too went out to play with other boys. While describing all this, Simran had become quite agitated. "Isn't all this usual for most of the serving Army Officers' families? What does the doctor think? Does she think all children of Army officers posted in field areas become paranoid? The doctor herself is crazy!" she had said and had thrown away the medicines Unmesh had bought for her, as per the prescription. She didn't take a single tablet.'

'Did Unmesh take her to the doctor again after fifteen days?' I asked Harish.

'No, she just refused to go. Two weeks later, when Unmesh insisted on this, she again flew into a rage and created an unsavoury scene. Unmesh then just gave up the effort.'

The sad story of that day's events flashed like a lightening in my mind. Yes, I could understand why Unmesh didn't have the heart to tell Col Satbeer that Simran had once again walked out on him in a fit of rage, after a quarrel.

Our journey into the past was interrupted by noises from the street. A vehicle had come and stopped outside our house. I looked out from the window. An ambulance had arrived. A man in a male nurse's uniform and two policemen came out of it. It was time to take the body for post-mortem.

Eight

A medical attendant jumped out and opened the rear door of the ambulance. Two policemen in uniform also came out and stood by the door. He pulled the stretcher out and said to the policemen, '*Chalo,* Let's get the body.' I followed them upstairs where Ratna, Veena and some relatives were sitting on the floor by the dead body. Unmesh was sitting close to her, his head on his knees. His face wasn't visible but his body could be seen shaking with muffled sobs.

The body was laid on the stretcher and then brought down by the medical attendant and a policeman holding it on the front end and Harish and Unmesh holding its rear end. What was irksome was the presence of a photographer taking snapshots of the stretcher being brought down. He seemed to be concentrating on capturing the faces of all the pallbearers including the two policemen. He took photographs when the body was being put in the ambulance and then took photographs of the people assembled there including me, my wife, relatives and neighbours. I was getting irritated by the flashlight of his camera. 'Is it a marriage procession?' I growled. But surprisingly Saxena, Veena's father, came closer and whispered in my ears, 'Please let him carry on. He is not a police photographer. I have engaged him.' Even though I hated the crazy idea of making a photo album which would perpetuate the torturous memories of the painful occasion, I let it pass as a fad of Saxena. People do have all sorts of corny ideas.

The body was placed inside the ambulance. The two police escorts and the medical attendant sat inside along with the body. Unmesh was to sit along with them. Just as he was going to get inside, a police sub-inspector came to me. He sought my permission to take Unmesh along with him to the police station. I asked him if he was arresting Unmesh but his denial was loud. He assured me that I need not have any apprehension and Unmesh would be back home by the time we came back from the post-mortem. I saw no reason to oppose this request. Unmesh accompanied the SI and sat down on the pillion of his motorbike. The stupid photographer found even his going on the SI's motorbike worth capturing in his camera. I turned my gaze away from Unmesh and sat down in the ambulance.

Soon the ambulance started rolling forward with Harish and Mr Saxena following it in our car. When we reached the post-mortem house, after half-an-hour's drive, we found Simran's father and uncle already waiting there with one more person whom I had seen in the morning and who I later found was a lawyer. We were not allowed to escort the stretcher as the body was taken inside a room. We remained outside. This time Col Satbeer and Manbeer stood good fifty yards away from us. They were sullen and morose. There was cold silence between us.

While the autopsy was being carried out, Saxena found out that afterwards the body would be handed over to Simran's father. The Suri brothers were not inclined to talk to us but we had to find out the details of the funeral arrangements. I avoided confronting them with any questions. Saxena took it upon himself to get the details from Simran's father. But all that he could evoke was an icy, 'We don't know. We will decide once we reach home'. He didn't add, 'We will let you know'. The message was clear; we were not welcome!

It was dark when we reached home. Our house wore a deserted look after our neighbours had dispersed. But there were two policemen seated in our lawn. My in-laws who had come from outstation were inside along with Ratna and Veena. They were curious to find out about the cremation but we had nothing to tell them. I was expecting a barrage of questions but my wife's very anxious voice took me by surprise when she said, 'When Unmesh was taken to the police station you were told that he would be back in an hour or so after some questioning. But he hasn't come back. What are you doing about that?' I realised that I had not even noticed Unmesh's absence in the deathly silence and gloom at home.

I was still undecided whether Harish or I should go to our sector's police station or I should request Saxena to go there and check about Unmesh when the doorbell rang. A few moments later, our neighbour Agarwal walked in, along with a person I had not met earlier. He introduced the person accompanying him as his brother-in- law, Rajeev. About 45-years-old, Rajeev had no distinguishing features to describe him. I wouldn't have bothered to pay much attention to him but became interested when I was told that he was an advocate practicing law in Kanpur and happened to be a houseguest with the Agarwals for a few days. In spite of being almost numbed by the harrowing sight of Simran lying stiff on the floor and by the depressing wait outside the post-mortem room, I was now shocked by the news that Unmesh had spent the whole day at the police station and had not yet come back. At the moment, this was my first concern. I mentioned this to Agarwal.

Agarwal's brother-in-law Rajeev, who had just been introduced to me as a lawyer, now spoke up for the first time. '*Bhai Sahib*, you don't know the *dav-pench* (tricks) of these *policewallas*. If you permit me, I will go to the police station and will find out what is happening. But you shouldn't expect that they will let Unmesh come home so soon. Your going there will not help. Your being an ex-Air Force officer is essentially a disadvantage in that they will hesitate in asking you for some *chai-pani* money. It is going to be a prolonged interaction with them not only today but for some time to come.So it will be good if I go there.' I couldn't have asked for anything better. It would indeed be better if Rajeev, who was a practicing lawyer, went there. I offered my car but Agarwal politely declined it. He would use his own car, he said. Rajeev brushed aside the offer of some money for use if required. *'Dekh lenge baad mein* (We shall see that later)', he said cryptically, and then both Rajeev and Agarwal pushed off.

I then rang up Harjeet, a batch mate of mine who lived in Noida. After giving him a brief synopsis of the events, I requested him to find out about the cremation. Harjeet's being a Sikh would be helpful in getting the information from the Suris, I thought. After getting over the initial shock, he promptly got ready to do my bidding. Seeking his help turned out a sensible thing to do. Harjeet came back within an hour with the information that the body was being kept overnight in a local hospital's mortuary. The cremation would take place in the afternoon next day, at the grounds along the Yamuna River. Harjeet also brought the news that her father had filed an FIR against our whole family, in the wee hours last night and expected all of us to be behind bars. But they planned to request the police to bring Unmesh (under police escort, of course) to Simran's funeral where, as is customary, the pyre would be lit by her husband.

We went into a huddle immediately. Saxena advised that Harish, Ratna or I should not even think of attending the cremation as the Suris could create a very ugly scene there. Unmesh, he was sure, would be allowed to attend the funeral even if he was under arrest. He felt that our arrest was imminent and we should make ourselves scarce if we wanted to evade arrest. This, he felt, was necessary to gain time to make legal preparations and settle things at the factories before we were arrested. Of course, it was not prudent to avoid arrest for too long as it would unnecessarily give the impression of a guilty conscience on our part.

I was totally flabbergasted. Simran's parents knew very well how happy she was in our family and how well she had been assimilated amongst us. Her marriage had been performed after parents on both sides had given their consent albeit under pressure! But once the decision had been taken, there had been great bonhomie between both sides. The marriage had been solemnised in both Sikh and Hindu styles with great fanfare. After the marriage there had been one single unpleasant incident in which Simran had gone to her parents place with a grouse against Unmesh and then too, they had nothing to complain of against anyone of us. It was Simran herself and Unmesh who had brought things to such a pass. Were her parents not familiar with her history of suicide attempts before her marriage? Couldn't they check up with our neighbours and servants about the whereabouts of each member of our family throughout that day? After all, we were all in the factory, seen by scores of people right till the evening when we had returned home. How could there be even an iota of doubt in their minds about its being a suicide? What had made them lodge an FIR, naming us as persons responsible for her death?

I blurted out all this in a fit of rage and despair, helplessness and anger. Saxena and my brothers-in-law listened in silence. When I stopped, Saxena gently patted me on my shoulders and spoke solemnly, 'Look Vinod, it is not a question of what you or the Suris think. If you look at it from their point of view, it is only natural for the parents of the deceased to try and get a full investigation done. All said and done, it was an unnatural death. Wasn't it?'

'Is it also very natural for them to put the blame on us? Harjeet said that they had named all of us in the FIR. Couldn't they just request, without accusing anyone, that the matter be investigated?' I said.

'No, unfortunately the law is totally blind. In all cases where a woman's death occurs due to an unnatural cause within seven years of her marriage, the police have to treat it as a cognisable offence. The police had to get the post-mortem done to ascertain whether the cause of death was self-inflicted injury or not. We don't really know what they have mentioned in the FIR. After all, Unmesh's name had to appear as her husband and your name had to be mentioned while referring to Unmesh as the son of so and so. Harjeetji has only confirmed that they have made a report at the police station. In fact, it cannot even be called the First Information Report (FIR) because it was you who telephonically reported the death to the Police Control Room first of all. So let's not jump the gun. Let's hope Rajeev would be able to obtain a copy of the FIR from the police station. Let us go through it and then coolly decide what should be done next. It is usual in such cases to blame all members of the groom's family for causing or abetting suicide', explained Saxena.

'I don't see the logic. We have maintained the most cordial relations with the Suris since our children got married. What can they achieve by implicating all of us? They know very well that we are incapable of such a heinous crime', I persisted.

'Vinodji, you are too straight a man. There can be many motives behind it. Let's hope it turns out to be different in this case. Often people who lodge such complaints are encouraged and prodded by other relatives to do so', said Saxena.

I was suddenly reminded of the horrific scenes created by the distant relatives of the Suris last night. The most vocal, loudest and ugliest were people we had not met even once in the two years since the Suris had become our relatives through marriage. The one who was totally silent and had only whispered things in Simran's fathers and uncle's ears was not even a relative. He was a lawyer and a friend of Simran's uncle. That was all Unmesh had told me about him when I enquired in the morning. He was the one who had led Simran's father, uncle and two, three other men in the morning, when CO Santosh Singh had informed me that they had gone to lodge an FIR. It was time for action instead of wailing over our fate. If it was indeed true that all of us had been named in the FIR for committing a cognisable offence, the earlier we made ourselves scarce the better it would be.

Nine

There had been no movement in or out of our house since Agarwal and Rajeev had left. We could see the two policemen in our portico where they had moved in from the lawn to avoid the cold. We were obviously under an undeclared house arrest. Harish rang up a close friend, Gopal, and informed him that he along with his parents would like to shift to his house for a day or two. Gopal had a three-bedroom flat a few kilometers away from our house and a heart large enough to offer all the help that he could. Harish, Ratna and I then stealthily crossed over the terrace of our house to land on our next-door neighbour's terrace. We came down the stairs into his house where we met a very surprised Sehgal—our next door neighbor. We had enjoyed good friendship and neighbourly relations with them. Sehgal had spent the whole of that morning and quite some time last night at our house. We asked him to call his driver and get us dropped at Gopal's house. We had to take him in confidence. He knew our predicament and was very sympathetic. He immediately obliged us. We wanted Veena to go to Lucknow along with her father for a few days but she flatly refused to seek peace for herself, leaving us in the lurch. A little later in the evening, Saxena brought Veena in our car to Gopal's house. She had brought along an attache case hastily packed with some clothes for Ratna and me. The policemen posted outside our house probably did not recognise Veena and, of course, Saxena was an outsider. My other relatives also left one by one, leaving our house in the care of our trusted domestic aid Raju. The policemen must have presumed that Harish, my wife and I were inside our house. Gopal did his very best to make us all comfortable in his house. My in-laws had dispersed in different directions as we all had many relatives in different parts of Delhi. Gopal was kind enough to lend his, and his wife's mobile phone's simcards to us. We had discarded ours and stored them for use when things returned to normalcy.

I was up early next morning and contacted the managers of our industrial units, including the one run independently by Harish. They were all very anxious and sympathetic. Harish used to sit separately in his office in his unit which was only half-a-kilometer away from our other two units. A whole lot of workers and staff had seen all of us in the factories throughout that day. While Simran had left in the afternoon in a cycle-rickshaw hailed by the security guard at the factory gate, the rest of us had left for home many hours later in the evening. Unmesh, who had visited another factory in the afternoon almost two hours after Simran had left, had been accompanied by a supervisor from our factory and the timings of their arrival and departure had been noted also at the guard room of the factory visited. At least our employees knew that none of us were present at home when Simran had gone back from the factory alone, but our disappearing from home at this stage would appear strange to them. I took my Senior Manager in confidence and briefed him.

We remained very worried about Unmesh who had been detained overnight at the police station without being officially arrested. Rajeev had been informed that the police considered it prudent to detain him at the police station and to escort him when he went to attend Simran's funeral ceremony in the afternoon, only for his own personal safety and security. They expressed their apprehension that Unmesh might be assaulted by some agitated relatives of Simran as they held him and his mother squarely responsible for Simran's death. To me it appeared sensible that Unmesh should attend the funeral ceremony under police escort. At least this would ensure that he came to no physical harm. It also became clear that Ratna too was a suspect in their eyes, though Rajeev was not sure if there were any specific allegations against Harish, Veena and me. I could not think of any reason or justification for this. In fact, Rajeev had been unable to personally see the FIR the previous evening and had inferred all this only from his informal chat with a sub-inspector. He informed me that he would be visiting the police station again after 9 o'clock and will obtain a copy of the FIR and bring it to me. But I avoided telling him my exact whereabouts and asked him to fax the copy of the FIR. Gopal gave him the fax number of a PCO very far away from his house. We waited with bated breath for the faxed FIR which was collected by Gopal after some time.

My jaws dropped as I read the FIR. It had been written in Hindi. The language was simple but full of spelling mistakes and the contents were atrocious and unbelievable.

To

The S.H.O.

Police station, Sector-90, Noida

Sir,

My daughter Simran was married to Unmesh Asthana, son of Vinod Asthana, resident of House No. E-308, Sector-90, Noida where she had been living along with her in-laws. We had performed the marriage two years back with much aplomb and had given them a very good dowry to the best of our capability. But about six months after the marriage, we came to know that the dowry given by us was much below their expectations. My daughter Simran's mother- in -law Ratna Asthana and husband Unmesh started torturing her. About one year back my son-in-law Unmesh came along with my daughter to my residence. My daughter had blue and black marks of beating on her face and was crying. My son in law Unmesh took out his engagement ring and threw it at me and said that their marriage was finished. My daughter refused to go back to his house and she was very nervous. She told me that she was being tortured physically and mentally. But then I gently persuaded her to try and adjust with her husband and in-laws and finally she went back to them. But recently she rang me up and said that her husband and mother-in-law were demanding a dowry of rupees five lakhs. I told her that I could not help her in this matter and she should solve it herself with her husband. Then my daughter had said that whatever happens to her in future she would not come to me to seek any help. On 19th November, I was in Jalandhar when I received a phone call from my brother informing me that my daughter had met a serious accident. I hired a taxi and immediately rushed. When I reached Noida I took my brother and some other relatives along with me and we went to my son-in-law's residence. There I was informed by my daughter's father-in-law that she had committed suicide by hanging herself from a ceiling fan. I am not convinced that it is a case of suicide. This is a result of my not giving dowry. I feel that she has been tortured and then murdered for the sake of dowry and now they are calling it a suicide.

Col. Manbeer Suri, Sector-3, Noida

Writer in Hindi – Prithvi Nath R/o 212, Sector-80, Noida

I had been reading the FIR loudly so that Ratna, Harish and Veena could also hear. My throat had become parched and my voice was failing by the time I finished reading it. I had stumbled, hesitated and given jerky breaks while reading but at the end I was livid with rage. My hands shook and my voice split as I uttered just one word—'Bastards!' Harish burst out in anger, 'Look at the shameless liar. My God, what depth can he sink to! What white lies he has spoken!' Ranta's reaction was of complete shock. She was dumbstruck. She snatched the fax copy from my hands to read it herself. Veena remained speechless. Tears started flowing down her cheeks. She had been silently crying throughout my recitation of the FIR.

I was finding the whole situation very surreal. I remembered the day I had met Manbeer Suri formally for the first time in connection with our son's marriage. Col Satbeer too had been present on the occasion. While Manbeer had mostly kept quiet, it was Col Satbeer who had done most of the talking as Simran's Tauji (elder uncle). He had asked me in a very round about manner as to what were our expectations for the marriage. I had smiled warmly and reassuringly told him that by God's grace we had all that we required to meet our needs. We considered ourselves lucky that Unmesh had liked a charming girl like Simran. What more could we ask for except her hand for our son. But we had one request, we would like the marriage to be solemnised in the Hindu style with the bride and groom performing the *Saptpadi* (seven steps around the sacred fire) or the *saat phere*. Col Satbeer had appeared a bit embarrassed and said, 'We have no problems at all but Simran's maternal grandparents very earnestly desire that the marriage be solemnised as *Anand karaj* in a Gurudwara'. He also explained that Simran's aunt and uncle (*Mausi and Mausa*) still had strong reservations and were unwilling to attend the marriage, even if it be solemnised in the Sikh style. But if the *Anand Karaj* be solemnised in a Gurudwara, it will win over all their other relatives and her maternal grandparents will be extremely pleased. I visualised no problem in agreeing to this. In my eyes, a Gurudwara was just as holy as a Hindu temple. So I had readily agreed but then Ratna, who was quiet till then had spoken, 'I think my parents will be happy if the *Anand Karaj* ceremony is followed by a *Saptpadi* ceremony at our place.'

Both the brothers and their wives were quite satisfied with this suggestion. It was mutually agreed that the marriage would be solemnised in the Sikh fashion in a Gurudwara in the afternoon. Simran would not go back to her parents place and in the evening the marriage would be solemnised as per our Hindu Vedic customs. The matter had thus been very amicably settled. The meeting had ended with lots of hugs and backslapping between both parties. Thus the only demand, if you cared to call it that, from our side was the solemnisation of the marriage as per Hindu customs too and that was the end of it. The ugly word 'dowry' had never been mentioned nor had any disguised, polite or camouflaged version of it been used to make any demands on the girl's parents.

We had been careful not to hurt the Suris' sentiments at any time by doing anything that could be misconstrued as 'showing off'. On the fourth day after her marriage, she had gone on a formal visit to her parents' home for a few days. Thereafter, not once had she expressed any desire to go there even for an overnight stay though she enjoyed full freedom to do so if she ever wanted to. She had all along been quite happy in our joint family. Then what the devil had happened to the Suris? How could they cook up such a rotten, baseless story in the FIR? It was difficult to believe that he could pour so much venom against us when our relations had been quite cordial till then.

But the reality had to be faced boldly. I could hardly deny that the shock received by Simran's father was no less than the jolt we had got. After all, he had lost his daughter in our home. He couldn't be in a fit frame of mind to think logically and behave decently. He must have written all this in a fit of rage. Probably with the passage of time, he would realise how unfair he had been in making such patently false accusations against us. 'Let's see what unfolds in the coming days', I thought as I looked out of the window at the white fluffy clouds in the sky. Silence prevailed for a few minutes after our angry outbursts, as I kept gazing out of the window. Gopal had not spoken at all since he had given the fax message to me. Now he tried to console me in a soft tone, 'Uncle, let's be happy that they have spared Harish and Veena. For that matter, there is no complaint against you either.' Yes, I had noticed this too. But I was not too sure that I had been spared. My name had appeared in the very first paragraph of the FIR.

I put on my reading glasses again and commenced a second

reading of the FIR. Yes, Gopal was right. My name appeared only as Unmesh's father. No mention had been made of any specific acts of cruelty or harassment for dowry by me, although vague allegations of harassment and a specific complaint of demanding dowry had been made against Ratna and of cruelty and harassment against Unmesh.

The realisation took me by surprise. Why this streak of kindness in his utterly brazen and venomous accusation against us. It could not have been a simple omission. Was it too heavy a burden on his guilty conscience that he had tried to lighten by sparing me? Probably by not roping in the whole family, he wanted his story to appear more credible. I wondered if it had any legal implication beyond my understanding. I told Harish and Ratna that I would discuss it with Rajeev. 'Rajeev is only visiting his brother-in-law for a few days; we will have to seek legal aid from a local advocate. The allegations are so grave that we have to obtain the best legal aid', said Harish. 'Uncle, why worry about all that right now?' chipped in Gopal. 'Col Manbeer has done the damage... It is definitely going to take time to sort this out. Right now we should concentrate on getting Unmesh back after the cremation. If he is under arrest, we will have to arrange the bail too. Let us see what happens at the cremation. Since Harish's name doesn't figure anywhere in the FIR, it could be safe for him to go attend the funeral.'

'That makes sense to me', I said. 'Gopal, you and Harish can go and attend the funeral. I guess, Saxena can also go there.

Ratna and I shall stay back. I will utilise the time to ring up my contacts and locate a good criminal lawyer to take up our case.'

Gopal and Harish left separately to attend the funeral. Gopal's wife went to the kitchen. Ratna and I were left alone in our room. How much had I longed for this solitude! We needed to be together to seek comfort in each other's arms. We were both heartbroken, sad and right now very angry. I hugged Ratna and kissed her on the temple. She shivered in my tight embrace. Her eyes were swollen from lack of sleep and the continuous mental and physical strain of the last thirty six hours shone on her face. It appeared to be drained of blood.

Ratna has always been a great moral support to me due to her gift of always looking at the brighter side of things. Shedding tears is not her weakness. I had never seen Ratna so sad, looking so vulnerable as she was looking now. I kept gazing at her tear-stained face while holding her in my embrace. Now her tears had dried up. Vulnerable? Yes! Defeated? No! She shuddered and swayed gently in my arms. I put my lips on her parched lips. She mumbled gently, '*Hato* (move along), what are you doing?' I must have heard these words after a gap of three decades in our blissful married life. A faint smile came to my lips. The irony of the situation irked me. My young son's bride had committed suicide, after having fought and won a prolonged cynical battle against her near-and-dear ones to wed her love. They had had a stormy but stealthy courtship. For two years they had avoided nosey acquaintances when they met each other, snatching a few hours together, he from his busy MBA studies and she from the watchful eyes of her parents. And now God knows from where this spark had come which had set fire to their conjugal love. I, on the other hand, after going through a typical arranged marriage of the most routine and uneventful type, was holding my bride of three decades in my arms. I was conveying my tender concern for her getting entangled in this poisonous web of conspiracy by putting my lips on her trembling parched lips. Her gentle protest reminded me of our predicament. I released her from my embrace, came out of the sitting room and picked up Gopal's phone to contact my friends in my quest for a good lawyer.

Later, Gopal rang me up and gave details of the cremation. After the body had reached the cremation ground, Unmesh had been brought there in a police Gypsy. He had not been handcuffed but two policemen were closely escorting him. He had been allowed to put his shoulders to the *arthi* (the bamboo stretcher on which a body is carried for cremation). The Suris had not created any fuss this time, though no one had spoken a word to Unmesh. Harish too had similarly been allowed to be amongst the four pall bearers, the other two being Manbeer and Simran's brother Anand. Not a word had been exchanged with Harish either. Unmesh had lit the funeral pyre and everybody had silently watched the body being reduced to ashes. Unmesh had been allowed to stand there while the flames kept leaping up. After the pyre had been consumed and the fire was just smouldering, Unmesh had been taken back to the Gypsy by the policemen but this time neither of the policemen even held his hand.

Saxena had also been present there. But nobody from Simran's side had spoken a single word to him. There were no other relatives from our side. Finally they had all dispersed. Harish informed me that he would return to Gopal's house after planning the arrangements for the *Shanti Hawan* (Prayer Meeting). He needed to contact the local Arya Samaj temple to organise the ceremony. Harish, who was in the habit of depending on me for detailed instructions and guidance in all major and sometimes even minor issues in the factory, had suddenly matured in the last two days.

Ten

Ratna reminded me that one of her distant relatives was practicing law and apparently had a flourishing practice at Delhi. One of my first cousins also was a senior advocate, practicing on the civil side at the Allahabad High Coutrt, but I felt terribly self-conscious in informing him that my son and wife were facing the prospects of being tried for dowry death, after our daughter-in-law had committed suicide in our house. There was no doubt that the news must have reached him by now, but the prospect of my telling him all this personally was very daunting. In any case, he was based in distant Allahabad. Our requirement was to engage a criminal lawyer in Noida or Delhi. I opted for not discussing my problems with my cousin. I contacted Ratna's cousin, Sanjay. Sure enough, the news had reached him too. He informed me that personally his forte was Income Tax cases but he would ask his colleague Tripathi, one of the topmost criminal lawyers practicing at Delhi High Court, to look after our case. The immediate requirement would be to seek bail. Later on, there will be a case under sec. 498A/304(B) IPC and Dowry Prohibition Act and this lawyer would take care of everything. 'But no one has been arrested so far', I quipped.

'Don't worry, you will all be arrested soon', Sanjay said. I was aghast at his choice of words. I hoped his friend would be more judicious in advising us on when to worry! I tried to find out what would this Tripathi charge as his professional fees. 'Not to worry on that issue. His fees are high, but you are family. *Baad mein dekh lenge* (we shall see later)', he replied very casually.

He asked me to visit his chamber with full details of the case and a copy of the FIR. He said he would arrange an extract from the daily diary of the police station. 'Is that a public document?' I asked. 'Oh! Please don't go into the nitty-gritty of a criminal lawyer's activities. There is nothing like a public or a non-public document. What is strictly non-public can be available, if you are not stingy. If you count your pennies, then even a public notice board can be out of bounds for you.'

'In that case I think I should leave a small imprest with you to meet the immediate expenses', I insisted. But Sanjay was very adamant in not accepting any money, at least in advance. 'Please stop bothering about such things *Jijaji* (brother-in-law). You need to stand by your family. Please concentrate on that. I will take care of everything. *Kharche ko baad mein dekh lenge*', Sanjay told me in very sweet and cordial tone. I was touched by his kindness and large-heartedness. I had hardly met him once or twice during the many decades since I had married Ratna, and here he was refusing to take any retainer for his colleague and he had called me *Jijaji*! I was lucky to have such help!

I then contacted Rajeev. I wanted him to go to the police station to bring Unmesh back home, after he had attended the funeral under police escort. Now that it was all over, I was sure he would be released. Rajeev was very annoyed when I told him that I had fixed up Tripathi to give us legal aid. 'Here I have been running around because I have regards for your wife just like I have for my sister, and you are running after Delhi High Court advocates. What can they do in Noida – which is in UP. I know the UP system best. I deal with it every day. Didn't I get you a copy of the FIR within a few hours of its being filed? Now let's see when your Tripathi gets an extract of the police diary. I will get it to you before 10 o'clock tomorrow morning. Why don't you have faith in me *Jijaji*?'

I was rather surprised at being called '*jijaji*' by Rajeev, so soon after Sanjay had addressed me in the same manner. But he clarified that he had the same regards for Ratna as he had for his real sister, Mrs Agarwal. No wonder he was addressing me in the same manner as he addressed his brother-in-law and my friend, Agarwal. Poor chap must have spent money from his pocket in getting the copy of the FIR from the Police Station and now he was going to get the extract from the police diary too. I must offer him some money to reimburse the expenses, I thought. But Rajeev would have none of that. *'Kyon sharminda karte hain Jijaji?* (You are putting me to shame). These are petty things. But if you insist so much, *baad mein dekh lenge*. Yes, one more thing! You must not get trapped into the claws of this Tripathi. All these Delhi High Court*wallas*' talk about bail is meaningless. What is the idea of first getting arrested and then seeking bail? Although I practice at Kanpur district courts, I maintain regular contacts with the best criminal lawyers at Allahabad High Court. Come with me, I will arrange anticipatory bail for your whole family from Allahabad High Court', he said very convincingly.

I had already started feeling guilty that I had not consulted him before fixing up the arrangements with Sanjay. Both Sanjay and Rajeev had won me over with their sincerity and genuine concern. Why not nip the problem of the imminent arrests in the bud by obtaining anticipatory bail from Allahabad High Court? I was now fully tempted by Rajeev's offer. But before making up my mind on this course of action, I thought it prudent to at least now consult my cousin practicing as a senior advocate at Allahabad High Court. When I rang him up, he very considerately allowed me to skip the gory details by saying that he had already got the news from some other relatives. When I asked for his views on my seeking anticipatory bail from the High Court, he said that there was no provision for anticipatory bail in the State of UP, though it did exist in adjoining Haryana state and the Union Territory of Delhi. Since the incident had taken place at my residence which was under UP Jurisdiction, there was no chance of our obtaining an anticipatory bail.

But Rajeev was adamant. 'I know your *Bhai Saheb* is a very well respected senior advocate of Allahabad High Court. But he practices on the Civil side where all that matters is deep and thorough knowledge of the law and its provisions. But criminal law practice is a totally different ballgame. It requires a lot of *daav-pench* and *jugaad* (tricks of the trade and improvisations). If you know how to manage things, you can manage the law also. I will take you to the best criminal lawyer in Allahabad and you will be amazed to see how he can extract oil from even a fistful of sand. And his fees will be nominal, if you come along with me', he said forcefully.

I didn't have much choice. I thought I might as well try what Rajeev was so confidently suggesting. So it was decided that Ratna and I would proceed to Allahabad by car. Rajeev asked us to start in the night and proceed in a hired car, rather than in our own car to evade arrest en route. He advised us to avoid staying at a hotel in Allahabad. We couldn't go and stay with my cousin, after I had decided to act against his advice on the question of anticipatory bail, so we decided to stay with a distant relative of Ratna who was also practicing in the District Courts at Allahabad. The car journey would take almost twelve hours. Rajeev planned to start by train the next morning, soon after obtaining extract of the police daily diary from the police station. I really did not understand why the daily diary was so important but Rajeev explained that it would help us size up and appreciate the future course of action the police would take. I proposed to postpone the journey to Allahabad for the next day so that he could also come with us. But he said it would not be prudent for him to travel in the same car with us because technically, Ratna and I were avoiding arrest. For his train journey, an air-conditioned first class berth was available in *Tatkal* booking for his journey to Allahabad. I offered him money to buy the ticket. Once again he said, '*Baad mein dekh lenge*'.

There was nothing else to do in the evening. I could not go for a walk, nor did I feel like watching my favorite news channel on TV. Both Ratna and I were too depressed to indulge in small talk. Being utterly exhausted, we hit the bed early. But we kept turning and tossing on our bed. Finally at about five in the morning, I managed to get some fitful and disturbed sleep. But even this was cut short at 10 am by Rajeev who gave me a jolt by faxing me the excerpts from the case diary, obtained from the Police Station which seemed to be lifted from a cheap crime novel. I was aghast at the flight of imagination of the sub-inspector who was in charge of the case. I read on: 'I, Sub-Inspector Khushiram, was informed by a reliable source at 10 am on 20th November that accused Unmesh Asthana had been seen standing at the bus stop of Sector 90, Noida with a bag in hand. Apparently he was trying to flee from his house. I reported the matter to the SHO, who asked me to draw arms for myself and with a party of six constables, proceed post-haste to the spot to arrest accused

Unmesh. Rushing immediately to the spot where the accused was waiting for a bus, we surprised him. Finding himself surrounded by our party, the accused did not offer any resistance. He was arrested and brought to the Police Station where he has been placed under Police custody.'

After the initial shock, I was amused by the funny side of this cock-and-bull story. I failed to understand why they had to give it such a dramatic twist when they had already taken Unmesh to the Police Station after informing me. The fool of a SI had mentioned the time of locating Unmesh as 10 am while Unmesh was helping in bringing down Simran's body and putting it in the ambulance till about 12 o'clock. The photographer, whose presence I had resented so much, had taken many snapshots of Unmesh as one of the stretcher bearers. I knew in some photographs Unmesh would be seen coming down the stairs with the stretcher while two policemen were holding the stretcher along with him. There would be another photograph showing Unmesh on the policeman's motorbike, sitting on the pillion while the policeman was riding the bike. The shot was taken from a short distance and the policeman's nameplate would be clearly visible. Also, along with Unmesh, other relatives and neighbours must be visible in the photographs taken when the body was being put in the ambulance. All the photographs must be automatically carrying the date and time of the event as is usual in digital cameras these days. Further, the inquest report signed by the Magistrate and other five witnesses also had recorded the time of the inquest as 10.30 am. The body had been sealed in a cloth bag and handed over to the policemen after that, and then it was taken to the ambulance which had come a good one hour later. So even if the case diary claimed that Unmesh had been ambushed and apprehended while trying to flee, how its timing could be shown as about 10 am when he had helped put the body in the ambulance after 10:30?

It was obvious that the police was dramatising events. What we had seen in the case diary could only be the beginning of a much-concocted tale to land us into serious trouble. I had initially thought that since no specific allegation had been made against me in the FIR, I should be able to move around freely. But now, after reading this concocted story in the case diary, it became clear that even I could not take any chances and must lie low. Gopal left with the copy of the FIR and the case diary, to seek Saxena's advice.

It was already afternoon when Gopal left. I had barely slept in the night for a few hours. Ratna had been equally disturbed and sleep had eluded her too. After she read the FIR copy and learnt that she had been accused of torturing Simran for dowry, she had become speechless. She kept reminiscing about the happy times Simran had spent in the kitchen, learning new recipes from her, how she always thanked God for fulfilling her desire to have a daughter by giving her two very loving daughters-in-law. And now, this was her reward for showering her love on her as her younger daughter. She kept sobbing while we planned our next steps. Harish fixed up someone's private car, which would be better than a taxi in case the police were on the lookout for us. By now I was feeling utterly exhausted both mentally and physically. Finally Ratna and I decided to pop some tranquilising pills and try and snatch some sleep.

We left for Allahabad in the evening. We had started just after sunset to avoid recognition during the journey. The cold winter night gave me a good excuse to put on a monkey cap, hiding most of my face. Ratna too wrapped a shawl around her head, leaving hardly any scope for anybody to recognise her, particularly at night. We remained tense as the car passed through two police checkposts while exiting Noida to join the Grand Trunk Road, now called National Highway No 1. But nobody took any notice of us. We stopped near Aligarh for some tea and refreshments at one of the all-night *dhaba*s which were lit up with coloured bulbs. Noisy diesel generator sets were shattering the silence of the night. Even at this hour of the night most of the *dhaba*s had trucks lined up along the road while their drivers were sitting on stringed cots and enjoying their meal of hot tandoori rotis, *daal makhani* and mango pickle served with raw onions. Ratna and I opted to have only some tea and biscuits. I managed with great difficulty to persuade the *dhaba* owner not to brew the tea in pure milk. Even after keen supervision of the tea-making, we had to contend with very heavily sweetened tea but it helped pass time while our driver had his dinner.

We had been very tense till then due to fear of being stopped by policemen and being detained as fugitives from law. But during the rest of the journey our anxiety subsided considerably. Unfortunately, poor Ratna had other concerns. She found it an abominable experience to go out from the car to relieve herself in the dead of the night by the roadside. The pitch-dark night would be penetrated by two beams of headlights of trucks whizzing past and the eerie silence would be shattered by the roaring truck engines every twenty or thirty seconds. Ratna would go cursing and protesting and hide herself behind some thick mango tree trunk and come back in a nasty temper, chafed with the indignity of it all which ladies were expected to suffer silently in such road journeys. But that was about the only excitement she faced during the journey. We reached Allahabad at about eight in the morning. It had been a fourteen hours drive but we had dozed through most of it due to the sheer physical and mental exhaustion of the last two days.

Eleven

Ratna's cousin Ranjan lived in a middle-class locality in the city. After reaching his house, we had freshened up and had our breakfast. We then sat down to discuss our problem with Ranjan. To our great surprise, he already had a solution for our problem, which he said would be explained by his friend and neighbour Sharmaji. What exactly did this Sharmaji do for a living, was not mentioned by him. He vaguely said that Sharmaji did all sorts of things. His specialty was 'contacts'. He had solutions for all sorts of problems, whether it was pension-fixation or getting a passport, an ageing daughter's marriage or a job for an unemployed son. When I asked him if Sharmaji was a legal expert too, Ranjan just laughed it off. 'When you can get all your problems solved illegally, where is the sense in sweating it out at a law college' he said with a mischievous wink. I was getting anxious and a bit annoyed with this introduction. I was itching to get ready and meet Rajeev. He had reached Allahabad by train and we were in touch on phone. I was to go to a senior advocate's residence by 11.30 am where Rajeev would wait for me. We would then discuss our application for anticipatory bail with this advocate. When I mentioned this to Ranjan, he got quite annoyed, '*Arre Jijaji*, why are you getting involved in all this tedious legal processes. You don't know these lawyers. It is their job to suck you dry once you enter their labyrinthine alleys. Our Sharmaji will take care of all this "*law-phaw-kanoon-phanoon*".' And as if on a cue, even before Ranjan could finish his sermon, Sharmaji entered his small sitting room.

Sharmaji did not look like a social do-gooder. Of average height, medium complexion and clean-shaven face, Sharmaji did not have any distinguishing feature to describe him. He was dressed in a neat, full-sleeved shirt, trousers and a brown jacket. What really distinguished him was the honey in his voice and his extremely polite mannerism. He almost bent double on being introduced and when he recovered his straight posture after remaining bent for a couple of seconds, said in a voice dripping with syrup, '*Jijaji*, you just don't worry. Just leave all your problems to me. Ranjan is more like a real younger brother for me and his sister is my real sister. I will ensure that no one touches you.'

'But Sharmaji, this is a legal issue', I protested. 'My wife and I are accused in a case of dowry death. Her arrest is imminent. What else can we do except to approach a court to prevent her arrest?' I said.

'*Arrey Jijaji*, you don't understand these things. Preventing these arrests at High Court-level is not a joke. These things will cost you a hell of a lot of money. My ways are different. I have already done my homework. It is a much cheaper way', Sharmaji said, his voice sounding very sad and concerned at my ignorance and foolishness.

'And what's that, may I ask?' I said impatiently.

'You don't know me *Jijaji*, but I am famous for my contacts. You name any field and I have a source there. Now, in your case, I have already found out that the Chief Judicial Magistrate at Noida belongs to Allahabad. He had studied here in school and university before he got into the state judicial service. I have already found out who were his best friends here and they are all in my pocket. You do one thing, get *Bahenji* admitted to a nursing home. Let the *policewalla*s arrest her. It will only be an arrest on paper while she enjoys the comforts of the nursing home. Now we shall submit a bail application for her and get her out within twenty-four hours on bail. You committed a big mistake in letting your son go along with the police. The same formula should have worked for him too. The *kharcha* (expenses) will be very minimal'.

'And what is that minimal amount?' I asked.

'*Arrey*, You give only rupees fifty thousand as of now, *baki bad main dekh lenge*. (Remaining, we shall see later).'

I was amazed at the brazenness of Sharmaji's proposal. But circumstances had exposed me to a whole new world. Who knows, there might be some method in this madness, I thought and decided to check it out with Rajeev. 'Sharmaji, I am not carrying so much of cash, will a cheque do?' I asked. The answer was quick and blunt 'Oh no, *Jijaji*, all this is a strictly cash game. I am sure Ranjan can help you', he said and looked at Ranjan. Ranjan opened his mouth to show his *gutka*-stained teeth in an apologetic smile and said, *'Arre, nahi bhai*, I don't have all that money even in bank, what to talk of cash.' This was a good opportunity for me to slip out of Sharmaji's clutches. 'Alright, Sharmaji, give me some time to find out if I can raise some cash here. I will revert to you in the evening', I said. Sharmaji assured me once again that all my problems would be solved as soon as I arranged the cash, finished his cup of tea and polished off the plate of biscuits that Mrs Ranjan had offered.

I then rang up Rajeev. It was only 9.30 in the morning but he had already reached the residence-cum-office of Thakur Balram Singh, Advocate, straight from the railway station where his train had reached at 7 am. I was not surprised when he said that he had already discussed my case with the advocate and had been assured of full success in getting the anticipatory bail. He told me to bring Rs 25,000 to meet the fees of the advocate. I decided to discuss Sharmaji's offer with Rajeev. But the moment I explained Sharmaji's plan of action, he blew up. 'What *Jijaji*? Why do you get involved with all types of frauds? It looks like you are bent upon throwing your hard-earned money down the drain. Now you are talking to plain and simple thugs who don't know the ABC of law.

Let me explain, once you are arrested under Section 498 B, the case will go to the District and Sessions Judge. The CJM has no role to play in granting you a bail; only the District And Sessions Judge can do it and in ninety-nine per cent cases, it doesn't come easily even at that level. Only the High Court can grant you the relief of bail. How is this fool's friendship with the CJM going to help you?' I hummed and hawed and then told Rajeev that Ratna and I will reach Thakur Balram Singh's residence in half-an-hour.

Ranjan was obviously unhappy with my decision. With a sullen face he explained to the driver the way to reach the residence of Thakur Saheb. The last thing he said to the driver was very reassuring to me, 'It is a big *kothi* at the beginning of the lane and is well-known in that area. You can ask anybody in the area to guide you to his house.'

Thakur Balram Singh's *kothi* was indeed big. He himself had a large frame and a booming voice and a face adorned with big graying moustaches. Rajeev had already told him about me and the first thing he said on meeting was, 'I am glad to meet a cousin of Mr SN Asthana. He is a very reputed senior advocate and highly respected at the High Court. I don't get to rub shoulders with him in the court as he is practicing on the civil side. That's also why he doesn't know the tricks of the trade of criminal practice. He might have advised you that in UP, there is no system of anticipatory bail. He is right theoretically. Now we will show him we have ways and means of bypassing such minor legal hurdles. You rest at ease, we shall take care of you.' Rajeev had obviously given him a more thorough briefing than I expected, including a word about the advice I had received from my cousin regarding anticipatory bail. Was there a faint smell of professional jealousy in his desire to show off his legal skills to my cousin who was a top rung senior advocate on the civil side? There was no time to indulge in such unnecessary conjectures. I grabbed the thin end of the rope that Thakur Saheb had dropped to pull us out of the whirlpool. I promptly unburdened myself of Rs 25,000 but when I gave it to Rajeev he demanded another Rs 5000 and explained that we would have to tip the *Munshi* (clerk) of the advocate and also to other petty officials in the court. I meekly did as advised.

I was simply knocked over by the efficiency with which Thakur Saheb's well oiled office system worked. After Ratna and I signed the *vakalatnama*, giving the advocate the power to represent us, Rajeev took from me copies of the FIR, Ratna's medical reports and sundry other documents and got them xeroxed. A young junior of the advocate prepared a draft application within the next half-an-hour. It was brought to Thakur Saheb. He made only some minor corrections in it and instructed his junior to rush to the High Court along with the application and its xeroxed annexures. I was informed that our application will be filed by 12 o'clock. Rajeev's proud and confident glance and smile asked me silently, 'See how efficient they are', and then he spoke, 'Only Thakur Saheb's cases are taken up like this on top priority. Had we gone to any other advocate, it would have taken a week at least to merely get our application filed at the High Court.You have seen nothing so far, you will get the Court's order on this application by the evening.'

I admired their cleverness in avoiding any mention of the word 'anticipatory bail' in the application. When I mentioned it to Rajeev, he very immodestly replied, 'Oh such an application is a routine job for us. I could have written it myself but unfortunately I don't practice in the High Court.'

There was nothing else to do, so we went looking for a restaurant near the High Court. There seemed to be a total absence of any decent eateries in close vicinity of the High Court though there were thousands of litigants, lawyers and their employees, touts, stamp vendors, typists etc in the crowd. Of course, there were many tea-stalls. *Chai-Samosa* and *Pakoras* seemed to be the most popular menu for lunch. We sat on a wooden bench in front of a dusty tea-stall operating from a thatched hut and shared our *samosas* with mongrels feverishly wagging their tails. I avoided looking at Ratna. I can take a lot of physical discomfort but I knew she wouldn't be able to eat anything sitting there.

We spent the afternoon sitting on the benches of different tea shops, reading local newspapers and sipping tea. It wasn't possible to occupy the bench for very long in a single shop. Time slowly dragged on. At about three o'clock Rajeev left us and went to enquire about the fate of our application. We did not have to wait very long. When he came back he had a grim expression on his face. Without saying a word he passed on a legal size paper to me with the order typed on it. I read it with a thumping heart.

The court order began with a synopsis of the case as mentioned in our application and then trashed our application disdainfully. It said 'we are not inclined to quash the FIR in the aforesaid case at the threshold in view of the very serious allegations against the petitioners. We do not find any cogent and convincing reason to stay the arrest of the petitioners till submission of the report under Section 173 Cr PC. The nature and gravity of the offence dissuades us to exercise discretion and restrain the police to arrest the petitioners. Hence the same is dismissed. However, taking note of the age of the petitioners and the fact that one of them is a lady with medical problems, they are advised to apply for bail in the appropriate lower court. The Court below would do well to decide the same as expeditiously as possible.'

Rajeev did not allow the grim expression on his face to linger very long and tried to lift my sagging morale. 'Let us look at it this way *Jijaji*. Thank God you did not fall into the clutches of that cheat Sharmaji who was charging 50,000. That too only as an advance to arrange a bail from the CJM. Now, at least, we know the attitude of the High Court on this matter so we have in fact saved a lot of money.'

I did not wish to prolong my agony so I asked him, 'What next?' He was quite smug. 'Not to worry. Both of you go back to Noida and get admitted in a nursing home. At this age, both you and Bhabhiji are prone to arthritis, high blood pressure, angina and what not. Any doctor can retain you there as long as you wish to. While you get arrested theoretically and take up the bail case at the District Court level.'

'What about Unmesh?' Ratna hissed. '*Arrey Bahenji*, unfortunately *Jijaji* let him go with the *policewalla*s without asking me. Otherwise I would have got him admitted in a nursing home then only. Anyway, now we will have to wait till he also gets his bail from the District Court. Don't worry at all. You go back to Noida. I will break journey at Kanpur for a day and sort out things at home. Then I will also get back and help you with your cases in Noida.'

I did not quite know how to get rid of this 'brother-in-law' of mine after having successfully avoided getting trapped by another one in the morning. Ratna took over at this stage. She always does whenever she finds me weakening. 'No-no, your clients and family must be missing you very much in Kanpur. I suggest you go back there. We shall go back to Noida and do as advised by you. We shall call you when the need arises. How can we forget all that you have done for us? We shall remain ever thankful to you', she said. It was time for me to take over and discuss the monetary aspect of his help. I said, 'We shall drop you in Kanpur on our way back. Please let me know, how much do we owe you for all the running around and for the out of pocket expenses?'

Rajeev's voice was dripping with honey, 'You are embarrassing me, *Jijaji*. I did whatever I could just because I consider *Bahenji* like my real sister. After all, she is a very close friend of my sister. You don't have to pay me but yes, I will accept reimbursement of actual expenses. I have some work at Allahabad so I will stay here till tomorrow. You may give me Rs 3,000 to take a cab for Kanpur tomorrow. And yes, Thakur Saheb had told me that the staff at the High Court had to be paid Rs 10,000 to take up the application today itself, otherwise you would have got stuck up here for God knows how many days. Then in Noida, I had spent Rs 5000 to obtain copies of the FIR and the case diary. Further, in Noida, I had to spend about Rs 2,000 on local conveyance. So you can reimburse three amounts. I do not need any payments for myself. It will be a sin to touch even a paisa of my sister for rendering her some help when she and her family are facing such challenges and calamities.'

I was speechless. I knew that a bus ticket to Kanpur from Allahabad would cost Rs 80, a shared taxi Rs 300 and an independent taxi Rs 1,500. And Noida had only cycle-rikshas and auto-rikshas in the name of hired conveyance. Nobody could spend Rs 2,000 on them in one day at Noida. I had given Rs 5,000 to him in the morning for the *Munshi* and other staff of the Advocate and payment of Rs 10,000 for taking up our application on the same day was pure poppycock. Thakur Balram Singh had never mentioned any such requirement. But having accepted so much of personal help from Rajeev, there was no way I could bicker. So I quietly took out a wad of Rs 1000 notes, counted twenty notes and thrust them in his palm. Rajeev did not waste any more time with me. He bent half way to touch Ratna's knees, made a half-hearted attempt to kneel down to my thigh level, then picked up his brief case and walked away towards a cycle-rikshaw.

Twelve

We were left high and dry in Allahabad. After Rajeev went back to Kanpur, we had the choice to go back to Noida the same night or to stay put at Ranjan's place. We were already exhausted. Ratna was now just too tired to undertake a fourteen-hour drive back to Noida. In my case, the anxiety about our future was even more excruciating than the running around. Our arrest as soon as we landed back at Noida was a distinct possibility and I was in no hurry to precipitate the matter. Yet, absconding for too many days would unnecessarily make everybody suspicious. We ultimately decided to go back to Noida after having a night's rest at Allahabad. We told Ranjan that we were driving back to Noida but shifted to a small but neat and clean hotel near Civil Lines to get a day's rest. In the evening, I contacted Saxena on phone and what he told me lifted my spirits up several notches.

Saxena and Ratna's sister, who also was an IAS Officer, had gone to the Superintendent of Police at Noida. They had lodged a complaint that the police was behaving in a most prejudiced manner against us. They produced the copy of the case diary and the photographs of Unmesh taken that morning, when at 11.30 he was one of the pall-bearers while the body was being brought down from the first floor. There were other photographs too. In one, Unmesh was seen standing near the ambulance door, in another he was seen lifting and placing the stretcher into the ambulance. In all these photographs many policemen could also be clearly seen. Then there was a photograph where a policeman was seen taking Unmesh with him on his motor bike. The policeman's face was clearly visible and a number of my neighbours were witness to the fact that Unmesh was present at our house all the while, till the ambulance moved away with the body. They had also witnessed Unmesh accompanying the policeman to the police station. The crude story narrated in the case diary was only an utterly whimsical flight of imagination. It was also pointed out that the witnesses who signed the Magistrate's inquest report were all outsiders who had come to our house with the Suris and not a single neighbour, relative or friend of ours present at my residence at the time of the inquest, had been asked to affix his signature on the inquest report as a witness.

Saxena happily informed me that the SP had promised to change the IO (Investigating Officer) of the case, although he had initially tried to laugh off the issue of the fabricated scene of

Unmesh's melodramatic arrest. He had said that this was the usual manner in which the police describes most arrests and no court took serious note of such description. Saxena felt that though there was no possibility of my arrest, Ratna couldn't evade arrest for long. He suggested we come back to Noida and assured me that by the time we reach arrangements would be made to admit Ratna in a nursing home.

Fortunately or unfortunately, depends how you look at it, Ratna indeed had been suffering from acute pain in her knees for the last six months. X-ray and MRI reports obtained three months back had revealed pronounced wear and tear of the knee joints due to the drying up of the cushioning jelly in the joints. She had been advised to take ostocalcium and pain relieving pills regularly. At that time she had been advised bed rest for two weeks. Subsequently, the condition had improved but she could not climb stairs without sighing in pain. This would be a good excuse to get admitted at a nursing home.

The telephonic chat with Saxena had a soothing effect on us. We felt somewhat relieved and were able to have a sound sleep that night. Next morning we started our drive back to Noida after breakfast. We reached Noida at 10 pm and drove straight to the nursing home where Saxena and Harish met us. Arrangements for Ratna's admission had already been made. New Light Nursing Home was not very close to our house but its Director, Dr Rathore, was known personally to me. No explanation was required at the nursing home. We were already a 'famous' family! Veena was waiting in the plush private ward room allotted to Ratna. They had come back from Gopal's house to our own. Unmesh, we were told, had been put under judicial custody in the local jail.

Harish informed me that earlier in the day, Police Circle Officer PK Gaur had visited our house along with three constables, after being appointed the Investigating Officer in place of Santosh Singh. Obviously, this was a sequel to the complaint made to the SP about the fudged case diary. Gaur had moved very rapidly. He had already talked to all our immediate neighbours, our two part-time maids and our domestic aid Raju, who had earlier too been taken to the police station. On that occasion Raju had then been kept in the 'cooler' throughout the day and grilled repeatedly by Santosh Singh about the exact time each member of the family had left home in the morning and returned in the evening. There were lots of questions about the treatment usually given to Simran by each one of us. Ultimately Raju had been let off and had come back by nightfall before we had left our home for Gopal's place. Now poor Raju had to face renewed grilling by Gaur too but he had remained unfazed and determined to give only a very truthful description of all that he had witnessed that day.

Harish came to the most important piece of news and said, 'CO Gaur asked me, "Why has your father also disappeared along with your mother? Tell him on my behalf that while the written complaint makes no allegation against him, I have also been verbally informed by Col Manbeer, whom I had met in the afternoon, that they considered Mr Asthana a decent man against whom they had no specific complaint. So there was no need for Mr Asthana to take so much of trouble to evade arrest. Sorry, but I can't say the same about Mrs Asthana whom we shall have to arrest in any case."'

'Didn't he threaten you or pressurise you to disclose our whereabouts?' I asked. 'No Papa, he was very civil. Maybe it's a result of the action taken on our complaint against the original Investigating Officer. In fact, I asked him why he was not disturbed by you and Mom evading arrest?' Harish continued, '...but he laughed at my question and said, "Why should we take so much trouble with our limited resources? What Mr and Mrs Asthana are doing is the most natural and common thing in all such cases. The only difference in this case, from normal dowry death complaints is that there is specific complaint only against the husband and the mother- in-law of the deceased. Usually the whole family is roped in. We take steps to locate the absconding accused only if we come across any specific piece of evidence of crime for dowry like letters, audio recordings or independent eye witnesses along with the complaint. But in this case, there are only allegations but no proof or documentary evidence of dowry demands. Your father is a government pensioner. How long can his wife evade arrest? He is an educated man and I am sure he knows that all his assets can be attached by the court. We know they will come back on their own. We also know their next step will be to get admitted in a hospital for the treatment of angina or some such complaint. We shall then confront them."

I had already started feeling relieved. 'No, it won't be angina. It will be arthritis and lumbago related complaints in this case', I said with a mischievous chuckle.

Veena spent the night in the attendant's bed provided in the private ward room allotted to Ratna. I and Harish went back to our house. Next morning, I was quite refreshed after a sound sleep. But my lightheartedness did not last long. Worries about Unmesh and Ratna soon confronted me again.

Thirteen

Ratna was now comfortably ensconced in the nursing home. All our relatives including Mr Saxena had gone back from Noida. There was a stream of visitors to see Ratna in her private ward room. The fear of 'getting involved' seemed to have bothered barely one or two of my friends. Both Ratna and I were dying to meet Unmesh. We had not seen him since the day he had been taken to the police station and later remanded to judicial custody at the district jail at Dasna. It would only be possible to meet him on Sunday—the visiting day. I had no choice but to wait. Ratna wouldn't see him even then.

I was planning to contact the police officer in charge of the case in the evening. I knew Ratna would be placed under arrest as soon as I told him her whereabouts. I wanted to give her at least one peaceful day without any disturbance. I fixed up a meeting with Sanjay at 5 pm before meeting the police officer. Sanjay, in turn, fixed up a meeting with the lawyer, Tripathi, who would take up our case.The next most pressing concern was the state of affairs at our factories.

The visit to my own office and factory was the most dreadful thing I had to do after going through the storm last week. I was terribly self-conscious. The factory had been closed for three days after Simran's death, as a mark of respect for the departed soul. We had been totally confused ourselves on the day when Harish had gone to attend the cremation. He had asked me whether our senior staff should be allowed to be present there. But we knew that Unmesh might be brought there under police escort and the very thought of our staff seeing him in that condition was unbearable. So we had not disclosed any information about her cremation. Even on the third day, when the workers reported for work, normal production had not been undertaken. All sorts of rumors had floated, some even hinting that the factories might be closed as our whole family would be arrested.

I had informed the senior manager on the phone that I would be coming to the office and he should ensure that I did not face a crowd of sympathisers keen to meet me. I knew it was only wishful thinking that my arrival in the factory would pass off silently, as if nothing had happened in the last week. Sure enough, the security guard at the factory gate itself had appeared to be giving me a questioning look as he saluted me and opened the gate to let my car in. As I walked towards my office on the first floor, I expected all eyes to be following me. I felt as if I would be surrounded by all the employees and they will start chanting 'what happened?' 'what happened?', like a mantra. The humming of the machines would stop and the silence will ask me 'what happened?' The screen of the computer will display the letters dancing and jumping and finally coming to rest to form the question 'what happened?' The ticking of the wall clock in my office will sound 'what happened?' 'what happened?', sixty times a minute. My peon will bring my briefcase from the car and while keeping it on the table, ask me, 'what happened?'

But nothing happened! As if on a cue, everybody had become very discreet. The receptionist just got up from her seat and even her 'Good morning Sir' was hardly audible. Our senior manager entered my office like a whisper and just stood silently for a moment before he asked, 'Sir, how is Madam?' I could not have been more grateful to all of them. Their kindest act could have only been to kill their curiosity and to carry on as if nothing had happened. They all did carry out the charade with great aplomb.

The earlier part of the day was spent in being updated with new orders and enquiries, production figures, sales numbers and so on. Later, as I was reminiscing on the events before I went to Sanjay's office to meet our lawyer Tripathi, I received a call from Ratna. She spoke very softly, as if whispering on the phone, 'They have arrived'.

'Who has arrived?' I asked.

'The police', she whispered back. There was no reason to get shocked over this piece of news. We knew it was unavoidable, yet there was an element of surprise in it. I had planned to inform the police about our arrival later in the evening. The Suris must have come to know about our return from some neighbour of ours or from someone in the factory and informed the police I surmised. But the news did not bother me much. It had to happen sooner or later.

I intimated Harish and proceeded immediately to the nursing home. A sub-inspector of police was waiting for me at the reception. He gave me official intimation of Ratna being taken under police custody. He had been told by the Nursing Home staff that she was bedridden due to a severe attack of arthritis and could not be released. Hence, the formality of placing her under arrest at the Nursing home itself had been carried out and a lady police constable had been put on duty in her room. I asked the SI, if the constable will remain inside Ratna's room or outside. The SI smiled, '*Arre Sahib*, these are small things. Give her something for *chaipani* (tea) and I will ask these nursing home people to give her a chair to sit outside the room.' I did not fail to notice that while he had suggested that I give something for *chaipani* to the lady constable, he offered to talk to the nursing home staff himself to arrange a chair for the lady constable outside the room. I took the hint and reached my pocket to take out my wallet. But he stopped me, '*Arrey Sahib*, no need to worry for these small things.' By now I had heard too many times, '*Baad me dekh lenge*' from my three lawyer "brothers-in-law" (somehow all three lawyers I had met recently had called me Jijaji) and I had reached that stage of my learning process about the system when I could hear *'baad me dekh lenge'*, without its being said at all.

Ratna took the presence of the lady constable outside her room in her stride. 'If this is all it means to be arrested, I don't mind', she said with a smile.

'Let me see—how long we can keep you here', I said. I had not realised then that the Suris would also throw the gauntlet by saying at the same time, 'Let us see, how long you can keep her there!'

That evening, I met Tripathi for the first time in Sanjay's office in Sarita Vihar. I had not expected his office to be so specious and plush. His own personal office had a wall-to-wall carpet, a big teak table with a high revolving chair for him and four plush chairs in front for his clients. There was a desktop computer and a fancy pen stand with a clock adorning his table. The walls were covered with bookshelves full of leather bound volumes of law books and journals. The adjoining conference room had an oval table with seating arrangements for eight people. This room too had a wall-to-wall carpet. A secretary's table with a desktop computer was placed in a corner. Then there was a large room with tables and chairs for three junior lawyers. Another room for secretarial staff had three tables with desktop computers. All the rooms were air-conditioned. A small pantry and a washroom completed the set-up.

I was impressed by Sanjay's set-up. Just two days back the

dusty, dirty chai shops and pan-cigarette kiosks outside the Allahabad High Court and the crowded spaces inside the court had filled me with revulsion. There, I had seen many lawyers dressed in fading black coats and crumpled once-white trousers moving outside the court on cycle-rickshaws, frequently shooting out jets of paan juice and red saliva from their tobacco stained lips on to the footpath and road. Looking at many of them loitering around or sitting on the benches at chai-shops, scouting for potential preys, I had wondered if they could afford to pay the cycle-rikshaw fare from their day's earnings. But Sanjay's law firm had an air of opulence. When I met Tripathi, I found him smartly attired in a well-cut coat and spotless white trousers with knife edge crease. His black shoes must have been dusted with a soft cloth before he stepped out of his car. He was about fifty years old with a bald head, shining alert eyes and a pleasant smile on his face. He greeted me with a firm handshake and as soon as the introductions were over, he came straight to the point. 'You are fortunate that the girl's side have only indicted her husband and mother-in-law. They have not roped in the whole family which is the norm in such cases. But I will give credit to the smart legal advice given to them; this departure from the rut gives a complexion of genuineness to the complaint.'

I interrupted him, 'I can assure you Mr Tripathi, that my wife did not give any chance to Simran or her mother to foster any grudges or grievances. My elder daughter-in-law's father has been a solid pillar of support and help to us ever since. If we were the types who tortured a daughter-in-law for any reason, or if my wife had a bad reputation as a mother-in-law, he wouldn't have been running around the last week to help us in every possible manner. So please take it that the allegations made against Unmesh and my wife in Col Suri's complaint are baseless', I said in a serious tone.

Tripathi smiled faintly. 'Mr Asthana, it is important for me to know if there is even an iota of truth in the allegations. I am glad you have made it crystal clear. Tell me, is there any truth in the incident narrated in the complaint which alleges that about a year back, Simran had gone to her parents after being thrashed by Unmesh and had only returned to your house after a lot of persuasion and cajoling by her parents?' he asked.

I gave him the full details of that incident and insisted that it was an isolated incident and nothing like that ever happened again. Besides, I had myself gone there and apologised to her parents and assured them that I would personally ensure that such an incident never recurred. Tripathi said, I appreciate your candor Mr Asthana. At least now, it is clear why they have not targeted you too. But do try to remember if there was any occasion when you or Unmesh or your wife made any demands on her parents which could be called a dowry demand. Maybe, your wife said something to the deceased which could be misconstrued as a demand for dowry.'

I felt he was ruffling my feathers unnecessarily and said, 'I was married to Ratna thirty years ago. Seeking dowry was a very common practice even in those days. Yet no dowry had been demanded or taken by my parents even in my marriage. I have talked to my wife and enquired if she had ever made any such statement to Simran or her parents which could be misconstrued. She insists that I should have no such fear and I in turn assure you of the same.'

Tripathi then asked me to narrate the events of that fateful day. I took pains to narrate in great detail the activities of Unmesh, Ratna, Harish, Veena and myself from morning till night on that unforgettable day. Then I gave a full account of the chain of events after the discovery of Simran's body till date. I also showed him all the photographs that the photographer arranged by Saxena had taken. Tripathi took his time in studying the photographs. After seeing other photographs of the interior of Unmesh's room and attached toilet, he expressed a desire to see the site of the incident. I readily agreed. Sanjay, Tripathi and a stenographer accompanied me to my residence. The suite on the first floor had been sealed by the police after the body had been removed from there on the morning after. After our return from Allahabad when Ratna was put under arrest in the nursing home, they had come and broken the seal and informed Harish that we were free to use the suite now.

Harish told Tripathi that no one had entered the room even after the police had desealed it. Tripathi spent more than thirty minutes examining the washing machine on which Simran must have stood to reach the fan. It was still standing at a tilted angle against the wall. He then asked for a stool and when it was provided, he stood on it to peer down at the upper surface of the fan blades. He looked at the broken latch on the toilet door. I informed him that the police had taken possession of the broken piece of the latch, the scissors along with its broken pieces and Simran's dupatta which was used as a noose and also its cut portion hanging from the fan. I was amazed at the thoroughness of the inspection done by Tripathi. It was obvious that he was checking the veracity of my version of the events. He then asked me to show the photographs of family parties, picnics, get-togethers and outings in which Simran featured, particularly those taken during the last one year. He looked keenly at those photographs in which Ratna and I, and Harish and Veena had also featured alongside a laughing, smiling Simran. That wasn't difficult. There were scores of such photographs. Tripathi also asked if any letters written by Simran to Unmesh were available. We had no idea. There couldn't be too many since she also resided in the same city before marriage and telephonic chats, rather than letters, were the norm nowadays. I told Tripathi that we shall check with Unmesh when we visit him in the jail on the coming Sunday.

Quite unexpectedly, Tripathi asked me, 'Have you received a telephone call or a message from her people?'

'No. Should I expect one?' I asked.

'Well, you haven't been here in the first place. So even if they wanted to talk to you, they couldn't. I was just wondering if you have received any message sent by them through somebody else', he said, looking intently at me once again.

'No', I said but my curiosity was aroused. 'After lodging a

complaint which is full of lies, would he have the courage to face me or talk to me? And what would we talk about?' I asked.

'Well, we shall cross the bridge when we come to it. You will find out for yourself', he said mysteriously.

After spending more than an hour at my house, Tripathi and Sanjay went back to their office. In spite of my repeatedly asking Sanjay about his fees, the only answer that I had been able to elicit was, *'Baad me dekh lenge.* No need to worry on that account.'

I made one last effort to get some idea why Tripathi expected the Suris to contact me, but all I could elicit out of him was, 'Never mind, I just had a hunch! But do let me know if they contact you.' My curiosity was not quenched but I left it at that.

Fourteen

The Ghaziabad district jail at Dasna turned out to be totally different from the picture I had carried in my mind of all prisons. It was situated a good twenty kilometer from the city, amidst a large carpet of bewitching yellow and green threads of flowering mustard fields and yet to ripen wheat harvest. As one approached it on a narrow road going through the fields, waves of breeze rippled through the plants as if rising waves of water were rushing towards the beach on a tranquil sea. In the distant background, emerged the eighteen-foot high solid brick walls like a backdrop of very tall curtains on a vast stage. The barbed wire and broken glass pieces embedded on top of the wall presented a strange contrast to the pristine scenery all around. One saw the imposing prison gates as one approached closer.

Behind the huge main gate of the jail made of very thick steel bars, was a courtyard open to the sky with the jail Superintendent's and his Deputy's office in one wing and a few rooms for the staff in the other one. One had to obtain a visitor's pass before entering the main gate. After going through these formalities, one came out of the courtyard quite unexpectedly into a vast open arena. It was like a huge park with well-manicured hedges of green shrubs and dozens of flower beds. Winter is the season in our region for flowering plants to be in full bloom and the gardeners in the jail had done a great job of creating a beautiful and cheerful environment in a place one would normally associate with all that is depressing. I had been expecting to see a wire net separating the inmates from the visitors through which they could exchange some conversation in the presence of watchful guards. But the scene here was like a boarding school's garden in which parents and guardians had come to meet their wards. Groups of people were scattered all over the area, sitting on the grass and talking to the inmates. Very few inmates wore jail uniforms consisting of a white shirt, white pajama and a red cap. Most of the inmates were in their normal civilian clothes. Later I was told that only those already convicted and serving their sentences were in the prison uniform while the undertrials put on their normal clothes. Most visitors had brought food stuff with them and groups of people sitting on the vast lawns and sharing food gave an impression of a vast public park with picnickers squatting all over.

I had gone along with Harish to meet Unmesh. Ratna had

been terribly anxious about Unmesh. I had tried to console her at the nursing home and told her that she will be out very soon on bail. She had said very confidently, 'Of course I will be out, what have I done to deserve this? Only my heart bleeds for Unmesh. I wish I could meet him. God alone knows what he gets to eat there. My poor child!' she had said and then two drops of tears had silently rolled down her cheeks. But she had soon controlled herself. Wiping her tears, she had said, 'Do take full sleeves pullovers, a muffler and woolen socks for him. It must be getting colder by the day. Here I am, sitting in the warm comfort of such a nice room. I wonder if he is properly clothed or has sufficient blankets in the prison. Can you take blankets for his use in the prison?'

'I am not sure if they will allow me to carry all this into the prison. I will find out when I go to meet him on Sunday', I had said.

But Ratna was hardly listening. She had given me a long list of items which I should carry for Unmesh and then she had given detailed instructions to Veena about the food items she should pack for Unmesh when I went to visit him on Sunday.

So, now I was carrying in one hand a tiffin-carrier full of *puris*, *paneer-matar subzi*, fried rice and *kababs*. In my other hand, I was carrying a bagful of fruits. Harish was holding an airbag containing pullovers, woolen mufflers and socks for Unmesh. All the items had been checked when we had entered the prison and we had not been allowed to carry the blankets inside. We were directed towards one corner of the open lawns and asked to wait there while Unmesh was informed about us. As we reached that corner and stood awkwardly, the uneasy feeling and shame of standing inside a jail to meet my son, arrested on an awful charge, slowly evaporated into thin air. Its place was taken over by worry and concern about his health, not so much physical as psychological. Unmesh had been a good sportsman. He had represented his school and college in the interschool and intercollege athletics competitions. He had been a good footballer and a middle distance runner in his school. Later he had given up these sports but had continued playing badminton and regularly did weightlifting and dumb bell exercises to stay fit. I knew he would be able to cope up with the physical discomforts in the jail but I also knew he would be shattered from within. All the tensions and anxieties of the police case, arrest and custody in the jail would be nothing as compared to the trauma he must be undergoing due to the loss of Simran whom he had loved with utmost intensity.

I had never been able to forget the day he had broached the subject of marrying Simran in the park outside our house. How deeply he had loved her; and how utterly devastating was the method she had chosen to bid farewell to him was the overpowering thought in my mind when we saw him approaching us along with a warder. He was looking thin and had stubble on his face. He had been walking at a fast pace, but as soon as he saw us he broke into a jog. The warder accompanying him did not restrain him and he came to us with a beaming face. While

Ratna and I had been away on the last visiting day, Harish had been able to visit him for a short meeting. Harish had been able to give him some money too. Apparently there was no real restriction on giving money to the inmates regardless of its being against the rules. Harish had told us that Unmesh had not talked much about himself in that meeting. Most of the time, he had only kept enquiring about his mother and me. This last meeting had been very tearful, Unmesh had kept on reminiscing about Simran. Ratna had asked so many questions about Unmesh but Harish had avoided giving us any details about him. Now that Unmesh was coming towards me with a broad smile, his happiness could not be restrained. How much Ratna would have wanted being here to see, touch and embrace Unmesh! Yet, I was mortally afraid that she too might very well join him soon as an inmate in the prison. While I was wondering if she would be permitted to meet Unmesh, if and when she too was 'brought' in here, Unmesh hugged me. My eyes became moist and I had to exercise utmost control to restrain my tears from rolling down. I did not want to demoralise him. I tried hard to say something funny to cheer him up, just anything to lift his sprits. But all the funny remarks, all the wisecracks, proved elusive like chicks one would fail to catch by shoving a hand inside a big coop. I basked in the warmth of that hug and could barely whisper 'How are you, son?'

I was trying to search in his sad eyes that chirpy son of mine whom I had always found full of fun, bubbling with energy, effervescent with the discoveries of happiness even in simplest things of life. He had been a very playful child and even in very normal situations, he could always find something amusing like green blades of grass reaching out from dark crevices in rocky mountain sides. But now the pain of losing his beloved wife had been compounded by the fears of an unknown, uncertain future. He was weighed down with the enormity of finding himself behind bars, the consciousness of being the first person to be in this unenviable position amongst all our friends, relatives and acquaintance. Coupled with this was the acute anxiety of being crucified for a sin that he could not have even dreamt of committing. The knowledge that his mother too had been roped in and was helplessly sinking in a quagmire of utterly baseless and wild accusations had burdened him with acute anxiety and pain. Pitched against these anxieties, fears, trauma and helplessness, his valiant efforts to hide his emotions behind a façade of a forced smile were futile.

After an embrace which must have lasted a few minutes, he bombarded me with a thousand questions about Ratna's health. He wanted to know about the efforts we were making to get her released on bail. But more than anything else, he was curious to know if there was a change in the attitude of his in-laws. Somehow, he had retained a feeling that the Suris had made those false allegations as an immediate fallout of their extreme anguish. Even this, he thought, was a result of the provocation by distant relatives. He was hoping that once the immediate heat and fury of the shock subsided, they would realise the hollowness and cruelty of their allegations. He insisted that I go and talk to the Suris face to face. He felt that as a family of Army Officers they were honorable people; what they had done was only in the heat of the moment and they would be unable to face me if I went and asked them as to how they had invented the baseless story of dowry demand and torture of their daughter for the same.

The visiting hour was coming to an end. I was getting impatient with the optimism with which Unmesh was pinning his hopes on the very remote possibility of the Suris changing their stand on moral grounds. Finally, I had to cut him short, 'Look, Unmesh, let's not waste time on a course of action which we can consider at leisure, from all angles. You had better tell us something about yourself. Your Mom will ask me hundreds of questions about you. I can't just go and tell her that we spent all our time discussing our strategy about the case which is yet to begin and which, according to what I gather from my lawyers, will drag on for many months.' I was trying not to sound harsh in nipping his enthusiasm.

'Papa, you can see the general atmosphere here is not too bad. It is in fact far better than what I expected. This place is full of people charged with very heinous crimes like rape and murder. But there are a surprisingly large number of young people, many of them from very respectable families too, who are facing charges under the Dowry Prohibition Act. People here are outright sympathetic to those who are facing charges of ill-treating or torturing their wives for dowry as almost all such cases are highly fabricated. In fact, most of such cases are of reverse tyranny, in which the estranged wife or her people have made false allegations. They usually withdraw their allegations after reaching out-of-court settlement with the husband's side. The general feeling here is that such inmates remain inside the prison only as long as they are not able to make the necessary financial arrangements', he said.

'But what about the treatment meted out to those whose spouse has died due to alleged dowry harassment', I asked with a bit of hesitation.

'The treatment given by the prison staff is entirely unmindful of all these allegations. They give the best treatment to those coming from wealthy and influential families. Most of the time one can buy comfort. Secondly, they respect education', said Unmesh looking a bit relaxed.

'That puts you at an advantage, doesn't it?' I asked.

'Of course it does. Right now I am in the highest category due to these considerations. Other inmates in my barrack know about my family background and have high regards for my MBA degree. Of course, all of them do not even understand what the letters stand for. One guy asked me if it was an acronym for MA and BA degrees combined in one. Secondly, I have amongst my friends two guys here who are held in high esteem. One is a journalist, holding a Masters in Mass Communication, who exposed some ministers in a sting operation on TV and is cooling his heels here after being dragged in a false case. Then there is another one from a well-known industrialist family, who mercilessly beat a so-called trade union leader for demanding hush money. They find me good company and I welcome their friendship, as they have been here for about a month and enjoy a good reputation and rapport with the prison staff', Unmesh said. He had finished the food we had brought while talking to us. Some *kababs* and sweets were still left. These he wrapped in a paper napkin we had brought and took it back for his two friends he had talked about.

The red-capped warder reminded us that the visiting hours were over. As we started packing the empty tiffin carrier, Unmesh took out a few sheets torn from an exercise book and gave it to me. 'I knew I would find the visiting hours too short and I had planned to utilise the time in finding out all that is happening at home and with Mom. I have written a long letter here to you and Mom. It will answer all your questions regarding my life inside the prison. You may read it at leisure', he said.

I took the sheets of paper, folded them and put them in my pocket. Harish and I grabbed Unmesh in a tight embrace one by one and then turned back. He accompanied us till the entrance to the open yard and then another hug followed before we parted.

We came back through the prison's imposing entrance after showing our rubber stamped back of the palms and entering the time out column in the visitors' register. Harish and I remained lost in our thoughts for a few minutes as he drove back, and then I took out the folded sheets from my pocket and started reading Unmesh's letter. The sheets torn from a school exercise book must have been obtained from some warder. Unmesh had tried to utilise every bit of the space available, leaving no margins. I read on:

Dearest Mummy & Papa,

This is to tell you how much I love you and miss you all and also to tell you that I am absolutely fine here. There is so much to tell you that I don't know where to start.

I miss Simran a lot. I am not only sad but very much afraid of the uncertain future that awaits me. I try to avoid thinking of her as it makes me very sad yet I just keep thinking and wishing if only it had not happened. Anyway, I am alright except for the void that is there without her and without you all.

Well, let me change the subject and tell you of my daily routine. Everyone here has to get up before sunrise and go out of the large cell for a head count. As I have been here now for more than a week and because of my good credentials like education and family background, I, along with another five, am left to remain inside while the head count outside the cell is on. We live in a large hall-type cell which accommodates about 150 people. Each inmate has been given two blankets—one to sleep on and the other to cover himself. Of course, we all sleep on the floor. I am friendly with the cell warden—a fellow prisoner, who is himself from an influential family, hence I have three blankets. I spread two on the floor and do not feel cold. The cell is very large and has huge windows of the size of doors with thick steel bars, thus it is very well-ventilated and bright. There is no problem of mosquitoes as we cover our heads with the blankets because of the cold breeze blowing through the cell. Don't worry, I keep myself quite warm with my three blankets and three layers of clothing. I have got used to sleeping with a pullover and a jacket on.

I get up around six because of the noise at the time of the head count, but leave the bed only half an hour later when the head count is over. After that I do heavy exercises with two inmates, both of them charged with multiple murders. They beat me hollow at ethnic exercise like *dand-baithak* but appreciate my enthusiasm. The cell in which I stay is only for fresh under-trials or those under investigation. Inmates are all shifted to other cells after two to three days here. I, along with the cell warders who are four in number, will continue to stay here. I, because of my education and they being very well built and physically powerful enough to be useful in case of any eventuality in this cell. I am happy to stay in this cell as it is well-ventilated. But the flipside is that I don't have many good companions.

After the exercise, at about 7 o'clock, I go to the hospital and get some milk and two slices of bread—thanks to the money that Harish handed over during his last visit. The food I buy at the hospital is actually meant for sick prisoners admitted there. Initially I felt guilty about buying the food meant for them but I soon realised that the warders, in any case, carry the food home, if they are not able to sell it. The prisoners, sick or otherwise, will never get it. The breakfast provided to the prisoners comprises two or three very dry, hard and muddy chapatis with a cup of lukewarm black tea without sugar.

In the first few days here, I used to wander around in the garden after breakfast. But looking at the flowers and birds and the sky makes me very sad. All the time I keep imagining that Simran will come back to me in some new form. I used to look at the birds in the sky as if they will talk to me. A very strong feeling used to overtake me that Simran will try and interact with me in the form of a bird. Fortunately, with the arrival of the journalist inmate in my barrack, good sense gradually prevailed and I stopped walking around alone. I now try and spend all my time with these two boys and feel normal in their company. We get locked again in the cell at 11 am, after another headcount. In fact, this business of head counts seems to be going on all the time. I have managed to get some novels through the journalist friend and read till I start dozing and falling asleep. The cell is opened at 3 pm. I get some lunch from the prison hospital through the warder boys. I give them the money to get the food and we share it. But the problem is that the mugs in which he gets the *dal* and rice are quite dirty and covered with an even dirtier cloth to prevent flies from dropping in. There are swarms of flies over the cold food; cold because it is prepared in the morning. Yet the very sight of the food that other poor prisoners get, makes our food taste very delicious.

Bribery is enforced like a divine right by the prison staff. All the prisoners are made to clean the floors and the toilets. One can avoid cleaning the floors by paying Rs 100 weekly and avoid cleaning the toilets by paying Rs 500. Those who pay Rs 1000 can avoid doing any work or can chose to work in the kitchen or hospital or the garden. Anyway, this system at least keeps the prison reasonably neat and clean as there are a whole lot of very poor undertrials who cannot afford to pay any money to avoid work. They keep cleaning the toilets.

I take my bath at 3 pm at the hand pump in a corner of the courtyard outside my cell. The bath under the afternoon sun helps reduce the sting of the very cold water. After the bath, it is once again time to walk around with my cell mates. At 6.30 pm, after another headcount, we are counted and shut in the cell. There is a black & white television in each cell, which shows only the *Doordarshan* channel. The TV is kept in one corner of the hall next to the blankets of the *lal topi wallas*—ie. the monitors among the inmates serving sentences who wear the red caps. Usually they are the *Dadas* of the cell. I have been avoiding watching the TV only because I would then have to sit along with them and will have to cultivate their friendship. But loneliness does not appear to be a better alternative and I have, of late, started mixing with them. The biggest problem is that most of them, including the warders, are addicts of smack/heroin which they smoke at night. Actually, they too seem to avoid talking to me as they imagine that I am very well-connected and could have access to the jail authorities. This happened because the jail Superintendent talked to me in English during his rounds on the day after I arrived here. Actually, he just asked a few routine questions and then somehow got interested in my story and let me walk along with him for good fifteen minutes, chatting to me in English. He had mentioned that he had seen many cases like mine sorted out after the deceased wife's parents extracted large amounts of money from the accused husbands. Surprisingly, even after suggesting that I should work out a compromise with my in-laws, he said that I should not be in a great hurry to go out on bail as a very short stay inside the prison will only hurt my in-laws' ego.

Incidentally, in the event of my stay getting prolonged, admission into the prison hospital can also be considered. Like every other comfort, it has a price tag attached. But it does not appear too attractive a proposition as the prison hospital is dark and cold. Besides, the company of sick prisoners (if there are any genuinely sick ones therein) will only be depressing. In fact, I will volunteer to work in the prison and pass my time doing some community service.

Ma, I would like you to be mentally prepared for at least a three months' stay for me here before I am granted bail. Wish I could speak to you and hug you!

I love you, Mom and Papa,

Unmesh.

By the time we came back from the Dasna jail, it was late afternoon. Visiting hours to call on patients in New Light Nursing Home were from 5 pm to 7.30 pm but I knew I would have no problems in meeting Ratna, whenever it suited me. I proceeded straight from the jail to meet Ratna, after dropping Harish at his office enroute. When I entered Ratna's room, the lady constable who was sitting in a corner in Ratna's room gave me a smile and tactfully retreated and occupied the chair outside the room. I was alone with Ratna. She was so keen to hear all about Unmesh that she barely allowed me to give her a tight hug and a kiss. She almost wriggled out of my embrace and started bombarding me with a thousand questions about Unmesh. The questions ranged from what Unmesh was looking like to the minutest details about his routine. I gave Unmesh's descriptive letter to Ratna. She kissed the neatly folded letter umpteen times, then opened it and got deeply immersed in it. Having read it once, she started reading at all over again. I waited patiently and after she had read the letter twice, I was ready to answer all the supplementary queries.

After I had spent about an hour-and-a-half with Ratna, Harish joined us. I left him with Ratna and went to meet Tripathi.

Fifteen

Tripathi had drafted the application seeking bail for Ratna and Unmesh, which he was confident of obtaining. He warned me, 'Mr Asthana, from now onwards, things will take their own time. The police have been granted two weeks time to complete their initial investigation. That time is now over. They will now seek extension of his judicial custody and will oppose our bail application. That is the norm even in open and shut cases. We should be able to get the bail from the District and Sessions Judge's Court, though in a very large majority of cases under Sections 498 and 304, the bail applications do get rejected at the District level and normally, the relief is obtained only from the High Court. In our case, the social standing and track record of the accused and their family, their educational and financial background and the apparent lameness of the accusations without any supporting documents or evidence being provided along with the FIR are all very strong grounds to obtain bail.'

I said, 'I am hundred per cent sure that the Suris just cannot produce any evidence at all, whether personal or documentary, to substantiate their allegation of dowry harassment.'

'No. All that is not going to be decided at this stage. That will come when the police complete their investigations and file a charge sheet against the accused in the court. Right now, it is only to be seen whether the accused will abscond if freed on bail or their personal security is better ensured by keeping them in prison. None of these factors pose any problems in our case', said Tripathi. 'Bail cases do not take very long to get decided. The pronouncement will be made by the judge immediately after he has heard both sides in the same session. Normally, a detailed judgment is not given. So nothing very spectacular is going to happen in the whole process.'

I became excited and very optimistic. 'That means Unmesh and Ratna should be free on bail within a day or two?' I asked.

'Unfortunately, no. It is usual to grant judicial custody in such a case for at least two to three consecutive fortnights. Besides, the actual conditions in the District Courts, particularly in Uttar Pradesh, are not very propitious for smooth and orderly working. Adjournments on very flimsy grounds, lawyers' strike, Court workers' strike, condolence meetings, unexpectedly declared government holidays, non-availability of the counsels or the litigants or even the judges and magistrates themselves on personal grounds on a given day, it all takes a toll. Fortunately, this malady though rampant in civil cases, is not so bad in criminal cases. Now tell me how is Unmesh doing in the jail? I hope he is not too depressed. In fact, Mrs Asthana must be very anxious about him.'

'He is facing it boldly', I said with pride. 'As for Ratna, she is feeling relieved after I told her at length about my meeting with Unmesh in the jail. Unmesh has sent her a letter giving a graphic description of jail life.'

Tripathi's smile was indeed very faint and very short. He again assumed a serious expression, 'I am glad he does so. It will prepare Mrs Asthana mentally if she herself gets shifted to the jail.'

I almost jumped with apprehension. 'Is that a real possibility? Do you think we won't be able to keep her at the nursing home till she is freed on bail', I asked.

'Well, I can't say I would be surprised if the Suris do not try and do everything possible to ensure that she goes to jail. After all they have gone a great length to harm you all and must be disappointed to learn that she is comfortably ensconced in the private ward of the best nursing home in Noida', said Tripathi.

I was taken aback. If Ratna was removed from the nursing home and sent to the jail, it could possibly break her indomitable spirit. This time, without speaking a word, my facial expression said it all. Tripathi's voice was very reassuring when he said, 'Let it not bother you too much. We shall cross the bridges when we reach them. Mr Asthana, justice may not always be bought but comfort certainly can be. As far as the stigma of arrest is concerned, it remains the same whether one is under arrest in a jail or in a nursing home.'

Tripathi's statements turned out to be quite prophetic.

The very next day, while I was in my office in the afternoon, I got a call from Ratna. Strangely, she spoke in a whisper, 'They have come to shift me from here to the jail.' I wondered why she was whispering. If anything, it should have been a shriek.

'Who has come?' I asked.

'The police, who else? You must come immediately. They seem to be in a great hurry. The lady constable has allowed me to use the phone one last time. After this call they will seize it. We shall be leaving in the next five minutes. Dr Rathore is here along with the police team and is very apologetic that he couldn't prevent this. But you relax. I am not nervous. In fact, I am happy that I will be able to meet Unmesh. Bye! Take care', and the phone became quiet. I clicked on her number again but just after a ring, her phone was switched off. I tried again but this time it said the number called had been switched off.

I rushed out, jumped into my car and drove frantically towards the nursing home. On reaching there, I learned that Col Suri had put up an application in the CJM's Court, complaining that Ratna was feigning illness to avoid going to the jail. The CJM had, therefore, ordered that Ratna would be shifted to Dasna jail where she should be examined by jail doctors and if needed, she would then be shifted to the jail hospital or the District Government Hospital at Ghaziabad. I was advised to wait till the next day before I went to see Ratna in the jail, as the jail authorities would not allow a visit on the same day after completing the formalities at their end. I went to the Accounts Section to clear the nursing home bill. It was a hefty bill; the room charges were as high as in the costliest hotel, at least in Noida, but the period of her stay had been very short. Other expenses for medicines and specialist medical care, never actually provided, had also been put in the bill. I was advised that I need not pay that amount. I went to Dr Rathore's office once again to thank him and asked him why he had prescribed so many medicines and such expensive specialist medical care for her arthritic problems which were routinely being treated without much fuss. He winked at me and said with a smile, 'This and our medical report will help you shift her from the jail to the District Hospital within the next two or three days. And I know the right people in the District Hospital to arrange a nice private ward room for her.' I breathed a sigh of relief.

I got into touch with Tripathi, He was not surprised to hear of the developments. He advised me to go and meet the jail officials and put up an application for shifting Ratna to the District Government Hospital. I was to attach New Light Nursing Home's medical certificate, bill and her medical history with my application. The next day was spent in doing exactly what Tripathi and Dr Rathore had suggested. After I pulled some strings, Ratna had to spend only two more days in her prison barrack. She was shifted to the District Hospital, where as hinted by Dr Rathore, it turned out to be quite an easy task to get her a private ward room and the assurance that she would not be sent back in a hurry as long as suitable remedial measures were taken by us! On Sunday, Ratna was comfortably occupying a room in the private ward of the district hospital. It was, in fact, a suite with a smaller room, a kitchenette and a toilet at the back. A lady constable was present inside the room. She promptly moved a chair outside the room and sat down there. Harish and I sat down and listened to the amazing tale Ratna told us about her two days in the district jail at Dasna. I am reproducing her story in her own words:

> New Light Nursing Home was plush, with shining floors, glass and chrome all around. I was seated in a wheel chair as soon as our car stopped in its portico and then quickly shifted to a beautiful garden-facing room. My blood pressure and other parameters were checked by a continuous stream of doctors and nurses, as if I were in a very serious condition! I stayed here for three days.
>
> On the third day, Vinod and Harish left after the visiting hours ended. A light dinner was served at 7 pm. As I was left all alone in the room, I tried to sleep but it kept eluding me for very long. Next morning again a stream of nurses, matron and doctors woke me up a bit too early for my liking. The room was done up and I was given a light breakfast. I was told to be ready to go for physiotherapy at 11 am. Some soup was served before that. It was lukewarm and tasteless and did nothing to

lift my depression. I told the ward boy sternly that I liked my soup piping hot. But before he could replace it, another female attendant brought a wheel chair, asked me to get in and moved it to the physiotherapy department, which was very impressive with a large array of gadgets. I was enjoying the warmth provided by the electrical heating pad placed on my knees, when my mobile phone suddenly rang. To my surprise, it was Dr Rathore, the Director of the Nursing Home. He gave me a shock of my life by informing me that thc police had arrived to take me to the prison. The police had already reached the reception. I suddenly felt cold and numb and almost stopped breathing. The nurse saw my strange expression and enquired if the heating pad was too hot. I wondered what to tell her. I rang up Vinod and tried very hard to sound composed but knew that my voice was a giveaway. But soon after informing Vinod, my defence mechanism started working. I slowly got over the shock. I reminded myself that it was a good opportunity to meet Unmesh. I was dying to meet him and hug him to soothe his anguish and pain. There was a knock at the door. A police woman entered the room and asked the nurse to take me in the wheel chair to the reception and thence to the police van waiting outside. I had managed to inform Vinod but he couldn't make it before the police van drove off to Dasna jail with two uniformed escorts sitting beside me.

When the vehicle stopped in front of the huge gates of the jail, my escorts got busy in collecting the documents kept in the van. I stepped out of the van. I was dressed in a good sari with a nice leather bag hanging from my shoulders. My make up was quite intact. I did not wait for my escorts and started walking towards the prison gate with such confident strides that the sentry standing with a rifle in his hands got thoroughly confused. His tone was polite when he asked me where exactly I was going. I gave a very concise reply, 'Inside, where else?' He was still gaping at me as I entered the small gate within the huge gates and found myself facing another gate with a huge padlock. The policewoman escorting me had caught up by now. The padlock was opened for her. I accompanied her and found ourselves in a big courtyard. I stood looking around as the policewoman entered details in a register. At the end of the courtyard, some inmates were sitting on the ground near a barrack-type structure. A female warder walked up to me and asked, 'So, you are the one who killed her daughter-in-law?' I was very annoyed and barked back, 'It was a suicide. I had nothing to do with it.' She nodded her head. 'Yes, this is what they all say. But I know ninety per cent of them are right when they say this in such cases. You won't be the only one here paying for other's greed.'

She showed me a thin jute mat spread on the ground to sit on. Soon, quite a few inmates surrounded me, gaping at me curiously. Without bothering to say as much as 'by your leave', a middle aged inmate caught hold of my leather bag, opened it and started examining the sunshades and make-up cosmetics kept inside the bag. I was hungry but it was past 3 pm and apparently there was no question of any food. I fondly remembered the lukewarm soup which I had rejected in the nursing home and here I was, now myself in a thick soup!

The senior inmate baffled me by giving a very deferential treatment. She offered me a glass of tea brewed in milk, instead of water. I gratefully gulped down the tea. I was dying to meet Unmesh and asked her if she could help me. She snapped her fingers to enquire if I had money. I showed her a hundred rupee note. She grabbed the note greedily and went and said something to the warder. Soon I was taken out from there to a distant barrack on the other side of a vast ground. I found Unmesh waiting outside. Tears welled up in my eyes when I saw him standing unshaven and unkempt, and looking so morose and weak. I hugged him, wishing I could erase all his anguish and pain. We sat in a green patch of the grass and started talking hungrily. He had brought a packet of potato chips for me, besides a blanket. He warned me that the nights would be too cold to brace with the two blankets provided in the jail, as one had to sleep on the floor and the barrack was in fact a vast verandah-type structure with two sides open and grilled with steel bars. A cold breeze started blowing as the darkness set in. The female warder asked me to wind up the meeting with my son. Soon it was dark. The inmates were lined up and counted. Then we were herded on the long verandah. I was so happy after meeting Unmesh that the prospect of a cold night, sleeping on the floor did not upset me. I did not know where to spread my blanket and was guided by the senior inmate who acted as a warder. She explained that inmates belonging to upper strata of society slept on one side and the less fortunate ones slept near the foul smelling toilet end. The blankets were spread on the floor, practically overlapping each other as the number of inmates was very large. I put on all my clothes and tried to cover myself with the blanket provided by Unmesh. The other two blankets provided by the warder were too foul smelling to be used. Next morning when I got up I found some inmates sweeping the floor and some others cleaning the lavatory. I was told that the lavatory cleaning duty could be avoided by greasing the palms of the warders.

The meeting with Unmesh the previous evening had greatly elevated my mood. I was assigned no task and was looking around curiously, trying to absorb the morning scene. To my surprise, I found quite a few very young children, adoloscent girls and young girls inside the barrack. They, I was told, had nowhere else to go, hence had been allowed to stay in the prison along with their mothers who were under custody. They were all squatting in various corners with sad and dull expressions on their faces. I tried to gather some of them near me. I wished to engage them in some game. But their expressions and response remained sluggish. I gave some money to the warder, requesting for a ball and some toffees. These were soon brought to me. This time I declared that we shall play a game of dog and the bone, and the winners shall get toffees as prize. Soon the numbers swelled and after a competitive game of dog and the bone, we moved on to the ball game of seven tiles. The girls were really thrilled. After the games, I shook hands with the winners and distributed toffees and there was almost a stampede of excited, happy and shrieking children. After some time the bell rang, announcing lunch time. All the inmates lined up with bowls in their hands. They got some boiled cauliflower with hardly any salt or spices, some watery dal, thick half-cooked chapattis and boiled rice of very rough quality. Some inmates showed me worms floating in the cauliflower vegetable. A further shock awaited me when I found all the 'upper strata' type inmates throwing away their vegetables and rice and retaining only the chapattis and dal. I was told that the chapattis would be dried up in the sun and used as a fuel to make tea, and the dal would be improved by adding some fresh vegetables grown by the inmates in a patch outside the barracks. After lunch, I sat down with the inmates who were by now treating me with a lot of respect. I listened to their tales of woes, many of them so horrifying that I forgot all my personal problems. Most of them had lost all hopes of ever going out of the prison. They had no idea when their case would be heard in the court next. There were many who had been there for years and the world outside seemed to have just forgotten all about them. And worst of all was the misery of those who were not sure that they would be accepted back in their family, even if they did manage to get released from the prison by some miracle. A young Bangladeshi woman came to me with an unexpected request. She gave me a phone number on a small chit of paper. She had been picked up by the police as an illegal immigrant while going back to her slum from her employer's house, where she worked as a housemaid. Her four-year-old daughter was left alone with an unemployed lout of a father. She wanted me to contact her employer on the phone number she had given, and request her to take care of her daughter. I promised to do so whenever I had an access to a phone. I was able to do so the next day, with the warder's help, little anticipating the question her employer would ask me. I stumbled when she asked me how I met her in the jail. I gulped and then readily invented a lie – 'I had gone to look up my maid in the jail. I met this maid of yours there.' The lady was quick to congratulate me for having the guts to go and meet my maid in the prison! She would have fainted, she said, oh so delicately, if she had to enter the prison and then she went on to congratulate me for doing this tough but voluntary social service!

The Suris were successful in not letting Ratna stay in the comfortable nursing home and had ensured her being shifted to the jail. But they would never have imagined that she would get moved to the private ward of the District Hospital from the jail so soon. Had they seen how much at ease she was in the District

Hospital, they would have raised a lot of stink again. Fortunately, they still had no idea, nor did I have any inkling earlier, that the District Government Hospital's private ward was in many ways far better than even the Nursing Home's. Here, in the private ward one attendant could stay with the patient all the time. Practically, there was no restriction of limited visiting hours. Cooking was permitted in the kitchenette, and if one wanted, one could get quite good food delivered from a number of restaurants in the vicinity of the Hospital. Orthopedic patients, particularly those suffering from arthritic pains, could be retained for pretty long. Nobody seemed to be in a hurry to throw out patients under arrest back to the prison. My elder sister volunteered to give company to Ratna as an attendant and when she arrived, Ratna declared that it was a going to be a wonderful holiday away from the pulls and pressures of running a home and a factory.

We remained anxious about Unmesh, but on our visits on Sundays we found that he too had settled into the prison's routine. But sadness oozed out of his eyes; his tormented soul remained lost in the memories of Simran. In comparison, all the inconvenience and sufferings of prison life became utterly insignificant.

Sixteen

The hearing of the bail application kept getting postponed for some silly reason or the other but ultimately the day arrived when we found ourselves sitting in the court of the District and Sessions Judge for the hearing. By now I had got used to the filth and dirt, the crowded corridors and dark dingy court rooms of the magistrates. Frequent power failure forced the proceedings to be carried out in almost dark rooms, with only a single battery-operated emergency light on the magistrate's table and another one on his reader's table. Fortunately, it was the cold month of January and the packed court room without a whiff of fresh air did not become as suffocating as it would become in the summer months. There used to be continuous murmur of voices within the courtrooms and the magistrates would get totally exasperated by continuously reminding people to keep quiet. A couple of policemen and a court orderly within the room would be busy reminding and cajoling people to keep their mobiles switched off. The courtrooms looked more like a weakly bazaar on the footpaths of Noida, rather than temples of justice which they were purported to be.

Ours was the first bail petition to be heard that day and when the court orderly loudly proclaimed, State of UP v/s Unmesh and Ratna Asthana, there was a sudden hush. Even the soft murmurs stopped. The court room was packed to capacity. A case of Dowry Death involving two well-placed, well-educated families and a young Director of a factory was naturally a big-ticket event. Two months ago, it had aroused a lot of curiosity after it was reported in all the Hindi newspapers and most English newspapers read in Noida, and public curiosity had not yet lost its sheen. Tripathi, his junior lawyer, Harish, I and a few close friends of mine were present in the court, while only the government counsel representing the State of UP was present to oppose the bail application. I did not see Simran's parents, brother or uncle in the courtroom.

A little after 10 o'clock, the District Judge made his appearance in the court room where his Reader and many lawyers were already seated. He was in his late fifties, with salt and pepper hair and neat attire. His sharp intelligent eyes looking alertly through dark-framed bifocals gave him an impressive personality. He took his high-backed chair on the raised dais and ordered the court proceedings to begin in the bail applications of Ratna and Unmesh. Tripathi walked up in front of the judge, bowed courteously and began his pleading for the grant of bail to the prime accused, Unmesh.

He began by stating that the petitioner was only 26-years-old, had never been involved in any offence and had been falsely implicated. He then gave a short detail of his academic achievements which ended with an MBA degree, his work experience in a leading private sector bank where he had been given excellent reports and was drawing a handsome salary before he resigned and joined his father's business. Then he went on to narrate the events of that fateful day when Simran had been found hanging in her room. The action of Unmesh's father (myself) in calling a doctor, informing the police, informing the brother and uncle of the deceased as her father could not be contacted and their never leaving the house in the next twenty-four hours was highlighted.

Tripathi went on to say that as per the prosecution, neither Unmesh nor the co-accused Ratna, were present after the incident and that Unmesh had been apprehended the next day by the police on the information provided by a source. This was a patently false claim. The police had been called up immediately by the father of the accused, after the death was discovered and thereafter, he and his whole family had spent the entire night and the next day at their house. The dead body was removed at 12 noon the next day. Many photographs, taken when the dead body was being taken for post-mortem, showed that the accused was present there along with his whole family. In fact, the accused appeared in the photographs while carrying the dead body on a stretcher in which two policemen could also be seen and subsequently another photograph showed him leaving the spot as a pillion rider on a policeman's motor bike. All the photographs showed the time and date as recorded automatically by the camera. Hence, the entire story of the petitioner being arrested by the police while trying to escape was concocted and false.

I suddenly remembered how irritated I had been with the photographer's presence and his activities. I had found it obnoxious that he was taking snaps of Unmesh carrying the stretcher down and to the ambulance, of our family members surrounding the ambulance and of Unmesh leaving with the policemen on his motor bike, while Ratna and I were talking to the sub-inspector. All these photographs were now produced in the court, along with the extracts of the police case diary to establish how the police had concocted a vicious story of Unmesh trying to flee his residence soon after the death. Tripathi then described how the parents of the deceased were opposed to her marriage to the accused from the beginning. Her parents' opposition to her marrying outside her community and her subsequent suicide attempts were disclosed. He mentioned the scar on her left wrist, which had also found mention in the post-mortem report, as an indelible evidence of her earlier suicide attempt.

Tripathi went on to establish that Simran was married both per Sikh and Vedic Hindu rights out of respect for her religion and had been very well-treated at her husband's home. Details of various functions, picnics and family outings were given with photographs of all these events, apart from details of her excursions and tours with her husband alone to show how cheerful and happy she looked in all those photographs. Documentary evidence of her earlier employment in a different company before marriage, and after marriage her subsequent employment in her husband's factory at a much higher remuneration, her independent savings bank accounts in which this salary was deposited, her independent credit cards and even bills of purchases made by her during the last six months for her own wardrobe and accessories were presented. This was to establish that she enjoyed full freedom in spending money for her own needs and desires and drew good salary from the same in-laws' factory, who had been accused of demanding money from her and her parents.

Tripathi then went on to establish how her father-in-law had quit the Indian Air Force to establish a very successful business. He gave a short history of how their family business had grown into three factories having a good total turnover. These factories had been set up by taking longterm loans from financial institutions, which had all been dutifully returned on due dates. That they employed a total of more than a hundred workers and had been contributing good amounts in sales and income taxes to the state exchequer was mentioned. He even gave figures from the Income Tax returns of the companies as well as personal Income Tax returns of Unmesh, his father, mother and brother to establish that the whole family was quite affluent. He established that the deceased was kept in the matrimonial home with absolute love and affection, had been given complete freedom of conduct and of visiting her parents whenever she wished (though she visited them only thrice during the last two years). But on occasions, she did show sudden and impulsive fits of anger on trivial issues, displaying her short temper and impetuous nature and then the details of her consultation with a psychiatrist and the doctor's prescription and her subsequent refusal to continue the treatment were given.

Tripathi then produced certain documents in Simran's own handwriting in which she had described herself as very short-tempered, stubborn, jealous, highly egoistic and as a 'crybaby', with a tendency to get a sudden surge of anger. This was how Simran had described various facets of her personality to a homoeopathic doctor from whom she had taken treatment and who wanted a self-description from his patients before prescribing the treatment. Tripathi had sorted this out from a bagful of personal papers, letters etc. of Simran, made available to him by Unmesh. He also mentioned that neither specific acts of violence or torture, nor any documentary evidence of dowry demands had been mentioned in the FIR which was quite vague in its language. Thus the story of dowry demands and ill-treatment of the deceased held no water. The post-mortem report also did not indicate any violence on the body of the deceased and supported the fact that it was clearly a case of suicide but that could be discussed later as and when a charge sheet was filed.

Under the circumstances there was no ground to show any complicity of the accused in the death of the deceased, nor was there any question of his or his family not cooperating with the police in its investigations. Thus, the accused Unmesh definitely deserved to be freed on bail.

Coming to the bail application of Ratna, which was being jointly heard with that of Unmesh, Tripathi highlighted some other points. He introduced Ratna as an educated lady with postgraduate degrees, who actively worked as a Director of the family's companies and paid a high income tax. She was in her late fifties and was suffering from chronic arthritis and osteoporosis for quite some time which had become acute of late. He produced documentary evidence to support these facts.

Tripathi now took up the psychological aspects of Simran's personality. Simran, he said, was an emotionally unstable person who used to get over-excited and altogether hysterical if she was denied what she desired. He described in detail the events at the Gurudwara that fateful morning and later on, the outbursts of Simran and retorts by Unmesh in the factory office due to which she had become uncontrollably angry and enraged even within the earshot of the employees within the factory premises.

Tripathi wound up by pointing out that the family business was being run with the active help of the owner's wife, son and daughter-in-law. One of them was no more and if the other two were denied bail, it would become impossible to run the factories.

This would affect a workforce of about a hundred workers directly employed therein. In view of all that had been explained, both Ratna and Unmesh deserved to be set free on bail.

There was a wave of murmur in the court after Tripathi wound up. One thing was sure; Tripathi was an excellent and forceful speaker. He had spoken very fluently in English in this court where normally only Hindi was spoken. Call it a legacy of the colonial spirit, or an expression of our deep-rooted inferiority complex, but English has an upper hand in impressing people. This is just a statement of fact. The judge had been intently listening to that long and forceful speech of Tripathi. He had not interrupted even once and had appeared to be paying full attention to every word. Now with a flourish of his hand he invited the District Government Counsel (DGC) to state his reasons for opposing the bail.

DGC Gopal Singh was known to be good at his job. Tripathi had warned me that he was an upright man who took his job seriously. He adjusted the white band around his neck, adjusted his golden framed spectacles, cleared his throat and then opened his tirade in a booming voice. He chose to speak in Hindi and spoke very fluently and confidently. He gave a short summary of the events and background as narrated in the complaint of Col Suri. And then he used the very information provided by Tripathi regarding the educational background and social and financial standing of our family to buttress his fear that such a family could very well try and influence the witnesses if the accused were granted bail. He also took up Ratna's health issue and said that as she was getting the required medical facilities in the District Hospital, therefore, she need not be freed on that account. He emphasised that Unmesh was in the prime of his youth and could very well abscond and hence must be kept in judicial custody till the case reached its final conclusion.

The government counsel kept on harping on these points and the judge had to remind him that he was repeating himself. I was glad that the photographs showing Unmesh and his brother and parents near the ambulance in the presence of policemen and later his going with the policeman on his motor bike had torn the police story of his absconding to shreds. So the fears of the counsel did not have feet to stand on.

When the DGC concluded I expected Tripathi to get up for a rebuttal but he kept seated. The proceedings had already taken about four hours. Tripathi alone had spoken for almost two hours during which he had submitted a whole lot of documents. I had been told that in bail applications, the judge usually passes his order immediately after the hearing. But we were in for a surprise. The judge reserved his order for the next day and the Court rose for the lunch break.

Ratna and Unmesh were taken back with Police escort to the district hospital and district jail respectively. Harish, Veena and I came back home after thanking Tripathi and appreciating his convincing and forceful presentation of the case. The next day brought immense joy in our tense lives when the judge declared that both Unmesh and Ratna were to be set free on bail. Each one had to offer two sureties of Rs one lakh each and were directed to appear in the Court whenever summoned to do so.

The wonderful news was conveyed immediately to the jail authorities by us requesting them to intimate Unmesh and Ratna accordingly. But we had to furnish two sureties each for Ratna and Unmesh. We did not have to look far for this. There were a whole lot of friends and relatives to oblige us. But the procedure was time consuming and it was 4 pm by the time we could complete the formalities. Then we had to rush to the district jail to convey the order and in order to release Ratna, the jail authorities had to send the order with their endorsement to the District Hospital. By the time we reached the jail, it was almost 6 pm and past the working hours of the jail office. Harish, Veena and I could not even meet Unmesh that day. It was like a bucket of cold water poured over our feverishly happy mood but we made it up by going to Ratna's room in the District Hospital and celebrating there. We offered sweets to the policewoman on duty in Ratna's room and to the hospital staff looking after her. A visit to the temple for thanks giving was postponed till Unmesh also joined us. Harish, Veena, my sister and I spent the whole evening in Ratna's room and returned home at about 10 pm. Sleep eluded me for many hours and finally, when I went to sleep in the wee hours, I kept on dreaming about Ratna and Unmesh.

Seventeen

Although the jail authorities had assured us that their courier would convey the bail order to the District Hospital as soon as their office opened on Saturday, we had by now a fair idea of how the system moved. So we did the needful to provide the motivation. In order to doubly ensure that there was no delay, I sent Harish early in the day to the jail to follow up on the delivery of the bail order through the official courier latest by 12.30 to complete the formalities, failing which Ratna's release would get postponed till Monday. Those in the jail office knew very well the importance an early dispatch of this order had for us and would ask for their pound of flesh. So I instructed Harish to 'motivate' the office staff further, over and above what had been done the previous evening. Within five minutes of this instruction to Harish, the confirmation came that the courier was on his way, cheerfully taking a lift in Harish's car. Of course he would claim travel allowance for this journey to and fro later, after accepting the return auto fare from Harish. Because of the rush to reach the District Hospital in time to manage Ratna's release, Harish had not been able to pick up Unmesh from the district jail. I had also gone directly to the hospital to ensure that no unexpected glitches cropped up in getting her released.

I synchronised my arrival at the District Hospital with that of Harish. As soon as we reached there, Harish went to the Hospital office with the courier and I rushed to Ratna's room. But I could have never imagined that I would find Ratna in such a foul mood. She was utterly annoyed and her face was red with rage. She was so angry that she took some time to cool down before she could describe the reason for her anger. When I heard her story I could not help smiling. What transpired was this. Ratna was very excited that morning with the prospect of her release. The policewoman on duty at her room, the cleaning people and the duty nurse who came in the morning had all been told by her excitedly that she was going home. But the orthopedic surgeon attending on her had been very curt when he came for his round in the morning. He did not share Ratna's enthusiasm and had just carried on with his visit to other rooms. After about fifteen minutes a male nursing attendant had come and conveyed his instruction to Ratna, 'Tell your husband to see me as soon as he can, otherwise you won't be able to reach home in a hurry.' Ratna was shocked and then she was furious. She knew very well the price that was being paid for her being retained in the hospital. An assurance had been given that she could stay there as long as we desired and there would not be a need for her to be sent back to the prison in a hurry. Apparently, a price had to be paid even for walking out of the private ward and not only for walking in. She now felt scoffed and slighted. She told the messenger that she wanted to see the doctor but he came back telling her that the doctor would not be able to see her before 1 pm and if she wanted to get released that day, her husband should talk to him.

Poor doctor! How badly had he underestimated Ratna! Furious like a hungry tigress, she had walked out of her room and found her way to the doctor's room where she found him chatting with some people. Without waiting for his permission, she had gatecrashed into his office and asked, 'Is this gossip session keeping you so busy that you cannot see me before 1 pm?'

The doctor was angry too. He had not assessed the opponent accurately. He growled, 'How can you walk into my office like this? I don't owe you an explanation for my activities.'

'Well, I am already in your office, so that's how I can walk in and I shall tell you why you owe an explanation to me. I am the one who has obtained a bail order from the Court. I am not going to stay here even for one hour beyond the time the order is delivered in the jail office.'

The doctor was equally furious now. 'Oh yes, you would! What is more, I will send you back to the jail. You can take your release from there and since it is a weekend, you will cool your heels there till Monday.'

'Oh really?' Ratna exclaimed. She pointed a finger at the doctor, 'You think I don't know at what price I am being kept here? How can you be so greedy?' She brought the accusing finger within an inch or so of the doctor's nose and screamed, 'You want me to expose you loudly in front of this audience? Don't you dare threaten me with another day's stay in the jail. I have already been there for a couple of days for no fault of mine. What difference would it make if I have to stay there for a few more days? I cannot earn greater notoriety by staying therein for two more days but I shall have the pleasure of teaching you a lesson on how to talk to a lady, or probably you think one who is even falsely implicated in a criminal case does not deserve to be treated like a lady!'

The doctor beat a hasty retreat from his own office. Ratna thought that he would come back with the Hospital Superintendent or some security staff. While she was contemplating what to do next, the clock in the doctor's office struck one and she came back to her room grumbling furiously. When she found me there, she ran into my arms. I hugged her and whispered in her ear, 'Harish is in the Hospital office, we are going out to pick up Unmesh in a few minutes.'

Only a few minutes later Harish also turned up at her room. He hugged her, lifted her up and pirouetted around, with Ratna happily and excitedly shrieking and flapping her arms in the air with mock anger. I would have given up a kingdom to do that myself even before Harish lifted her up. But my middle-class upbringing made me too self-conscious to express my joy with such gay abandon, with many strangers watching us. Harish did not spare me. He chuckled loudly and said, 'Papa, don't be such a prude. Ok. Don't kiss Mom but at least give her a tight hug! Everybody knows she is your wife. Nobody would object.'

I blushed deeply at the suggestion from my Bollywood-inspired son. But I replied to the banter in the same spirit, 'Yeah, I know you want me to set a precedent so that you can be quite free with your wife whenever you wish!'

Once Harish put her back on terra firma after a few pirouettes, Ratna swayed for a few moments like a palm tree in high winds. Once she became steady she extended her hand coyly and quite self-consciously uttered just three words, 'How are you?'

I was too overwhelmed emotionally to respond to this. I just held her hands and gazed into her eyes, drinking in her happiness with my eyes till Harish again mockingly said, 'Alright! If that's all you are going to do, let's go to pick up Unmesh.'

While Harish was escorting Ratna to the car, I dropped in at the doctor's office, where he had come back. He looked at me sheepishly. I thanked him without showing him that I knew what had happened there a few minutes earlier.

We did not take long to reach the district jail and once there, we did not have to wait for any more formalities and paperwork. Somebody was sent to fetch Unmesh from his barrack. I expected him to be back in a few minutes with Unmesh probably coming on a run but was disappointed. Unmesh took more than twenty minutes to reach us. It was Ratna's turn to take the lead in hugging him. She held him so long in a tight, silent hug that Harish had to mock her once again by saying, 'Yeah, we know who holds all rights over this property but how about giving a chance to us poor bystanders too.' Ratna did not react to the mocking suggestion. She just held on to Unmesh, as if clutching a mast in a ship amidst a storm. After what was an endless wait for me, when she ultimately released Unmesh from her vice-like grip I found she had done something quite uncharacteristic of her. Second or third time within the last few cruel months; her cheeks were tear stained.

But what surprised us most was the expression on Unmesh's face. There were no smiles; there were no tears. He was grim, with a faraway look in his eyes, apparently burdened with painful memories of Simran. Harish and I did embrace him but he remained very subdued. The trademark effervescence was totally missing. Ratna was too overwhelmed to note this but Harish and I exchanged silent glances. It didn't take Unmesh long to collect his few personal belongings from the prison office. We were soon seated in the car, heading for home.

Home was at least an hour's drive. I wanted Unmesh to get over whatever was going on in his mind before Veena welcomed them both at home. I gently broke the silence by asking him, 'You took quite some time in coming to us from your barrack. Your friends must have been bidding farewell to you.'

Unmesh looked at me and replied, 'Yes, I got a farewell and

what a pain it was!'

'Why? Had you become so fond of your two journalist and businessman friends?' I asked.

'No Papa, they didn't take much time. What took time was a very painful encounter with another inmate. I had tried to preach and reform him a few days ago. As it is, I have been feeling very guilty about my privileged and painless stay in the jail but the shock I just received has burdened me with an unbearable feeling of guilt.'

'Why? Would you please stop talking in riddles?' Harish butted in a bit impatiently.

'Are you feeling guilty about the rash act of Simran? Don't we know that it was her troubled psyche which was responsible for what happened?'

'No, it is not about Simran', Unmesh was forthright. 'Her memories were very painful to me till the time I was too self-centredly engrossed in my own problems. But as time passed, I slowly started getting aware of the painful realities all around me, of the hundreds of unfortunate victims of the system languishing in the jail. Only a few of whom were really guilty of the crimes they were charged with. They were accused of a whole gamut of crimes ranging from murder, burglary, rape, minor thefts, violence and even dowry harassment and dowry death. Many women prisoners were accused of prostitution. I first used to observe them from a distance. Later I started watching them closely. I then got talking to them. Only then did I realise that their single biggest crime was POVERTY. So many of them have been locked up on false and trumped up charges, pressed by their richer oppressors and adversaries, in cahoots with the heartless police who couldn't pick any flesh from their starved bodies. A whole lot of them are so illiterate and ignorant that they don't even know on what charges they have been shunted into the jail. Many of those who are aware of the charges have no idea as to when their cases will come up for a hearing or how long will they languish on false and fabricated charges. And most unfortunate are the ones who are aware of the charges but are too impoverished to afford a lawyer.'

'But the government provides free legal assistance to those who cannot afford it', I mumbled, though I knew very well that I was on a very slippery wicket. Not only I, even Unmesh knew that I was being very naïve in making this comment. One does read about a number of NGOs existing with the very laudable objective of providing legal aid and succour to the unfortunate undertrials but they are so few and the sheer number of the needy so humongous that they remain only as effective as a drop in the ocean. Moreover, usually the N G Os loose their missionary fervor rapidly after receiving grants and aid from their sympathisers, mostly in foreign countries.

As expected, Unmesh just overlooked my remark and continued in his sad voice, 'What a mockery we make of the socialistic pattern of our republic inside the prison! Papa, initially I used to buy milk stolen from the prison hospital and delicacies smuggled in by the prison warders themselves, but after watching the poor among the prisoners somehow swallowing insect-infested watery dal and half-cooked and burnt chapattis, I started finding it impossible to even nibble the smuggled and stolen food I used to buy. I now feel myself sunk up to my neck in a heap of guilt. While I used to enjoy my leisurely walks in the prison garden along with my journalist and industrialist friends, those languishing in the jail for even minor thefts used to clean the stinking, choked toilets because they couldn't buy release from the malodorous task. Mummy moved to the private ward in the District Hospital because we were lucky enough to be able to afford it. What about the women who first got caught for prostitution and are now busy cleaning toilets; both times for the same reason; no money to eat and no money to bribe.'

The mention of purchasing comfort for Ratna and Unmesh made me feel very uncomfortable. Unmesh was telling the truth and truth is the most dreadful weapon to face. I could have insisted that since Ratna and Unmesh had been victims of false charges under a draconian law, I was justified in spending money to at least buy comfort for them but somehow, I lacked conviction deep within. The fact was that even if it was indefensible on moral grounds, I would have purchased comfort for them. If it was called bribing, so be it. Why should they, who had committed no crime, suffer? I tried to make Unmesh feel less guilty by directing the conversation away from Ratna and himself. I said, 'Agreed that your innocent mother bought comfort by bribing the doctors, but what makes you so sympathetic to scums like prostitutes?'

Without raising his voice Unmesh replied gravely, 'I am sympathetic because earlier I had never viewed prostitutes, thieves and burglars as human beings. It was drilled into me that they were worse than vermin. But why? I can hardly believe that anyone becomes a prostitute for pleasure. Only poverty drives them into it if they are not coerced into it by deceit. By the way, I have pondered over this question for many restless hours in the prison. What is wrong in their selling the body if that is the only thing left to sell for filling their empty stomachs? This entire holier-than-thou attitude has been created by those who have never heard the angry rumbling of an empty stomach. When a rikshawpuller pedals his rikshaw, when a coolie lifts your baggage on his head, when a masseur presses and massages your feet, don't they too sell their body? Calling it "selling the body" is only a figure of speech. After all, he doesn't give away his arms and legs, nor does the prostitute.'

Ratna was finding his talk nauseating. She suddenly interrupted loudly, 'Enough Unmesh, enough! Will you stop this nonsense? You have spoilt the fun of this meeting by talking utter rot!'

'You call this rot? You Ma? You, who has seen the reality herself through a zoom lens?' he retorted.

'But enough is enough Unmesh!' chipped in Harish who had been maintaining a stoic silence so far. 'At least, your homecoming should be on a happy note.'

'No, Harish. Let me just tell you how painful was the parting note I received from another inmate. The sting of his parting remark was unbearable. It will chafe me for ever.'

'What parting remark? Don't talk in riddles', said Harish.

'Alright, you asked for it. Now listen! I have already told you that the filthiest task of cleaning the choked Indian style lavatories was given to those who couldn't afford to pay any bribes. But there was one youngster, barely eighteen, who paid no money and enjoyed maximum comforts and the best food. Do you know in what currency he paid the warders? By offering his services as a passive homosexual! One day I tried to tell him that he should not debase himself like that, but he was adamant. He told us that as an orphaned pickpocket, he was beaten severely by his gang leader when he turned up empty-handed. One day, when the torture became unbearable, he hit his boss's head with a brick in a fit of rage and was shocked to find him dropping dead. Since then, he has been languishing in the jail. Here too he suffered like a dog as he had no money to pay for the bribes. One day, a warder proposed to spare him all the torture in exchange for sexual favours. He discovered that getting sodomised was the key to all sorts of luxuries like edible food and escape from lavatory cleaning. And now, when he had learnt how to have a cushy time, who was I to sermonize him. I stopped in my efforts to make him mend his ways.'

I was feeling utterly embarrassed, listening to this sordid tale, that too in Ratna's earshot. She was very uncomfortable at first, and now positively angry. I was about to interrupt Unmesh and ask him to shut up when I noticed Harish looking at me in the rearview mirror. He nodded his head very slightly to hint that I ought to exercise restraint and keep quiet. I followed his advice.

Unmesh stopped his monologue, but continued again after a very brief pause, 'Do you know what were this boy's parting words to me just before I came to you all? As the news spread that I was leaving, he came to me and said, "Congratulations, Big Brother! You are the first inmate I have seen getting out of this jail within two months on bail in a case of dowry death. And I have been here for some time. Isn't it good to have money to buy anything, even freedom from jail?"'

'I tried to convince him that I was innocent and was there on trumped up charges and my people had not paid any bribe to the judge for granting bail to me. But he said, "It is all the same, whether you have the money to pay to the judge or to a big lawyer to fight your case. Ultimately, it is money that has seen you through and let your mother rest in a private ward instead of rotting in the jail. I have come to tell you that I shall continue getting sodomised till I save enough money to hire a lawyer who will steer me out of this hell."'

We were all speechless with embarrassment. I and Ratna were shocked to see how coarse Unmesh had become in his language during these two months he had spent in the jail, how unmindful he had become of other's sensibilities when broaching upon crude topics in civil company. There was now complete silence between us in the car. Only Harish had a tranquil expression on his face. Unmesh once again got lost in his thoughts till he saw the car approaching our locality and then he suddenly came out of the trance and mumbled, 'Ma, Papa, I am sorry. I have hurt your sensibilities. I have been seeing life in all its nakedness; its sordid and unspeakable secrets laid bare to me. I find myself a changed man. I know you must have found my words shocking but my language too has become affected by the company I had. I promise, I would try and undo what the jail has done to me.'

Ratna and I kept quiet. We had reached our house and the car came to a halt in front of it. A beaming Veena was standing in the lawn with two huge bouquets in her hands. The hard expression which seemed to have frozen on Unmesh's face vanished in a jiffy. He smiled.

Eighteen

With Unmesh and Ratna back at home, our lives once again found a semblance of normalcy but the sword of Damocles still hung over our heads. Tripathi told us what to expect next. The Police would carry out further investigations and then file a charge sheet after some time. I asked Tripathi, 'What charges could they possibly make now? Isn't it an open and shut case that Simran committed suicide in a sudden fit of anger? There can be no evidence of any dowry demand as there really was none. Couldn't the police just submit a request to close the case?' Tripathi explained why there was absolutely no chance of the police closing the case. Unlike every other crime in which the onus is on the prosecution to prove the guilt of the accused who is considered innocent till proved guilty, the draconian Dowry Act prescribes that when a woman dies an unnatural death within seven years of her marriage, it shall be considered a dowry death and the husband shall be considered guilty. The onus is entirely on him to prove that he is innocent. The Dowry Prohibition Act thus turns the Indian jurisprudence upside down. Of course, it pertains only to unnatural death which was relevant in Simran's case.

'So what do we do now?' I asked Tripathi. 'Just wait till the chargesheet is filed by the police and then fight it out in the court'

'Well, half the battle is already won because you did convince the District and Sessions Judge that the case was baseless', I said.

' Oh! just forget about the bail order. It has served its purpose and is of no further use', said Tripathi and then asked, 'Have you heard anything from the Suris? Are you in touch with them?'

'No. I did try to contact Col Suri but he would not pick up my phone. This was immediately after Ratna was put under arrest while in the nursing home.'

'What did you want to say to him?' asked Tripathi.

'I wanted to confront him and ask him how could he tell such a sordid lie when we had never demanded a single paisa as dowry. I also wanted to find out if he knew about the suicide attempts that Simran had made before marriage or Mrs Suri had kept that a secret from him. The latter was a distinct possibility as according to Unmesh, Col Suri had not been personally present on at least two such occasions. If he was made aware of her earlier suicide attempts he would probably not hold us responsible for her success in the final attempt. But that was not to be. I could not get him on phone at all', I said.

'What did you do then? Did you drop the idea?' he asked.

'No. I just couldn't drop the idea. The wish to confront him kept getting stronger and stronger in my mind. I was thinking of it day and night, particularly as both Ratna and Unmesh were under arrest and I had a lot of lonely moments when Harish and Veena were busy. So, one day, I decided to take the plunge and just dropped in at their house without any prior intimation. To my surprise I found Mrs Suri at home. She had apparently not gone back to Jalandhar after the tragedy. I wondered if she had resigned from her job or merely extended her leave, but I kept my curiosity under check and clarified to her that I had come to talk to Manbeer. Unfortunately, I learnt from Mrs Suri that he was out of station and Anand too had gone to college. She was alone at home', I said.

'Did you pose your questions to her?' he asked.

'Yes, I did. But she just refused to answer my questions. She started sobbing and kept on sobbing and crying during the entire fifteen or twenty minutes I spent there. I asked her how they could mention dowry demand in their complaint when they knew it was a white lie. Didn't she know very well that Simran was in the habit of getting sudden fits of anger?Had she completely forgotten her earlier suicide attempts?But she did not answer any of my questions and kept on repeating that they had spent considerable amount of money on their daughter's marriage, even if no cash was given as dowry and now they had lost all that and their daughter too. Then I asked her what exactly did she mean by considerable amount of money spent on the marriage including all the gifts that were given to Simran. As far as Unmesh was concerned, only a gold ring had been gifted on his engagement and a gold *Kara* and a suit length during the *Anand Karaj* and finally a wristwatch on his first visit to their house after the marriage. So how had they made huge expenses during the marriage?'

Tripathi interrupted me, 'Mr Asthana, the way you listed these three items and emphasised that there was no other major gift in cash or kind to Unmesh, and if any gifts were given in the marriage they were given to the bride, was brilliant. Did she say anything about their expenses?'

'Yes, she got carried away and between her sobs she mentioned that though we had not demanded any dowry, yet in all, they had spent five to six lakh rupees in the marriage, but she didn't name any specific gift to Unmesh or to our family besides what I had mentioned.'

'Great! So what did you do then?' he asked.

'I asked her what specific acts of harassment and persecution of Simran was carried out by Ratna or by Unmesh after that forgettable fight he had with Simran one year ago. But I couldn't get her to admit anything. Her silence only confirmed that she had no specific grouse of persecution against Ratna or Unmesh, but she avoided saying that. I then got exasperated and bid her a good day and walked off', said I.

Tripathi now added, 'I wish you had carried with you one of those pen-size mini tape recorders concealed in your pocket and recorded this conversation.'

'In fact, I did carry one and did record this conversation', I said, probably with a glint in my eyes.

'Oh, absolutely great! Who gave you the idea? By the way, was the recording clearly audible?'

'Well, it is clearly audible. I have friends in one of Noida's giant Film Studios, with state of the art recording facilities for film music. I took their help in getting it transferred on a CD which reproduces it as crystal clear as I am talking to you now', I said.

'Brilliant! Mr Asthana! Preserve it very carefully. Let me warn you, it won't be long before you will have another opportunity for a recording session. And it would be wise if you return all the items received by Simran and Unmesh or any of you during the marriage', Tripathi added.

'I have already returned all the items going right down to even her slippers to the Suris. The very next day after I met Mrs Suri, I hired a tempo and dumped the double bed and bedside table, the only item of furniture received as a gift. Then there were two dinner sets, two tea sets, a mixie and a vacuum cleaner. I also heaped all her clothes, from the heavy saris right down to the undergarments. These were handed over personally by Harish to Simran's brother Anand. All the items were listed in an inventory made in two copies. They accepted all the items but did not wish to sign a receipt, but when Harish made it clear that he would not hand over the jewellery unless a receipt was signed, Anand consulted his parents and then gave a signed receipt on the duplicate copy of the inventory.'

'Were his parents present when the items were returned?'

'"Yes, they were inside their flat but only Anand came out. Harish did not enter their flat and they never came out to talk to him', I added.

'Ok, Mr Asthana. You are indeed a wise man! Keep your wits about just like this. You have a long battle ahead. One more question by the way. Do you agree with their estimate of five to six lakhs spent on the marriage as mentioned by Mrs. Suri?'

'Thanks for the compliment, Tripathiji. I can't verify the accuracy of the stated expenses, but the figure of five to six lakhs does ring a bell. It is the same amount that we have been accused of demanding from the Suris as per the FIR.'

'Well, I am sure you will hear from them now.'

'Why so? So far, Suri has only refused to take my phone calls, what would bring about this change of heart?'

'The changed situation will bring the change of heart. Mr Asthana, you probably don't know that in ninety-nine per cent of similar cases, bail is denied to the accused at the District level. Relief does come in most such cases only at the High Court level but that takes a long time due to the surfeit of such cases, procedural delays and overloading of the High Courts. Thousands of accused, mostly innocent, languish in jails for months and at times years before they are able to obtain bail from the High Court. Now try to visualise the impact of all the events on the morale and the psyche of the complainants after their FIR was lodged.

Right in the beginning, they have witnessed the removal of the original investigating officer who concocted the story of Unmesh's arrest while trying to flee. Then they saw Mrs Asthana spending all that period under arrest in a first class nursing home or in the private ward of the District Hospital instead of languishing in the district jail. Then came the biggest blow of all in the shape of the bail order which came at the District level itself. Mind you, this happens only in one per cent of such cases. All this is enough to convince them that you are a mean adversary. If they wanted to extract their pound of flesh, there could not have been a more opportune time than immediately after rejection of the bail application at the District level, when your sagging spirits would have been down in the dumps. But since that was not to be, now is the time for them to make the best of a bargain quickly turning sour.'

'I don't quite get you. Are you trying to suggest that they have filed the FIR basically to blackmail us?' I asked a bit surprised. 'They are basically decent people. I can't imagine their falling to such depths.'

'Look, you know them far better than I can surmise. But if you have not concealed anything from me, there can be only one reason to make all those false accusations and that is to make the best out of a bad bargain. They may have initially lodged the FIR under pressure of their relatives and in the grief of their loss. But they have by now had sufficient time to regret indulging in such falsehood. The heat of the moment must have long evaporated.

But their persisting with the effort to put your family in such deep trouble clearly indicates their sinister designs. Look at Mrs Suri's breast beating over the amount of money which she claims to have spent in the marriage. I do see a distinct possibility of their reverting to you with a demand to mitigate at least their financial loss.'

During our association with the Suris, during the last almost three years since Simran had joined as an employee in our factory, we had found them to be honourable and self-respecting people. They were not very affluent but they had never displayed a streak of meanness or unbridled greed in their conduct. It pained me to such an extent to see that Tripathi could put them in such poor light that I underwent a role reversal and started defending Col Suri. 'Look Tripathiji, why can't we put ourselves in their shoes? After all, they have lost their beloved daughter. There can be no limit to their pain and anguish. She had appeared quite happy and contented in the morning before our house guests. Then, if she suddenly committed suicide before evening, won't her parents find a sinister design behind it?' I asked.

'In spite of her troubled past and previous suicide attempts?' asked Tripathi.

'Isn't it possible that since the suicide attempts had been made in his absence, the harried mother kept it a secret even from her husband. he could have blamed her for not taking adequate care of their daughter by being too engrossed in her own career. After all, he was leading a lonely life himself in the hope and belief that their children would be looked after better by their mother this way', I retorted but my voice lacked conviction.

Tripathi chuckled, 'What a wonderful imagination you have! Is it possible to keep such secrets in such a small family? That too, with tell-tale scars on her left wrist?'

'Alright, even if they knew of her earlier suicide attempts, how could they forget the previous incident in which Unmesh and Simran had fought each other violently? Agreed that things had been quite smooth in the last one year, but can they totally rule out a situation in which they had another violent quarrel and Unmesh involuntarily hurt her so badly that she died. For example, if she was screaming and he put her hand on her mouth to stop it and in the struggle, the neck vertebra was broken and then an attempt was made to give it the appearance of a suicide? Try to think from the point of view of an aggrieved parent and you will not rule it out as an impossible hypothesis.'

Tripathi objected, 'What about the post-mortem report which clearly states that the death is due to hanging but the vertebra was not broken. He clearly calls it a case of self-hanging. The exact details and cause will come out when the doctor who carried out the post-mortem is examined in the court. But if the death occurred due to hanging in a closed bathroom, bolted from inside and attached to a room which itself was locked from inside, how can one doubt a suicide?'

In a reversal of roles, I continued acting as Suri's lawyer, 'But only we know that both the rooms were bolted from inside.

How do they know about our alibis and about the absence of anybody else at home at the time of the death. At the moment, isn't it quite natural for them to suspect something fishy?' I said in Suri's defence.

'How can you be so naive Mr Asthana?' Tripathi was sarcastic. 'Couldn't they have lodged an FIR just stating that they suspected foul play and then demand a thorough police probe? Did they have to weave a story full of falsehood? Did they have to invent harassment and persecution of the deceased after her marriage? Did they have to invent a hypothetical figure of five to six lakh rupees being the amount demanded by you? And if at all this was stated in the heat of the moment, didn't they get enough time to cool their tempers while Unmesh was cooling his heels in the jail and Mrs Asthana was in the hospital living the ignominy of being under arrest? Mr Asthana, it is amazing that you are unable to see their devious designs even when their evil intents are shouting from the roof top. In my profession, one gets an opportunity to study human behaviour in its myriad forms, from the most sublime to the most sordid. And from what I have seen of cases under Sections 498A, 304 B and the Dowry Act, the intention in ninety-nine per cent cases is to blackmail and to suck the groom's family dry. Just wait and see! I am ready to lay a wager that the crux of the matter will be revealed to you very soon in the shape of demands that even you may find difficult to meet.'

I had not quite expected Tripathi to be so negative and so blunt. The discussion had become unpleasant and I beat a hasty retreat.

'Okay, Mr Tripathi. Agreed, I do not have as much exposure to such things as you have. But is it really such a common place thing as you make it out to be?' I said, my tone no longer so vehement.

'You will shudder to learn, to what extent people are suffering due to the legal provisions in such cases. In fact, I am presently handling another case in which an innocent young man, Deepak and his mother are being subjected to immense mental torture and the blackmail has brought a well-off family to the brink of financial ruin. The next hearing in their case is due just day after tomorrow. I think if you hear their plight, you may be benefitted in some way', replied Tripathi.

'Go right ahead', I said and braced myself to hear the tale of Deepak's misfortune.

Nineteen

Deepak was the only son of a widowed mother–Mrs Khanna. His father had held a good government post and had built a nice two-storied house in Safdarjang Enclave. Today, it is a prime location in New Delhi and the house has a market value of crores. After the untimely death of Mr Khanna, the family pension and rent from one floor of the house was sufficient for Mrs Khanna to lead a moderately comfortable life and to give a good education to Deepak. He grew into a handsome young man, got a decent job in a private sector firm and remained a very dutiful and caring son. After settling into his job, when his mother wanted him to get married, he willingly agreed to let her choose a bride for him. They advertised in the matrimonial columns and were flooded with good proposals. The mother took great pride in selecting the most beautiful girl for her son. Both

Deepak and his mother had a soft corner for the girl as she too was the only daughter of a widowed mother, though much less affluent than them. The girl was a graduate and was working as a front office executive at a five star hotel.

Their marriage was solemnized with much fanfare. The young bride remained on leave for fifteen days after which she resumed her duties. She was getting a handsome salary, which mitigated the inconvenience of her odd working hours which often involved working in the night shift beginning at 9 pm. Deepak usually came home from his office by 6 pm and went to drop her at the hotel at 9 pm. Jyoti did not want Deepak to enter the main gates of the hotel and always got down at the road beside the main gate. She told Deepak that she was getting a handsome salary and did not want her colleagues to see her husband coming on a scooter to drop her.

Deepak assured her that he would save enough money in two years time to be able to buy a car and Jyoti excitedly told him that when she also chipped in with her earnings the waiting period would be only one year. The newly married couple appeared to lead a blissful life, full of love and fun, till one day a friend of Deepak who had attended their marriage said, 'I saw Bhabhiji in Templeton last night. Has she changed her job?'

'No. Of course not, she is still working in the Cosmopolitan', said Deepak.

'Oh! Is that so? Well, I might have been mistaken. After all I have seen her only two or three times earlier', said his friend. But

Deepak knew that his friend wasn't all that dumb and was just being polite. A small seed of suspicion was sown in his mind. Next day he asked Jyoti if she had visited Hotel Templeton, probably on duty last night and she laughed it off as a silly question.

That evening when Deepak went to drop her at the hotel for her night shift duty, he asked Jyoti if he could leave the scooter outside on the road and walk with Jyoti to see her place of work in the lobby of the hotel which was famous for its grandeur and splendor. Jyoti did not appear very keen. She said that the management did not encourage the employees to bring their family members to the work place. When Deepak insisted, she agreed on the condition that she would not introduce him to her colleagues and would pose as if he was a stranger to her. Deepak agreed and they entered the imposing lobby of the hotel. They appreciated its modern interior, decorated with fresh floral designs and a large MF Husain painting, the beautiful thickly cushioned chairs and sofas placed under its glittering chandeliers and glimmering candelabrum. After a quick round, they came back to the front porch. Jyoti had been steadfast in not introducing her husband to her colleagues and had avoided even looking into their eyes. Deepak remained unmindful of the dazzling reception area and the lobby; he kept on wondering how even Jyoti's colleagues did not show any signs of recognition and camaraderie in their eyes. The seed of suspicion grew bigger.

That night, when he dropped Jyoti outside the hotel, he drove off even before she started walking in. But he only went a hundred yards away, parked his scooter and walked back. He stood behind a tree on the other side of the road divider, from where he could observe the hotel's entrance. Barely a few minutes had passed when a gleaming luxury car came and was parked adjacent to the hotel's entrance. A few more minutes passed and Deepak got a thousand volts shock when he saw Jyoti coming out of the hotel gate, going to the car, talking to the man in the driver's seat for a few seconds before entering its front door and sitting next to him. The car drove off. Shocked though he was, Deepak ran to his scooter, intending to follow the car but it was parked too far. The car got out of sight before he could even start his scooter. Deepak was fuming and fretting. He called Jyoti on her mobile but it was switched off. He was helpless. After reaching home, he kept pacing up and down his room throughout the night in sheer desperation. He did not go to pick her up from the hotel in the morning.

When Jyoti came home and found him unshaven and dishevelled with eyes red due to sleep deprivation, she very casually asked him if he was unwell. Deepak lost all self-control. He grabbed her by her hair and gave two-three stunning slaps on her face. Jyoti went wild with rage but not with fear. When Deepak started abusing her and called her a whore she shot back, 'And what are you? Aren't you a pimp who goes to drop his wife on a rotten scooter every evening, so that she could work all night to enable him to buy a cheapy car? Who cannot afford to give her a meal better than roti, dal, sabzi? Who cannot dream of spending even one night in a luxurious room which will claim half his month's wages? How dare you beat me, you crawling insect? I will teach you a lesson you will never forget!' She walked out of their house in rage, more tempestuous than Deepak's. His mother had come running when she had heard the torrents of abuse from both of them. She was aghast and speechless. Her ignorance of the reasons for this violent explosion was, in fact, a boon. She would have been devastated had she learnt the sordid facts. Deepak was dumbfounded. He refused to share his secret with his mother. He did not go to his office and kept wondering, what his next step should be.

But by not going to his office, he made the job of the policemen very easy when they came to arrest him on the basis of an FIR lodged by Jyoti and her mother. Deepak and his mother were speechless when they were told that a case under Section 498 and Dowry Prohibition Act had been registered for harassing, persecuting and beating a newly-married girl for not fulfilling dowry demands. The allegations were made both against Deepak and his mother.

I had never expected Tripathi to give me such a horror story. I was reminded of the story of Khalil Zibran in which a man felt sorry for not having shoes only till he saw someone with no feet. It was my turn to go speechless now. After a pause of a few seconds, I managed to ask, 'What happened after that? Did she realise her mistake and withdraw her complaint after her temper had cooled?'

Tripathi chuckled, 'No, Mr Asthana. *Hell hath no fury like a woman scorned*, even if she is a slut. Tempers may cool off but deliberate devious designs only harden with passage of time. Just for your information, I have been able to obtain bail for Deepak's mother on account of her advanced age, poor health and being a helpless widow, that too after she had cooled her heals in the jail for more than three months. I was not so lucky in the case of Deepak. He is still languishing in the jail.'

'So, how is this woman going to prove allegations of dowry demand and harassment?' I asked.

'Oh! You still haven't grasped the absurdity of this draconian law. Well, nobody has to prove the demand or the persecution. It is for Deepak and Mrs Khanna to prove that they did not demand dowry. The first thing that the bitch had done was to get herself medically examined in a government hospital and get a certificate from the doctor that there were tell-tale marks of being thrashed on the face, with a bleeding lip, a swollen eye and many a torn hair from her scalp. Once the FIR is lodged, along with such a medical certificate, the police have no choice but to prosecute the man without bothering about any provocation for such violence. As soon as the news becomes public many women's rights voluntary organisations jump into the fray. My client, on the other hand, has no proof to press any charges against her character. I wish he had not been so impetuous and had employed a Detective Agency to gather tangible evidence of her foul conduct and sought an annulment of the marriage. But that momentary loss of self-control is going to cost him a fortune', said Tripathi.

'What do you mean by a fortune?' I asked.

'Well! He doesn't have much beyond a house and a scooter. She doesn't want the scooter!'

'What the hell! Does he lose his house for this?' I gasped.

'Yes, Sir. I had no way out but to seek a compromise and this is the price demanded by the daughter and mother duo. I now have to go for an out-of-court settlement rather than just deny their allegation during the trial.'

'You mean, the Khannas will be on the road, if not in the jail?' I asked.

'Not exactly! In all such cases, the initial demand is for the moon but prolonged negotiations finally bring it down to the earth.'

'So where do you think this will end!'

'Well, I have finally suggested that the house be sold and half the proceeds be given to these women, to seek Khannas' release from their clutches in this case as well as to obtain a divorce by mutual consent.

'How can you encourage this blackmail? Doesn't it amount to extortion? Do you really want them to swallow such humiliation and torture silently?'

'Mr Asthana, you had better direct your questions to the lawmakers who have remained blind to the Act's foul consequences. The higher judiciary has been repeatedly pointing out its shortcomings, but to no avail. Listen to this observation by Delhi High Court in Savitri Devi's Case.' He picked up the *All*

India Reporter and started reading out from a book-marked page, 'This law is hitting at the foundations of marriage itself and has proved not so good for the health of the society at large. There is a proven tendency to come out with inflated and exaggerated allegations, roping in each and every relation of the husband. If one of them happens to be of higher status or of vulnerable standing, he or she becomes an easy prey for better bargaining and blackmailing.'

Tripathi sounded both forceful and defeated in the same breath as he said, 'Why, even the Supreme Court has gone to the extent of calling Section 498A, Legal Terrorism. But the lawmakers have remained deaf to all the wailing of its victims, as well as the criticism of the judiciary.'

There was defeatism and anguish in his voice as he continued, 'I am not a lawmaker. I can only fight for the law's fair implementation. If its misuse is inherent in its language, I can only suck my thumb. It then becomes my duty to advise my clients to buy peace if they can afford it. If they are too poor to afford a compromise, then and only then do I advise them to fight it out. But the legal procedure is too sluggish and good lawyers demand such high fees. The price of self-respect and fight for justice turns out to be very high in the long run. And believe me, it is usually a long run of seven to eight years.'

'Tripathiji, your hint is quite broad and the horror story of the Khannas is frightening enough for me. But I have not received any demand from the Suris', I blurted out.

'Well, I am sure they were waiting for the outcome of the bail case to determine how much they can extract from you. The events so far have been in your favour and are discouraging enough for them. You will definitely get a good discount from them due to the outcome of the bail case. I don't think they will demand the moon.'

'Could it be the magic figure of five to six lakhs, which has been mentioned so many times?'

'No. My guess is that they will begin at ten times that amount but the ultimate figure will depend upon your negotiating skills', said Tripathi.

'You mean, your negotiating skills?' I said suggestively.

'No. I mean what I say. It will be your negotiating skills. There are reasons why I won't take up this task.'

'What are they?"

'Well! In all probability, the demand will come through a third party and not their lawyer. I won't participate in the discussions and negotiations because I want you to carry out your sting operation in the meeting, with your pocket tape recorder. It will be professionally wrong for me to do such recordings myself, especially if the negotiations are with their lawyers. But you have been roped in this war so unjustly and their demands are so unethical that a sting operation by you will be fully justified.'

'That seems to be an easy solution! Why not counter-blackmail them with the tape recording for extortion, rather than surrender to their extortion?'

'Because the shortest route to peace in your family life is through an early closure of the case. By opening one more front by exposing their recorded demands, you will have to fight prolonged battles on two fronts. Don't expect speedy justice. The average life span of a case under Section 498 is five years, which can stretch up to seven or eight years. Besides, there is every possibility of only a third person making the demands on their behalf. These days, everybody knows about sting operations. It will be difficult to hold the Suris responsible for demands made on you in a third person's voice, whose identity cannot be proved. Even if they are naive and foolish enough to talk to you directly, shame and guilt will force them to put their demand for money in disguised and vague terms. So it is up to you to decide whether you want to immediately buy peace of mind or prolong your agony by fighting injustice.'

But suppose I fulfill his demands, how can he go back on the words used in the FIR? Won't it be perjury in the eyes of law?'

'Ha-ha-ha! Asthana Saheb, what are we lawyers for? If every written statement withdrawn, modified or denied later gets classified as perjury punishable by law then our courts will have no time for any other type of cases. As regards verbal statements made to the police, they are as ephemeral as a painting on the surface of river.'

'But what shall I do with the tape recorded conversation? If, as suggested by you, I do try to buy peace by surrendering to their blackmail, and am yet unable to get Unmesh and Ratna out of their clutches, will the tape prevent double crossing?'

'Exactly! On the other hand, they can safely assume that you won't publicise the contents of the tape after both Unmesh and Mrs Asthana are declared innocent by the court. After all, if perjury is established, the case will only drag on much longer. So, I don't think they will be extra careful to prevent any sting operations by you. Yet, they may or may not come out in the open and talk to you directly.'

'That means, I have to preserve the tapes till the court declares Unmesh and Ratna not guilty?'

'Yes, and even beyond that. I can't explain right now, but unforeseen eventualities do turn up in life. I can't predict that it will be useful to retain the tapes but you never know. And, in case the Suris step out of the lawyer's shadow and make their demands directly to you, you absolutely must retain the records for posterity', insisted Tripathi.

'What do you mean by posterity?' I asked.

'I can't predict all the possible eventualities. But let's take just one case. Your wounds are very raw now but after a couple of years when time heals them, you may think of Unmesh's second marriage. After all, he is so young, why should the innocent boy suffer all his life? At that time, once the court has declared them innocent of any wrongdoing, the conversation on these tapes will convince anybody that your family became a victim of the rash behaviour of a diseased mind, the greedy demands of her blackmailing parents and the inherent cruelty of the mindless law.'

'Oh! The law!' I said with disdain.

'Howsoever much you may hate some of its mindless provisions, the Dowry Prohibition Act, we must admit, was created with very noble intentions. With all the cases of bride burning and beastly torture of young brides by greedy husbands and in-laws, our legislators had to do something to tame them. Exemplary punishment was the need of the hour. It is unfortunate that in doing so, the law has swung to the other extreme where innocent people are being harassed and tortured even more than the poor brides and their parents', Tripathi tried to pacify me.

I butted in sarcastically, 'Well, it gives a good opportunity to briefless lawyers also to fish in troubled waters.'

Tripathi was not very happy with my remark. He agreed, but reluctantly, 'Yes, you are not very wrong. Our society has changed too rapidly in recent years. Women enjoy considerable freedom in selecting their life partners now. But often, the couple does not have proper understanding of each other's nature and character. Minor misunderstandings often get magnified manifold, when their respective parents jump into the fray and start taking sides. Voices of sanity then get drowned. Occasionally, it may lead to violence. Once that happens the spark becomes a wild fire. Incidents of physical violence, often a result of momentary loss of self-control by the husband, provide adequate grounds to land not only him but also his parents and near relatives behind bars. Yes, it does then provide a great opportunity to briefless lawyers to make a quick buck.'

Tripathi was so cynical that his tirade was not going to stop in a hurry. He continued, 'It also provides great opportunity for self-styled feminists and their NGOs to locate preys for easy blackmail. The rampant corruption in the lower rungs of the judiciary acts as a catalytic agent in the harassment and plundering of the hapless boy and his family. Absolute powers of arrest by the police and the magistrates, as the offense is both cognizable and non-bailable, give them an open field for sucking the blood of often innocent victims.' I was amazed to learn that the dowry laws were full of holes like a sieve, but Tripathi had still not run out of ammunition.

'And, that's not all. There are hundreds of cases in courts where Section 498 has been invoked by girls to get out of inconvenient marriages, at times forced upon them by parents. Sometimes, there can even be an old boyfriend lurking in the wings to share the booty collected by the girl from her husband who finds an easy outlet in a mutual settlement to get out of her clutches. This is an unfortunate fallout of the marriage and divorce laws which have made getting a quick divorce so cumbersome and difficult. What can be a quicker way than blackmail, leading to a divorce with a huge bounty as a bonus in the shape of a settlement? Many poor but greedy parents also happily join in such blackmail.'

It was getting a bit too complicated for me to grasp fully. 'How can there be an out-of-court settlements when Section 498 is a non-compoundable offense. Doesn't that mean that having made it once, the petitioner cannot withdraw his complaint?' I asked.

'Well, you are right theoretically. But in practice, the courts do adopt a lenient attitude when there is no dowry death and harassing the bride for dowry is the only accusation.'

I realised that Tripathi would go on and on due to his strong feelings against this law. It was getting late. I had to stop him and take leave for the day. I said that I would go home and give a serious thought to his suggestion that I should willingly accept a compromise if Manbeer offered me a chance by demanding money. But I had serious doubts. I did not really expect him to stoop so low to conquer. 'Only time will tell', was my thought even on the way back home.

Twenty

After that prolonged discussion with Tripathi, I had become prepared to buy peace but the expected call from the Suris did not come. A few months passed in utter suspense for our family. The police too was taking its time in completing its investigation. Soon after Ratna and Unmesh had obtained bail, the new Investigating Officer, Gaur, a Deputy Superintendent of Police, had called me to his office. I went there full of apprehension, but he talked quite courteously. He asked me some questions about the conjugal life of Unmesh and Simran, then about her relations with Ratna. The meeting lasted barely half-an-hour, at the end of which he politely allowed me to leave. I hesitantly asked him, 'How come, you never quizzed me on my equation with Simran or her parents?' He replied with a disarming smile, 'Because there is no mention of any harassment by you in the FIR. Your name figures there only as the father of Unmesh Asthana. You will be glad to know that both Colonel and Mrs Suri told me, when I interviewed them, that they held nothing against you as their daughter always held you in high esteem.'

I had learnt from my neighbours that police officials had visited them and asked them many questions about our nature, our equation with Simran and whether they had noticed any tell-tale signs of unhappiness on Simran's face, during her short married life. They had particularly asked many questions regarding any unusual activity, if any had been noticed at our house on the day Simran had been found dead. Our neighbours had made only favourable comments and the police had not recorded anyone's statement as they were all laudatory.

Ratna and Unmesh had already spent a lot of time answering questions asked by the police while they were under police custody. Simran's and Unmesh's suite in our house had been sealed by the police after the investigating officer and his men had spent considerable time in taking photographs in the bathroom and the bedroom. They had searched all cupboards, drawers and even under the mattresses. Like us, they too had not found a suicide note anywhere in the room. Then one day, the policemen had come and removed the seal on the lock of Unmesh's suite on their own.

After this, a couple of months had passed and then one day Ratna and Unmesh received summons from the Court of the Addl District and Sessions Judge. The charges had been framed and accepted by the court for hearing, which was to begin after four days. I informed Tripathi accordingly.

The much-awaited telephone call, from someone who introduced himself as a lawyer acting on behalf of the Suris, came only three days before the trial of Ratna and Unmesh was to begin. He gave his name as Kohli. He said that he wanted to discuss something urgently with me and invited me to his house in Noida. I expected that the Suris would be there and I acquiesced to the request. The meeting was fixed for 7 pm next day at his house in Sector-15A, the poshest and richest locality of Noida.

I had become convinced by Tripathi's forceful suggestions that I should buy peace, if it was affordable, rather than spend years fighting a prolonged battle to prove our innocence and protect the family's honour. I had spent many sleepless nights pondering over it and in trying to convince Ratna, who hated the idea of abject surrender to blackmail, that discretion was better part of valour. Money spent on buying peace would be money well spent. I knew Harish's young blood would boil with rage, but it became necessary to take him in confidence and tell him that I was ready to succumb to blackmail, as advised by Tripathi. When I told Harish about our decision, he reacted exactly as I had visualised. But ultimately, he yielded, grudgingly though.

Twentyone

Kohli's nameplate outside his imposing bungalow on a quiet tree-laden street in that posh locality of Noida proclaimed that he was a Senior Advocate practicing at the Supreme Court of India. The security guard at the gate escorted us to the entrance to the house, from where we were shown into a large-sized, tastefully decorated drawing room by a servant. We settled down in a leather sofa. Kohli entered a moment later and introduced himself. He was tall and elegantly dressed in a white full-sleeved shirt, black pants and black leather shoes.

Coming to the point without further ado, he said, 'I had expected one or two members of the Suri family to be present for this meeting, but at the last minute they were held up because Col Suri has fallen ill. In fact, he has been quite sick for the last few days. He was hospitalised due to a heart condition. Two of his cardiac arteries have ninety per cent blockage and he needs a cardiac surgery to fit stents to enlarge his choked arteries, or a bypass surgery as a better and longer lasting solution. Being a serving Army Officer, he is entitled for free medical facilities, but the facilities in Military Hospitals are not very good and the family feels that he should undergo that procedure at a good private hospital.'

Kohli then veered the conversation towards the spiraling costs of good medical facilities in the country. Delhi had the best cardiac surgeons in private hospitals but even a quick procedure like fixing of the stents would cost at least three lakh and a bypass surgery would very well cost double the amount. The figure of six lakh flashed in my mind while Harish and I kept listening silently to Kohli's monologue. He grieved over the necessity to get the operation done in a private hospital because of the deplorable state of facilities available in government civil and military hospitals and sought my views in the matter. But as I knew where this discussion was ultimately going to lead, I refrained from opening my mouth. Of course, Harish's transparent face was silently screaming. Thankfully, he just exchanged a glance with me and kept quiet.

Kohli was not one to be discouraged by such aloofness. He pressed on with his well prepared speech. 'Do you know the expenses add up to eight to ten lakh if one includes the amount spent on buying all the medicines for pre and post-operative care, once the operation is over?'

My continued indifference did not dampen his spirits. His residence was opulent, both outside and inside. It costs a lot of money to maintain such houses, and obviously his services did not come cheap. Regardless of how much he charged Col Suri for this mediation, one thing was clear. He was putting up a wholehearted effort to provide value for money to the Suris. No amount of indifference from his small audience of two, dampened his enthusiasm. He pressed on again, 'Just think Mr Asthana, what cruel blows fate has dealt to the Suri family. After spending a huge amount of money on Simrans marriage, they are now in no position to spend money on a decent treatment for Col Suri.' Suddenly, Kohli's voice became very soft, intimate and persuasive. He carried on gently, 'I feel that the Suris have been very impulsive in mentioning dowry harassment in their FIR. I have heard about the reputation your family enjoys and shudder to think what great damage has been done to it by Suri's allegations. I see no reason why every effort should not be made to clear those blots.'

I realised that he was now coming to the point and I could not keep sitting like a dumb doll. I finally opened my mouth and asked, 'So, if he realises his folly and you also feel like redeeming our family's reputation, what is preventing him from doing so?'

'Let me reiterate Mr Asthana, it is not my contention that his allegations are baseless and totally false. I am not here to sit in judgment on that. The only opinion I hold is that the earlier this unsavory episode is closed, the better it is. Whatever happens in the court, the Suris will never get their daughter back. The longer they indulge in legal proceedings, the harsher will be the chafing in their own hearts. It is for this reason that I wish to nip the imminent litigation in the bud.'

'All right Mr. Kohli, whatever your motives and reasons are, once again I ask the same question, what is preventing him from withdrawing his allegations?' I asked.

'That's a very good question and brings us to the crux of the matter. I am sure you know Mr Asthana, Section 498 is a non-compoundable offence, which means that the complainant cannot withdraw his allegations', he said.

'So, it closes the door for any further discussion, doesn't it?' I said in exasperation.

'No, it doesn't Mr Asthana. The one thing good in our country is that nothing is impossible here. The laws lay down many things, but in practice, they are openly defied and nothing happens. There are many doors from which complainants making allegations can get out. The judiciary is not blind to the very harsh nature of the Dowry laws, and does not really mind if the parties reach an out-of-court settlement. So, it turns a blind eye when the complainant, presented at the court as a Prosecution Witness, turns hostile. It has the powers to try him for perjury but it never does so.'

'I see. Are you trying to say that the Suris are willing to turn hostile, when presented at the court as Prosecution Witnesses?'

'No, I am only saying that I will definitely persuade them

not to be afraid of the perjury provision in law. That is what they are worried about now, after I convinced them that prolonged litigation is bad for them too, particularly in his present state of health.'

His sickeningly smooth and syrupy persuasion was frustrating. I knew all this would lead to the demand for a sum of money. How much will that sum be was my only concern. But Kohli was bent upon giving a veneer of respectability to this blackmail. He would not come to the point straight. I did not want to sound rude and impatient. I couldn't have said, 'Thanks a lot Mr Kohli for introducing a semblance of decency in this farce.' Instead, I asked, 'If the courts do turn a blind eye towards vacillations and perjury, what is holding the Suris back?'

'Simple, Mr Asthana, very simple.' Kohli now gave a broad smile, probably with the satisfaction of knowing that he had won half his battle. 'Everything is possible and everything costs money. And it costs so much of money that poor Suris just cannot afford it. The judge, the Government Counsel handling the prosecution, the police investigators are all potential sources which can put a clog in our wheels. The Suris will need a good lawyer by their side to guide them as to how far they can go in denying their allegations. All this costs money.'

'Well, how much money does it cost?' I asked bluntly.

'Wait Mr Asthana, it is not only others who need money. You know Col Suri himself needs money to get a decent treatment for his serious medical problem. As it is, the loss of his beloved daughter has aggravated his heart problem.'

'I see. So now he is placing a price tag on his departed daughter.'

'Please don't be sarcastic Mr Asthana. You will not gain anything from indulging in sarcasm and badmouthing.'

'It is not sarcasm, it is realism! Anyway, what sort of compensation has he in mind?'

'Well, to get out of the clutches of law, which can land both your wife and son for three years in jail at least, rupees three lakh will be required for each of them. This, I reiterate, is the amount which will have to be fed into the system and not into Suri's pockets, as his personal gain. Then, as I have told you, Suri's medical expenses add up to ten lakh. Mind you, his medical problems are rooted in the unfortunate death of his daughter.'

I was livid with rage but trying hard to keep cool. I countered, 'I don't understand. How am I responsible for his medical conditions? He lost his daughter only about three months ago. Are you trying to say that ninty per cent blockage of his three arteries took place within this period? Doesn't he know that his daughter was suicide-prone? She had made suicide attempts earlier too. Doesn't the whole family know that she was quick-tempered and rash?'

'Calm down Mr Asthana', said Kohli.

'I am as calm as I can be. Please answer my questions', I protested.

'Well, his heart problem might have been in the offing for

a longer time but you can't deny that such a shock certainly aggravates a heart condition. You may say that the deceased was suicide-prone, rash and short-tempered but first of all these are difficult to prove in the court. Secondly, it will prolong the litigation quite a bit. Then you will be spending a lot of money in bringing top class psychiatrists as witnesses at the court to support your contention. Also, if you knew she was suicide-prone and short-tempered, why did your son marry her at all? If he did notice these shortcomings in her mental makeup later on, why didn't he seek a divorce? Mr Asthana, please don't try to challenge my contentions on legal points. I am a successful lawyer and I don't want to brag but if I am brought in the court, I will tear your objections to shreds. Mind you, even my services don't come cheap. If the Suris are forced to hire me, then even if you decide later to seek a mutual settlement, my fees too will get added to their demands.'

I was taken aback by his justification of the blackmail. Finding me speechless, Harish decided to butt in. At last, he had been convinced by Kohli that we should buy peace. He now spoke, 'Sir, the amount of sixteen lakhs is not a joke. It is a huge amount'.

It was Kohli's turn to be sarcastic, 'Oh really? Never mind, you tell me, is this sum too huge for a family owning three factories and five cars?'

'Yes it is. You forget that ours is a joint family. We own one house between three families vis-a-vis one house independently owned by Col Suri and his dependent college going son. Three factories actually mean one small-scale unit for each cellular family. As regards cars, they are all financed by banks. We bought them because the interest on the loans, maintenance and depreciation give us income tax relief. They are all mortgaged to the banks. Even for our factories' working capital, we have tied up with financial institutions. Which institution will finance your demand of sixteen lakh?' Harish stopped, but not before impressing me with his presence of mind and control on the rage which must be burning like a fire within. Not surprisingly, Kohli too had not expected such a forceful elocution from a young man who had been sitting so quietly all this while.

'Well. I understand your difficulty too', said Kohli and continued, 'I know that Asthana Saheb also is a first generation entrepreneur. It is easy to understand that there would be charges on your properties held by financial institutions. The figure mentioned by me is only a suggestion. If you accept it in principle, we can negotiate a mutually agreeable sum'.

Thus begun the phase of stark, shameless haggling on the sum that I would have to pay to wriggle out of the totally false accusations made against my wife and son and the distasteful bargaining ended at an agreed sum of rupees ten lakhs.

'Now, what exactly are we gettin in lieu of this sum of ten lakhs?' I asked Kohli.

'You will be getting total denial of all accusations of dowry demand, harassment and persecution by your son and wife.'

'What about the accusations that their daughter was hanged?'

I asked.

'Don't you worry, Mr Asthana. Once they withdraw all accusations of dowry demands, there is no offence under Section 498 (A). As regards Section 304 (B), here the prosecution has to prove that the accused are guilty, unlike 498(A), wherein the poor soul has to prove his innocence. Without any dowry demands, there remains no motivation for murder by the mother-in-law or husband. The post-mortem report suggests self-hanging by the deceased. Each member of your family has watertight alibis of being present in the factory or office throughout the day, till late evening whereas the death occurred in the afternoon. There is no sign of struggle and violence on the body or in the room. Armed with these facts, any lawyer will tear the prosecution's case to shreds. You really don't need to waste your savings on lengthy litigation', Kohli said convincingly.

'So how and when do I pay the amount? Obviously it will all be in cash', I butted in.

'Of course, it will be. You pay it only on the day Col Suri is called in as a Prosecution Witness, to be followed by his wife and son and any other close relative of his.'

'All right. I shall pay the amount after his appearance at the court.'

'No, Mr Asthana, you will have to pay before he enters the courtroom.'

'What is the guarantee that I won't suffer another shock?'

'You will not pay the amount to him. It will be paid to

his lawyer and your lawyer may fix a member of the local bar association as the third interlocutor, to keep the cash till the promised statement is made in the court.'

'What do you mean by "his lawyer"? Won't you be there?'

'Oh no, Mr Asthana, you won't be meeting me after today. My job as a mediator is over. I don't practice in District Court. I shall inform you on phone and his lawyer will get in touch with you a day earlier. In the meantime, you may arrange to keep the cash ready.' There was nothing more to prolong the meeting. We took leave of Kohli, I with a sense of relief and Harish with burning rage and deep hatred, both for the system and for the Suris.

Ratna was furious when I told her that the price to be paid for buying respite from the clutches of law was a million rupees. 'Why do you call it an escape from the clutches of law? It is clutches of these utterly unscrupulous and greedy parents that we are trying to get out of. What has made you so weak Vinod? Why should you go down on your knees to beg mercy from those who want "blood money" for their daughter's impetuousness?' She said, her deep anguish reflected in her voice.

'Ratna, it is not fair on your part to dump the whole blame on my head. I didn't run to Kohli, as soon as I got a call. We knew what was coming. We had discussed these things at length and only then taken a decision. Now be sensible, don't renege on your own decision', I said and added, 'Look, aren't you yourself sick of being falsely blamed for what you never did? Is it now my turn to take all the blame for a decision taken by the family, by consensus?'

'Yes Vinod! I know. I am sorry', she started sobbing. I was taken aback. It was the helplessness of the situation and our utter desperation that was oozing out of her tormented soul in the guise of tears. I held her in a tight embrace and just kept quiet. It soothed her and her sobbing stopped gently.

Harish was angry. Extremely angry. We had both kept quiet all the way back home after that humiliating haggling with Kohli. I knew it would be discreet not to discuss any further with Harish on the subject, otherwise he would blow up.

It was quite late in the evening by the time we had come back from the meeting. It took me another half an hour to console Ratna and soothe her deeply hurt ego. It was past 11 pm when I rang up my father-in-law to inform him about the latest development. I explained how Kohli had justified the agreed amount. He listened patiently and very briefly said that we had little choice in the matter.

It was close to midnight now, but my elder brother had been waiting in Hyderabad to hear the outcome of the meeting. He too did not take long in supporting the arrangement. The very long day finally ended past midnight. I was so exhausted that I sank into deep slumber within seconds after I hit the bed. Ratna and Harish must have tossed and turned in their beds till the wee hours. Both were sad at our helplessness!

Next morning began with my briefing Tripathi on all that had transpired the previous evening. He chuckled from time to time as I narrated how Kohli had built up his case to persuade me. Finally, when I mentioned the figure of a million bucks I expected him to whistle in disbelief. But nothing of the sort happened. He said that the price wasn't too high to reach an early closure of the case. 'He must himself be arranging such deals as the bride's counsel in other cases', I thought. After all, whosoever wins, the lawyer is never at a loss. But in the very next sentence he proved my assessment of all lawyers as greedy vultures, wrong. 'Asthana Saheb, I would be glad to assist you at any time with my suggestions and views, but I advise you now to hire a local lawyer practicing at the Noida courts.' Without waiting for me to ask why, he continued, 'You see, once the complainants deny their allegations, there is no need to engage a top-rung lawyer.'

'But I hardly know any lawyers at Noida courts', I said and went on to add, 'I would need a very reliable person, who can be entrusted to safeguard the large sum of money kept with Suri's lawyer, till they honour their commitment'.

'You worry too much Mr Asthana', Tripathi chuckled. 'Even thieves have their honour. Cash changes hands much more safely in such deals even as cheques keep bouncing in aboveboard deals. Secondly, the amount is really not as large as you think. Just imagine how many times more you would have gladly agreed to pay, if you were really guilty of such crimes. It is an everyday affair for lawyers to handle very large sums as interlocutors. They know it is wise not to kill the goose that lays golden eggs by earning a reputation of dishonesty.'

I then went around the Noida courts and met many touts, lawyers and litigants. The senior lawyers had at least shanties to sit in, a few had modest brick and mortar offices, but the majority of lawyers were sitting on wooden benches and moulded plastic chairs chained to the wooden tables, laden with dog-eared files. Most of the lawyers had their mouths full of tobacco gutka, others puffed cheap cigarettes. A few, probably with better-off clients, sipped tea from dirty thick-ribbed glass tumblers. I narrowed my search to the ones who had at least an office to sit in and a few law books lined up on open wooden brackets fixed to the wall.

Chaudhry Karam Vir Singh, MA, LLB proclaimed the black wooden name-plate hanging above the door of his office. He was a lawyer, apparently in his early sixties, who impressed me by his sober looks, horn-rimmed glasses and neat dress amongst the crowd of shabbily-dressed lawyers roaming around the District Court premises, out hunting for prospective clients. I knew it was useless to enquire about his reputation from the touts or hangers on, and certainly meaningless to ask other lawyers. I decided to take the plunge and check out the man myself. It would be easy to check on his trustworthiness for handling a million rupees. After all, according to Tripathi, they all routinely handled much bigger sums.

Even today I keep thanking God for my inspired choice that day. When I introduced myself to Chaudhry Sahib—that was what others were deferentially calling Chaudhry Karam

Vir Singh—I found out within a few minutes that he was a knowledgeable lawyer. I started discussing my case with him, starting with the nature of the allegations. But he surprised me by saying that he knew the essentials of the case and was updated with the fact of Ratna and Unmesh getting the bail. When I expressed my surprise, he said with a very faint smile, 'Yours is a very well-known case. Your lawyer's presentation was indeed very convincing. I was there along with many of my colleagues that day. So I am aware of the basic details.'

I was wondering where to begin when Chaudhry Sahib hit the nail on the head by asking, '*Kya, samjhauta ho gaya?* (Have you reached a compromise?)' I evaded a direct answer and asked, 'Why? Is that the norm?' Chaudhry said in an even voice, 'Of course, it is. Especially where the accused is financially strong enough to buy peace.'

'I didn't know such things were being done so openly', I said.

Chaudhry smiled as he reassuringly said, 'That is what makes it an open and shut case! Without it, the case would drag on and on.'

Before giving Chaudhry the details of the sum to change hands, I asked him about his fees. He won my admiration by giving a straight answer instead of saying, '*Baad mein dekh lenge* (We shall see later)', as I had heard from every other lawyer so far. I was worried that his fees might go up if I first disclosed the big amount agreed in the deal. But, after learning about his fees when I told him that the agreed sum was a million rupees, he too remained quite unmoved, like Tripathi. Apparently it was no big deal for him either. Chaudhry called me to his residence in the evening with all the relevant papers. He wanted to see all the photographs, letters written by Simran and Unmesh to each other, medical records of Simran and Ratna, a copy of the bail order, copies of the inquest, the post-mortem report, the FIR copy, in short any and every document connected with the case. I asked him if he expected the Suris to renege even after getting the demanded amount. He assured me smilingly, with the phrase I had heard from Tripathi too, 'Even thieves have their honour!' Then he carried on, 'You see, Mr Asthana, we have to keep ourselves ready for any eventuality. You must realise that if they simply deny and negate all they have said earlier in their complaint, they can get caught for misleading the police. They have to justify the reason for lodging a complaint, even if they withdraw allegations of dowry or harassment or cruelty. If there is no justification at all for lodging an FIR against you, later on, you can take them on for lodging a malicious Prosecution Case and claim damages.'

Having engaged Chaudhry as our lawyer, it was necessary to show him all my cards. I told him about the tape recorded conversations, one with Mrs Suri and another, very long recording, of the meeting with Kohli.

When I met him in the evening at his residence, Chaudhry went through the list of documents and sought time to study them. But he was keen to listen to the recordings. When I played the tapes, he too was impressed with their clarity and appreciated my foresight in taking help from such a famous recording studio. He was very satisfied with the recording of my conversation with Mrs Suri but he was unhappy with the fact that the second recorded conversation was only with Kohli, who wasn't Suri's lawyer officially. He said, 'I wish you were able to record the demand for money, the haggling over its quantum and the final agreement in the voices of Col Suri and his family members. Do not miss an opportunity to do this, if you get a chance even now', he said.

'Now? After everything has been settled?' I asked. 'Well, I too don't see much chance of that happening right now. But I am just asking you to do it, if they make any additional demands', said he and continued, 'Asthana Saheb, once money comes easily through blackmail, people don't mind repeating the doze as greed is difficult to satisfy once and for all. Even after the matter is decided at the District Court and the charges under dowry death etc are dismissed, they may try to pressurise and blackmail you further by innocently demanding further probe into the question of it being a suicide or not. They can approach a Court of Appeal for this. Although criminal revision petitions take ages to be heard, your recordings will be a great weapon in your hand to reveal the real intention behind their petition. So do preserve this recording as a very precious possession, and certainly do record the conversation if any further demand is made.'

I promised to do so and that was the end of our discussion. I paid him an advance as a retainer and he said that he would get in touch with Kohli to fix up the third interlocutor for receiving the cash from me on the day Col Suri would be called as a Prosecution Witness.

Twentytwo

We did not have to wait very long for the trial to begin. It was held in the Court of the Additional District and Sessions Judge. The judge was a balding man in his late fifties. He looked impressive in his high-backed chair placed on a high platform, and his baritone voice displayed authority. To begin with, the District Government Counsel presented the Prosecution's case. He merely reiterated the facts and accusations mentioned in Suri's FIR. He then demanded that the two accused, Unmesh and Ratna, be awarded the maximum punishment laid down under Sections 498 (A), 304 (B) and Sections 3 and 4 of the Dowry Prohibition Act. He also explained that under Section 113 of Indian Evidence Act, the Court had to accept the 'Presumption of Dowry death' and it was for the Defence to prove and establish the innocence of the two accused, as the bride's death within seven years of her marriage was an undisputed fact.

The DGC did not indulge in any theatrics. Our lawyer remained a passive listener throughout. At the end of the DGC's presentation, the judge gave a date for the next hearing when the prosecution would start presenting its witnesses.

The next date of the hearing was to be given by the Reader (Peshkar), sitting adjacent to the judge's dais with a number of files and a register on his table. He asked Chaudhry and Suri's lawyer as to when did they want the next hearing? It was amusing to note that both the parties wanted an early date. The earliest available date was on the Monday next week, just six days later. Both the lawyers noted the dates in their files and both of them took out a hundred rupee note each and quietly slipped it into the pocket of the Reader. Later, I asked where was the need to grease his palms when both the parties had agreed on the same date. Chaudhry just smiled and said, 'It is the usual practice. He may not have been very useful today, but he can harass any litigant by giving inconvenient dates. So he has his nuisance value. Now please give Rs 200 to my junior, Vikram.' This was a young man in his late twenties, whose only role had been to carry the files for Chaudhry. He gave me a thankful smile as I gave him the money. In the coming few months, I would realise that such petty 'tips' from Chaudhry's clients were the only income for the young lawyer, who had spent three years earning a law degree after his graduation.

I went back to Chaudhry's chamber while Ratna and Unmesh

left for home. Chaudhry rang up somebody and within a few minutes, two middle-aged lawyers turned up in his chamber. I recognised one of them as Suri's lawyer, who had been present in the courtroom earlier as their sole representative. Nobody from the Suri household had come to the court. He introduced himself as Inderjeet and dialed a number on his mobile. As the phone was attended by the person on the other end, he thrust it in my hands and said, 'Here, take it Sir, and talk to Kohli Saheb.' Kohli's voice was quite familiar. After making polite enquires about my well-being, he informed me that Inderjeet was Suri's lawyer and the money was to be handed over to him on the next date when Col Suri would be called as the first Prosecution Witness. He confirmed that he had discussed the matter with Chaudhry and they had together agreed on the third interlocutor, Mr Rana. The money would be kept in Chaudhry's chamber in the joint custody of Inderjeet, Rana and Chaudhry and I was welcome to leave one more friend or relative of mine to safeguard the money, which would be handed over to Col Suri, after he had given his statement in the court. When I insisted that I would like to give it personally in Col Suri's hands, he firmly rejected my request. 'The money will be given by the three lawyers to my client or any representative sent by him. There will be no direct contact between you and my client.'

Chaudhry was following my conversation with Kohli. He gave a nod and said softly, 'Don't worry, it is ok.' When I returned the phone to Inderjeet, Chaudhry said, '*Tension mat lo* (don't worry)

Asthana Saheb, the money will be handed over only after he says in the court what Kohli has promised to us.'

I then looked at the lawyer accompanying Inderjeet. He introduced himself as Rana. We shook hands and then parted, to meet again on the next date.

On the next date, I carried the million rupees neatly stacked in a brief case. I brought my factory manager Satish along with me, besides Ratna and Unmesh. The money was handed over to Chaudhry, Inderjeet and Rana. Satish stayed with the brief case in Chaudhry's chamber. And then Ratna, Unmesh, Chaudhry, his junior and I walked to the Additional District Judge's Court.

Ours was the first case to be called. After the judge entered the courtroom, Ratna and Unmesh were made to stand on one side. The judge was kind enough to instruct Ratna to take a chair and sit down.

And then Col Manbeer Suri entered the courtroom as if on a cue. He probably had been waiting in Inderjeet's chamber and was called on phone. This was the first time I was meeting him, after that horrible day of Simran's death. He seemed to have aged during the last three-four months, with many more grey hair in his beard. He avoided making an eye contact with me. He was accompanied by his wife Jaspreet and son Anand. Jaspreet was dressed in a grey salwar suit and Anand was in a quiet T shirt and jeans. They all bore grim expressions on their faces. Jaspreet and Anand looked at me. I gave her a courteous nod, but she and Anand quickly averted my gaze and looked elsewhere, as if they did not recognise me at all. My heartbeat went up and I started wondering whether the arrangement would work out as planned.

Suri was called in as Prosecution Witness No. 1, after the court was called to order by the judge. He identified himself, took the oath and started speaking in a grim tone. After giving the basic details about his daughter's marriage, he suddenly dropped the bomb by softly saying, 'Unmesh and his mother Ratna, who are present in this court and whom I recognise, were quite satisfied with the gifts and never harassed my daughter with dowry demands.' Manbeer Suri stopped here for a moment. His voice was choked as he swallowed saliva, coughed and then continued after a pause, 'My daughter died on 20th November 2004. She died at her in-laws' place.' Once again he became quiet. The DGC helped him in making his statement by probing him with gentle questions, to which he replied, 'It is true that a year after the marriage, Unmesh brought Simran along with him to my residence after a squabble, but it is an incorrect accusation that Simran had marks of injury or beating on her face or that my son-in-law had treated her cruelly, nor did my daughter refuse to go back to her husband's home.'

'It is totally incorrect to say that my daughter told me that her in-laws had demanded a dowry of Rs five to six lakhs, hence the question of my not being able to pay the money did not arise.'

'I cannot say whether my daughter was killed by Unmesh or his family members. I approached the police with a request to investigate the case as, after all, the death occurred in their house.'

At this stage, the DGC got up to interrupt. He did not appear agitated. He had perhaps already heard of the proposed arrangement on the grapevine. Whatever be the case, there was not much melodrama in his voice when he requested the court to declare Prosecution Witness No. 1, a hostile witness. After that was done, he requested permission to cross examine Col Manbeer Suri, which was readily granted.

But the cross examination could not shake Manbeer from the stand he had chosen to take. Ultimately, the DGC requested that the original FIR produced in the court be shown to Manbeer and when this was done, he asked, 'Do you recognise this document, which is numbered 5A/1 to 5A/4?' When Suri replied in the affirmative, he asked further, 'At the end of this report, the scribe's name is mentioned as Prithvi Nath. Who is this Prithvi Nath?'

Suri gave a strange answer. He said, 'Yes, I recognise this Document and I recognise my signature affixed at the end. But I don't know any Prithvi Nath.'

The DGC's tone was a little harsher this time. 'The name Prithvi Nath is mentioned herein as that of the writer. The document bears your signature and yet you claim that you don't know any Prithvi Nath?' It was a question and not a mere observation, and Suri replied, 'Somebody present there asked me to get the FIR written as it was getting late. I was too dazed to even think coherently. On this stranger's suggestion, my brother, wife and son helped him with the relevant details and he wrote this FIR. When he finished writing it, I just glanced through the first page and the last paragraph on the last page and affixed my signatures wherever I was asked by him to do so.'

The DGC interrupted sharply, 'You just claimed that you read only the first page and the last paragraph of the last page in your FIR. Then what are your signatures doing on the cuttings and overwriting on page 2 and 3 of this document?' He thrust the documents at Suri. It was the FIR produced in the court by the police. 'Look at the cutting in 3rd line on 5A/3, the cuttings in second and tenth lines on 5A/4. All these cuttings bear the same signatures as put at the bottom of the last page, which you have just recognised as yours.'

Suri received the documents in his hands, gave them a cursory look and said, 'Yes, they are all my signatures. Actually, I had been advised by a policeman present there to affix my signature at all cuttings and over writings.'

The judge, who had been listening patiently so far, now interrupted. 'You are a Senior Army Officer. You have affixed your signatures on this application and have authenticated all corrections and cuttings by putting your signature in so many places. And yet you are denying all that is written therein. Do you understand how serious can be the consequences of willfully telling lies after taking an oath to speak the truth in this court?'

Suri appeared rattled for a moment but soon regained his composure and said, 'Sir, I was under severe trauma at that time. I was hardly in control of my senses when I signed these documents.'

The DGC butted in, 'Is that how an Army Officer of your

seniority behaves under pressure? Is personal loss sufficient ground to affix your signatures on page after page and then deny your statements later?'

'My personal suffering was not the sole reason for the confusion', Suri said and continued, 'This document has been written in Hindi, a language I am familiar with but not very proficient at. The words used here are not my own. Besides, I had no reason to suspect that the scribe will write so many imaginary things well beyond what I told him.'

The DGC now turned aggressive, 'If the husband of the deceased and his mother never harassed or troubled your daughter, why did you suspect a foul play?'

Suri had apparently come prepared to answer this expected but awkward question, 'I had seen the fan at the scene of the incident. I did not see any marks on the fan to suggest that she had tied her *chunni* to the fan to hang herself. Hence, I suspected foul play.'

The judge chipped in now, 'Are you making these statements here under some sort of pressure or mental tension?'

'No Sir, I am making these statements of my own free will and there is no pressure on me.'

The DGC's voice boomed, 'Is it just plain lying or merely going back on your words?' Suri could not look into his eyes nor could he face the judge boldly. Somehow, he managed to say softly, 'I am not lying.'

The DGC then became sarcastic. 'So, you have reached a

compromise and made some sort of arrangement with the accused.

'There is no compromise. There is no arrangement', mumbled Suri. The DGC finally gave up in exasperation. A visibly pleased Defence Counsel, Chaudhary, declined to seek a cross examination of the witness and the proceedings for the day were closed.

For obtaining the next date as per our convenience, the usual currency note was deposited with the Reader. Who was I to crib about a hundred rupees required to be paid to the Reader when a million rupees had changed hands!

After the day's proceedings were over in the court, I asked Chaudhry if Suri had personally collected the money. He smiled and said, 'No, it is the lawyer's job to receive or give such sums on behalf of the clients.' He dialed Inderjeet's number, who came on the line to confirm that Chaudhry's junior, my factory manager Satish and Rana were all present when Suri's lawyer collected the amount on his behalf. I was getting curious as to why Suri had not collected the money personally or sent his son or brother to do the same. Chaudhry reassured me that there was no reason to worry, as Suri had denied all allegations of dowry demand and torture before the judge. I said, 'We should have given only half the amount today. The other half could have been given after Mrs Suri, Suri's brother Satbeer and his son Anand had also made their denials in the court.'

'Don't worry about state capitals when Delhi itself has been conquered', said Chaudhry with a loud chuckle.

Twentythree

I was not very tense on the next date when Mrs Jaspreet Suri was called to the witness box. Mrs Suri had got emboldened from the demonstration given in the court by her husband on how to swallow one's own words. After taking the oath, she practically gave the same story as her husband had given. The DGC wasted no time in getting her too declared as a Hostile witness. The answers to the DGC's questions came forth without much hesitation. She disowned any responsibility for lodging of the FIR by coolly saying, 'I was so shocked after seeing my daughter's body that I just didn't know anything about the FIR and its contents.' She too boldly denied that she or her husband had entered into any understanding or arrangement with the Asthana family. When reminded of her oath, she said without batting an eyelid, 'Yes, I remember that I have made a commitment on my Holy Book to speak the truth, only truth and nothing but the truth.'

I was disappointed when Chaudhry, as a Defence counsel showed no interest in cross examining her. His economy of effort was commendable when there was no incremental return.

Mrs Suri was followed in the witness box by her young son Anand. I knew how close he had been to his departed sister. Col Suri had many postings in non-family stations or 'field areas' as they are called in the Army. Mrs Suri had spent a considerable part of her married life serving as a school teacher, not unusual for Army wives staying away from their husbands. The underlying reasons were many, financial compulsion being only one of them. The desire to make some use of their academic or professional qualifications and the wish to nurture one's own independent personality unfettered by the looming shadow of the husband, were all factors which had made working women out of most Defence Officers' wives. But often, it was at the cost of a healthy psyche in their children. Devoid of the father's presence most of the time during their childhood and adolescence many of them tended to develop complex personalities. The mothers did manage to run the household, often assisted by batmen or *Sahayaks* who were in fact provided to help the officers for the upkeep of their uniform and so on but whose misuse as domestic help had become rampant. A Sahayak could hardly provide the parental affection, love and care to such children. No wonder, children in such families often grew up into restless, obstinate, short-tempered adolescents and youth. Thank heavens, Simran at least had an extremely affectionate brother in Anand.

He was two years younger than her, but as often happens in families where the father is mostly away due to service exigencies, he assumed the role of an elder brother, a protector to the only sister, the 'man' of the family so to say. I wondered how much more stubborn Simran would have been, had she been an only child of parents too busy with themselves. I thought of the father whose family dreaded sharing their concerns and kept secrets from him in fear of his short temper. Simran had told Unmesh that her mother had been a strict disciplinarian who often could not differentiate between the roles of a loving mother and an efficient teacher. It was Anand who provided her the much-needed respite from the rule of law, who applied the soothing balm to a soul hankering for parental affection.

My wandering mind suddenly reverted to the courtroom where a very sad-looking Anand was standing in the witness box. Our eyes met and the sad eyes suddenly blazed with anger. Obviously, he was convinced in his heart of hearts that our family was solely responsible for Simran's suicide. I was not too sure if his mother had made him privy to the secrets of Simran's failed suicide attempts before marriage.

I saw a distinct possibility of his hating the arrangement made by his father to become a millionaire. It wouldn't be a surprise if he rebelled against a father who, after taking an oath on the Holy Book (*the Granth Sahib*) to speak nothing but the truth, had reached a settlement with us after coolly pocketing a very large sum of money. If Anand was as emotional and innocent as could be seen in his honest eyes, there was every chance of his not toeing the line treaded by his father. And what would happen then? The very thought was unsettling.

I listened with baited breath as after taking the oath on his Holy Book, he identified himself and then started speaking. After giving details of Simran's marriage with Unmesh, he said, 'My parents were never pressurised for giving any gifts by Unmesh or his parents. My sister appeared to be quite happy and contented after her marriage.'

The DGC couldn't help prodding him in the hope of getting some incriminating comment out of him. 'Did Unmesh not beat her up often?' and Anand said in a confident voice, 'No, my brother-in-law loved her immensely. There may have been an occasional quarrel but it would be wrong to say that he beat her up often.'

Two things happened simultaneously. I could resume normal breathing and the DGC instantly demanded that Prosecution Witness No. 3 also be declared Hostile. The judge readily obliged, without enquiring if Anand too had reached a compromise with the defendants.

The DGC now started the cross examination of Anand. He tried to rattle him. Obviously, he expected that Anand, a young boy, inexperienced in the ways of the world and having the glimmer of honesty and innocence in his eyes, would succumb to the fury of his questions. But after rejecting the dowry story,

Anand gave a very accurate description of all that he had seen and heard on that fateful day.

His statement, recorded under Section 161 Cr PC was read out to him and he said in a firm voice, 'I did not make any statement blaming Unmesh or his mother for my sister's death.'

'Then why would the police officer attribute such statements to you?'

'This question can best be answered only by him.' The DGC realised he was banging his head against a wall and wound up his cross examination. In his turn, Chaudhry also wound up after asking a few inane questions.

The usual fees were paid to the Reader and the next date given for the hearing. We knew that the next witness the Prosecution would produce would be Manbeer's brother Col Satbeer Suri.

As expected, Col Satbeer Suri was produced as witness No. 4 in the court by the Prosecution on the next date. Thanks to three prime witnesses turning hostile one after another so far, we were no longer very tense. Most of Satbeer's statement was only a repetition of what the earlier three Prosecution Witnesses had stated. But when he also said that occasionally there were quarrels between Simran and Unmesh and on one occasion, Unmesh had thrashed her, the judge interrupted to ask, 'What were the underlying reasons for this quarrel?'

Satbeer was apparently not expecting any interruptions from the judge. He said, 'I never asked them why they fought or why he beat her up.' And then, as if touched by a sudden spark of inspiration, he added, 'I think it can only be because Unmesh had a violent streak in his character.' But having somewhat slipped here, Satbeer remained quite careful in stating further that there was no demand for dowry.

By now, the familiar drill of the witness being declared hostile and his cross examination by the DGC, followed. Once again, I found Satbeer trying to put a twist in his tale to a certain extent when he was asked the reason for lodging a complaint with the CO, if no dowry had been demanded and no harassment was inflicted upon the deceased. He said, 'I had earlier witnessed elsewhere a scene of suicide by hanging from the ceiling fan. I had noticed over there that the fan blades were bent and there were tell-tale signs on the fan. But there were no such signs here and there was dust on the fanblades, so I became suspicious.'

'If a *chunni* is hung from the top of the blades above the central point of the fan and then it hangs from there between two of the three blades, will it necessarily bend the blades or leave marks on them?' asked the DGC.

'It may or may not. I don't know.'

The DGC did not press any further and left the field for Chaudhry, who asked, 'What makes you think that Unmesh has a violent streak in his nature?'

'I was told by Simran.'

'Can you prove that this hearsay statement is not a figment of your imagination and she did actually tell you this?'

'We don't keep proofs of all that we say to each other in our day to day conversation', Satbeer said defiantly.

'How could you be sure that there was dust on top of the ceiling fan blades? Did you climb and see from the top?'

'No. But there definitely was dust on the fan blades. That's why I feel it is wrong to say that she hanged herself from the fan.'

'Were you the only person who found the fan blades covered with dust?'

'CO Singh and Simran's grandfather also saw that the fan blades were covered with dust. I can't say that about Anand or my brother and sister-in-law, as they were emotionally too disturbed to notice that.'

'How old is Simran's grandfather?'

'He is 89 years old.'

'At what time did he notice the fan blades?'

'It was at about 11.30 in the night.'

'How bright was the light in the bathroom at that time?'

'It had a light bulb, I think, of 40 or 60 watts', he said, looking a bit confused.

Chaudhry suddenly declared that he had no more questions to ask.

Satbeer was the fourth Prosecution Witness to have turned hostile. I was greatly relieved of the tremendous anxiety I had, whether the Suri family would keep the promise made by Kohli on their behalf. I had not been able to talk to any of them personally. All four of them had averted their eyes and remained so cold and aloof that it had been impossible to talk to any of them when they visited the court. But I was not fully satisfied with the statements made by Simran's uncle in the court. He had tried to raise doubts in the court's mind, if it was indeed a suicide. I was unhappy with his insinuation.

Chaudhry saw the expressions on my face and gave me a reassuring look. He spoke very softly in my ears. 'Now the case has no legs to stand on. Why are you looking so worried?' I realised that my face was too transparent. I did not want everyone to notice what Chaudhry had been quick to see on my face. I came out of the court while the next witness was being called in, smoked a cigarette to release the tension that had built up during Satbeer's testimony, and went in again.

The next witness, Prosecution Witness No. 5, Mr Rudrapratap, the City Magistrate, had already made his statement when I reentered the court after spending a few minutes outside. He made a simple, short statement explaining how the *panchnama* (inquest) was made and afterwards the body was placed in a bag, sealed and handed over to constables Ram Pratap Singh and Sripat Yadav of Police Station Sector-90, Noida to be taken for post-mortem, along with the necessary documents raised by him.

Neither the DGC nor the Chaudhry had any questions to ask of the City Magistrate. The next date was announced by the Reader after the usual formalities were over.

On the next date, Head Constable Baldev Yadav was presented in the court as Prosecution Witness No. 6. He gave his statements after the administration of oath. He explained that in the early hours on the day, following the day of death, he was on duty at Police Station, Sector-90, Noida in his capacity as the *Pradhan Lekhak*. He produced the contents of the relevant pages of the General Diary of the police station in which arrests of Unmesh Asthana and Ratna Asthana had been recorded. A copy of the written information provided by Unmesh regarding the death of his wife was also produced before Baldev Yadav, which he verified.

I did not expect much action from Chaudhry but he chose to cross examine this witness. He did it quite forcefully to highlight many procedural lapses in the police paper work. The witness appeared quite shaken as he said in response to Chaudhry's cross examination, 'Yes, all the papers of the GD (General Diary) dated 20.11.02 are unnumbered. Yes, these papers are plain paper and do not appear to be reproduced from a printed register. This is because we did not have adequate stationery in the office.'

'Yes, the pages without serial numbers have not been authenticated by any police officer.'

'Yes, it is true that the pages pertaining to date 20.11.02 are stapled together while they are loose for the other dates.'

'No, it is wrong to say that we are in the habit of removing or adding pages in the General Diary at our will.'

'No. it is wrong to say that the dates for any of the entries in the General Diary have been entered at a later stage in the same writing and by the same pen.'

'Yes, all the General Diary pages were changed and they bear a serial number and the seal of the office of the Senior

Superintendent of Police.' I could not help smiling as I appreciated Chaudhry's observations and cross examination by giving him a vigorous nod.

And now came the turn of Prosecution Witness No. 7 whose words would be very crucial. It was Dr Vijay Gupta, the surgeon who had carried out the post-mortem examination on Simran's body.

Dr Vijay Gupta took the oath, gave his credentials as an surgeon posted in the District Hospital, and gave the day and time of the post-mortem. He then described his observations, already recorded in the post-mortem report. The most relevant observation was that there was a ligature mark of 27 cm x 1 cm on the neck in front. It extended from 4 cm below the right ear to 7 cm below the left ear. There was a 7cm long gap in the ligature. And the second important observation was that there were old scars of apparently some sharp instrument on the left wrist. These were three linear scars which were 2.5 cm to 3cm long. Then, based on the observations that the trachea, brain and both the lungs were congested, there was no fracture of the hyoid bone in the neck, the stomach and uterus were empty and the internal organs were all intact, he concluded that in his opinion the death occurred due to asphyxia caused by self-hanging about 24 hours earlier.

The DGC now pulled a rabbit out of his legal hat in the form of two books on Forensic/ Medical jurisprudence—one by Mody and the other by Lyons. He took permission of the court to submit a comparison of medical inferences from the post-mortem report and from those given in Mody's and Lyons' forensic medicine books. He requested the judge to go through a chart, prepared with the help of these books, showing the comparative inferences made by Dr Gupta and those made in the book regarding the condition of the neck, vertebra, spinal cord, hyoid bone and the ligature marks on the neck and concluded that it was not possible to accept the assessment of Dr Vijay Gupta that it was definitely a case of self-hanging.

The DGC finished his cross examination and subsequent submission. Defence Counsel Choudhry then began his cross examination, in answer to which the doctor's statements were as follows :

'No, there were no marks of any injury on the dead body other than those described by me in post-mortem report as the ligature marks on the neck and the old linear scars on left wrist. Not only in my opinion is it a case of self-hanging, it is also the opinion of Dr Varun Tomar, the second doctor, who has signed the post-mortem report in full concurrence of my opinion and observations.'

When prodded further by Chaudhary, the doctor explained why he thought it was self-hanging.

'The hyoid bone was intact, which indicates that it wasn't a hanging done jerkily by somebody else, by strangulation or as in judicial hanging, but was suicidal in nature. Also, in suicidal hangings, the rope tends to slip upwards on the neck and the chances of its fracturing the vertebra or the hyoid bone are very much reduced. The neck may get extended in length, if the body is left hanging for a long time. In the case of suicide, the ligature mark extends from the front of the neck up to the ears on both sides as happened in this case too. The ligature mark apparently was made by the *chunni*, deposited in the court and shown to me.'

I had found all these details too technical but was glad to see that Chaudhry was quite satisfied with his cross examination.

On the next date the Prosecution produced Santosh Singh the very same police Circle Officer who had arrived at our residence on that fateful night and had later been replaced by CO Gaur as the Investigating Officer.

Santosh Singh was required to give an account of all that he had seen and done till he was replaced as the IO by Gaur. He did this but now he lacked the zing that I had seen in him on that fateful night. Chaudhry made him look uncertain and shaky in his cross examination which went like this:

'Did you record the timings of starting and closing your investigation in the documents presented before the court?'

'No, I did not.'

'Did you record in your report or in the General Diary of the police station the date and time of recording the statement of Col Manbeer, Col Satbeer or Anand Suri, who have all denied making any statements to you?'

'I did record their statements but erred in not recording the date and time when they were made.'

'Did you give a copy of the FIR to the city Magistrate or ask him if he had a copy of the same when he was conducting the inquest?'

'No. I did not give him a copy of the FIR, nor did I check up with him if he had a copy while conducting the inquest.'

In response to the next question, the witness appeared very flustered and shaky. He said, 'The *chunni* and the scissors were not sealed by me. They were enclosed in a bundle which was sealed at the police station. The seal is that of the SHO and not mine.'

In response to the next question, he lost his cool and gave an angry retort, 'No record was kept in the General Diary or the Case Diary of the telephone number on which the intimation of Unmesh Asthana's arrest had been given to his parents.'

'No. It is wrong to say that the accused was arrested well before the time the arrest has been shown.'

'No. I did not take any statements from the neighbours of the accused or the neighbours of the complainants.'

'It is wrong to say that I never maintained a case diary.' It was a regular rapid fire of *No-No-No* by the witness, and every time a "No" was heard, the unsmiling face of Chaudhry seemed to be taunting him. I started feeling sorry for the hapless Santosh Singh by the time Chaudhry wound up and allowed him the much-needed respite.

The next witness, CO PK Gaur, the officer who had replaced Santosh Singh as the investigating officer of the case, clarified that Vinod Ashtana's name was mentioned in the FIR only in his capacity as the father of the accused and he did not hold Asthana personally responsible for the tragedy. He had arrested Ratna after he took the statement of Mrs Jaspreet Suri. The DGC declined to ask any questions nor did Chaudhry subject him to any worthwhile cross examination.

After this, the other Prosecution Witnesses were the two constables who had taken the body for post-mortem and the photographer who had taken the photographs that day. They only narrated the events already described earlier by many others. Neither the DGC nor the Defence Counsel troubled him with any more questions.

The DGC declared that he had no more Prosecution Witnesses to present before the court. I heaved a sigh of relief. The battle seemed to have been won. But the last act of the drama was still to unfold in the presentation of Defence Witness by Chaudhry. The court had seen enough activity for the day and the next date was given.

It was already almost a year since that night when Simran's one rash act of sheer mindlessness had wrecked such havoc upon us. Probably, with the closure of the case and honourable acquittal of Unmesh and Ratna, I would be able to forgive her. With this hovering over my mind, the four of us—Harish, Ratna, Unmesh and I reached the court on the day the defence counsel was going to start his pleadings.

The Court proceedings began with the court permitting the defence counsel, Chaudhry, to call Defence Witness No. 1,

Unmesh Asthana. Unmesh had already been briefed by Chaudhry to give a full description of events starting from the day Simran had entered his life so determinedly, till the day she cynically walked out of it. He did so with courage and apparent honesty. When describing his arrest and interrogation by the police, he said in a voice choked with emotion, 'It is true that in spite of our deep love for each other, we had an occasional quarrel. But it is utter travesty of truth to say that this was because of a violent streak in my nature. It is the contemptuous remark at the Gurudwara, and then on the phone, by the very same heartless people who are blaming me now, which infuriated her and rekindled the dormant suicidal tendency in her.'

His cross examination by the DGC followed and occupied a major part of the day. Most of the questions were aimed at discrediting him and establishing that he wasn't a very loving or caring husband. Narrating all the questions and the answers thereto will be repetitive, so I am narrating only some of it, to show the extent to which the prosecutor could go to present a distorted image of facts. The DGC asked, 'Your counsel has produced a big bunch of letters written by Simran and yourself to each other. Doesn't it prove that you two were often not at speaking terms, even though you stayed in the same city?'

'Our love blossomed when she took up a job at our factory. Later, I left home and lived in the Institute hostel for completing my MBA. Most of the letters were written by her during that period. It is indeed cruel to misinterpret this as our not being on speaking terms when they were written.'

In reply to the subsequent questions, Unmesh explained that her parents had taken away her mobile after they saw so many phone calls from him. They pressurised Simran for quite some time but gave in after her suicide attempts. He gave an account of her suicide attempts, but the DGC insisted that the scar on her left wrist was an old injury sustained in her childhood and the second suicide attempt was only a figment of imagination.

He suggested that actually Unmesh's ill treatment and anger led to the bitter fight on the day of her death. This was stoutly denied by Unmesh. He forcefully said 'Would you call my suggestion for making a smaller offering in the Gurudwara an act of cruelty and illtreatment? Can anyone fulfill every wish of one's wife?' Although said innocently, this remark evoked a bit of laughter from those present. After this, Unmesh was asked detailed questions on the events in the Gurudwara and the factory on that day, which he answered without hesitation.

After the appearance of Unmesh as a Defence Witness, Chaudhry called in the constable of the Noida Police who had first received the telephonic information of Simran's death, to substantiate that I was the first person to report the death to the police as entered in the occurrence register maintained at the control room.

The trial was over as far as Choudhry was concerned. The DGC wound up the proceedings with his final summing up. But the withdrawal of all accusations of dowry demand and dowry harassment had indeed knocked the wind out of the case. The testimony given by Dr Vijay Gupta had driven the last nail in the coffin of the Prosecution's case.

Yet the sword of Damocles was going to hang over our heads for a bit longer, as the judge reserved the judgment and gave a date ten days later. Our most harrowing wait so far began now.

Twentyfour

I wonder if believers await the final day of judgment in their graves as anxiously as we did for the judgment in our case. While Ratna continued with her ritual silent prayer before going to sleep every night, I found myself wondering endlessly whether I should go begging for mercy before the same unseen unknown power which had brought us to the brink of disaster for no fault of ours. The long wait finally ended one day. Chaudhry sounded confident about the day of judgment when he reminded me to be present along with Ratna and Unmesh in the court of the Additional District and Sessions Judge the next day. We reached there well in time the next day. I was surprised to see that no member of the Suri family had turned up in the court, though I saw Suri's lawyer quietly slipping in. The DGC was already present in the courtroom. The judge maintained a poker face as he opened the folder lying in front of him and started speaking in an even tone, 'This court declares both accused Unmesh Asthana and accused Ratna Asthana NOT GUILTY. They are both honourably acquitted. Their personal bonds as well as their guarantor's security are hereby released. A copy of the detailed judgment can be obtained from the court office.'

We all rose as the judge got up from his chair and exited from the rear door leading to his chamber, and then we rushed to the Reader. He gladly accepted the five hundred rupee note thrust in his hand by a beaming Chaudhry. He obligingly said, 'The copy of the judgment can be collected tomorrow. You may, in the meantime read the judgment from this original file while the lunch recess is on.' He handed over the file to Chaudhry.

The courtroom had become vacant now except for our group. We all surrounded Chaudhry and his junior Vikram. Chaudhry gave the file to Vikram, who then started reading the judgment loudly. But it was a lengthy document running into several pages. Vikram started skimming over the text and instead of reading it verbatim and he started giving a short synopsis.

Vikram said, 'To begin with, the judge has given a summary of Manbeer Suri's complaint followed by a synopsis of the statements made by Prosecution Witnesses. The testimony of Dr Vijay Gupta has been given in toto to explain why he was convinced that it was a case of selfhanging. Thereafter,the statements of various defnce witnesses have been dicussed.

'After this, the judge has described the statements given by all the Defence Witnesses, reproducing the statement of Unmesh in its entirety and a gist of the statements given by other Defence Witnesses. The judge has now come to the crux of his judgment, giving his analysis of the evidence produced before him. Here he has gone into great detail.' Vikram stopped here for a moment and handed over the file to Chaudhry.

Chaudhry also avoided a verbatim reading of the judgment and read only the important lines. Coming to other witnesses the judgemnt says, 'the four witnesses who turned hostile are so closely related to the deceased that their personal knowledge of all intimate facts cannot be questioned.The serious quarrel between the spouses mentioned by them took place good one year before the death.A single incident, that too not soon before her death, cannot bring the death within the ambit of dowry death.

'The Uncle of the deceased has viewed her death with suspicion, merely on the basis of a superficial examination of the scene of death without claiming any training in forensic science. Having examined the doctors' testimony, the post-mortem report and the comparison chart submitted by the prosecution, I am unable to agree with the prosecution's contention that the death was not caused by self-hanging.

'The Prosecution has not produced any evidence on the basis of which the accused can be said to have committed the crime under Section 304 B by demanding dowry. All the factual witnesses have denied the demand for dowry. If we look at the conduct of the two accused and their family, we shall note that they reported the death to the Police Control Room, informed the relatives of the deceased without any delay, contacted the Uncle of the deceased when they could not contact her father on phone and they got the scene of the death photographed at their own initiative. They could have normally fled from the scene, had they carried a feeling of guilt in their hearts. But their activities and conduct establish their clean conscience.

'No exernal presures have been proved to establish any abetment to suicide. Similarly a guilty conscience (*mens rea*) and motive must be proved beyond doubt. The cause should not be too remote from the effect. In the present case, the rejection of psychiatric treatment by the deceased, the extremely emotional tone of her letters and her bringing her family around to let her marry outside her religion show that the deceased was a strong-willed girl. In order to achieve her aim and fulfill her desire, she took up a job, left the job, put her family relationships at stake and yet displayed full faith in her religion right till the very day of her death. All these facets of her character show that she was a strong-willed person. She was not a simple village girl who would accept insults, harassments, torture and would ultimately commit suicide under such stress. Nor has any witness or evidence been produced to infer that she had been tortured or persecuted to the extent that she had to commit suicide. Coming to a suspicion of murder, there must be a serious purpose and a strong motive. No one can be punished on the basis of mere suspicion. How can any such conclusion be reached when the complainant's own testimony is full of contradictions?

'In view of the foregoing, this court declares both accused Unmesh Asthana and Mrs Ratna Asthana not guilty. They are both honourably acquitted. Their personal bonds as well as their guarantors' security for the bail are also released.'

My heart was thumping with excitement. Ratna was beaming away to glory. And Unmesh? He was expressionless. He was looking at a sparrow sitting on its nest in a skylight in the wall. I remembered the day in Dasna jail when he had said, 'I walk around on the ground outside my cell, looking at birds and imagining that Simran has assumed the form of a bird. I imagine that she will come to me and say, "Sorry. I never intended to hurt you so much!"'

Twentyfive

Life could never be the same for us as it was before this turmoil. The void created in the life of Unmesh stared at all of us. Only time would tell whether the deep wounds of our tormented souls, sullied reputation and tarnished social standing would ever heal. Even if they did, they were bound to leave behind indelible scars, like those left on a wrist after an unsuccessful suicide attempt by cutting the veins.

I kept wondering whether the real culprit was the departed soul? Sometimes, I thought she was herself an innocent victim of her love-starved childhood, brought about by parents, too absorbed in their professional lives and too stiff in imposing their own values on her. There must have been a deep grudge hidden in the depths of her mind, which expressed itself from time to time in such uncontrollable spasms of rage even over innocuous remarks or action of others that she lost the ability to rationally appreciate the consequences of her actions. Or maybe, she was just a pampered daughter of doting parents, too dumb to understand the implications of her rash actions on the lives of innocent bystanders. Although such had been her joy-de-vivre, so warm were her perpetual smile and spontaneous laughter, so open and gracious was her affectionate nature that I had loved her like my own daughter, yet her impulsiveness had singed our lives and scorched Unmesh's soul. He had loved her with total abandon. He had ceaselessly campaigned for her till she had been accepted as his bride in our small, happy family. He was now drowning in the deep sea of immense pain, entirely because of her mindless rashness.

The dichotomy did not end here. I remained confused and perplexed about my feelings for the Suri family, particularly Manbeer Suri. Was he just a tormented father who had lost the most precious possession he had? Or were they like greedy, callous and apathetic soldiers of an invading army who robbed amidst death and destruction? Hadn't they stooped so low as to demand a price for their daughter's blood? Were they too shocked and scandalised by the death of their darling daughter to appreciate that she alone was to blame for her death? Or was their accusation of a murderous plot only an act of revenge, a thirst for drawing blood for blood?

The answers would probably be revealed if I once again confronted them after the legal battle was over, after their lust for lucre had been quenched and after the judge had answered their myriad doubts in his lengthy but lucid judgment. I was itching to encounter them, even if only to put this dichotomy at rest forever. The desire to meet at least Manbeer Suri kept smouldering inside my heart. The opportunity would present itself one day.

And the day came. Quite unexpectedly.

Noida has an Armed Forces' Polyclinic which provides medical facilities to retired Servicemen. That day, when I went to the Polyclinic, five patients were already waiting for their turn, comfortably ensconced in easy chairs. There was only one vacant chair. And you guessed it right, I found myself seated next to Manbeer Suri.

Our eyes met. But he didn't shy away this time. He had avoided meeting my gaze in the court room during the year-long trial. It was natural after he had spun such a sordid yarn of dowry demands in his FIR. I thought that his inability to look into my eyes was only a sad indicator of his guilty conscience, torturing him for making a cool million by blackmailing us with his patently false accusations. Now, what chafed most was the fact that the man still had the temerity to look into my eyes with his chin up.

He had aged quite a bit during the last one year. The beard was no longer salt and pepper. It had become fully white. He was a veteran soldier and did not fail to reciprocate when I wished him a good morning. The opportunity that I had been seeking was now within my grasp. I decided to grab it by trying to strike a conversation.

'What brings you here? Nothing serious I hope!' I enquired softly.

'No. Only a routine problem.' His answer was short.

'God knows when we shall meet again. Let me tell you how sad we are with what happened. We all share your grief', I persisted with the conversation.

'Thanks. We know your feelings for her. She respected you and often talked about you', he said very softly.

'Then how could you even imagine that we could harm her?' I asked.

'You tell me! Put yourself in our shoes and tell me if you would not suspect something fishy, if she looked quite happy till a day before her death and then died all of a sudden?' he answered back.

'But what made you spin that yarn about dowry demand?' I protested. He hesitated for a moment and then mumbled, 'That complaint had been lodged when we were in a state of shock. Didn't we withdraw those allegations when sanity was restored after the initial storm?'

'And why not? Particularly when the arrangement made was to your full satisfaction', I retorted with a lot of sarcasm in my voice.

'What are you talking about? What arrangement?' His voice shot up suddenly. So far we had been almost whispering to each other, as we were sitting in the patient's waiting room. Now the sudden manifold increase in the decibel level attracted the attention of all other patients waiting there. Many inquisitive eyes turned towards us.

I became conscious of the impact his agitated reply had made in the quiet room. But I was in no mood to let go. I must sort him out today I thought.

'We cannot talk here. Do you mind if we go out for a little chat?' I whispered.

He abruptly got up from his chair in response to my suggestion and moved towards the door. I followed him. We came outside the clinic and found solitude under the shade of a peepul tree spreading its shadow on the ground below.

He was the first to speak now, 'What arrangement are you talking about?'

'Don't act so coy! I am talking about the cool amount you pocketed for agreeing to withdraw your false stories in the court', I hissed back.

'Have you gone crazy? What amount are you talking about? What price did we extract?' He was seriously angry now.

But I was not the one to be cowed by his display of anger. 'The huge amount you made us pay. The big chunk you coolly collected from Kohli's man in the court premises on the day you enacted your turning a hostile witness scene.' I replied vehemently.

'Who is this Kohli you are talking about?' he growled, but he genuinely looked puzzled.

'How funny! You seem to be suffering from amnesia. I am talking about Kohli, the Supreme Court lawyer who lives in Sector-15A. The one who negotiated the price of your retractions on your behalf', I said angrily.

'I really don't understand what exactly you are trying to say. Advocate Kohli, who resides in Sector-15A, is an acquaintance of my elder brother. But he, along with his wife, was out of India, visiting their only daughter in the USA from ten days before the day I retracted my accusation. When did you meet him?' He looked genuinely puzzled.

'I met him three days before the day you came in the court as a witness. That makes it well in the middle of the period he was in the USA?' I said sarcastically and continued, 'And now you will claim that you never discussed the case with him nor were advised by him to withdraw the allegations.'

'Of course! I did meet him along with my wife and elder brother. It was he who asked me if my daughter had really been pressurised for dowry or harassed by your wife and son for the same. When I told him that, that was one sin you or your family had never committed and I, therefore, wanted to withdraw these allegations, he asked me what was preventing me from retracting the same? I told him that I was worried about the legal consequences of perjury. I was afraid that I will get into trouble for signing the statement in the FIR and then refusing to verify the same at a later date. It was he who supported my desire to withdraw these allegations. He briefed me on how to go about it, without getting into legal trouble. He never asked me to extract any price for it. And even if he had suggested something as sinful, I and my wife in particular, would have refused to say under oath taken by placing our hand on the *Granth Saheb* that we had not accepted any gratification or reached a compromise with you. I had taken his advice and acted on it only to amend a mistake I had made earlier. That's all! But what baffles me is your claim that you met him at his house in Noida on a day when I know for sure he was in the USA. Who exactly did you meet at Sector-15A? And yes, that is where our Mr Kohli lives.'

It was now my turn to be totally flabbergasted. I had known Manbeer for more than five years now. I was sure he was incapable of telling such white lies with such a straight face. I had to unravel the mystery. I asked him, 'Did you discuss all that in the presence of a third person?'

'No. Only my wife and brother were present at his residential office when we discussed our problem with him', he said incredulously. But then, after a moment, he remembered something and added, 'But his office door was not closed. Our conversation could have been heard by one of his juniors, Mr Trehan, who was sitting alone at that time in the room adjacent to his office.'

'Can you describe what this Mr Trehan, sitting within earshot that day, looks like?' I asked.

'Well, he was Kohli's junior for a long time and is not exactly a young man. He is in his fifties and now he has started practicing independently at the High Court in Chandigarh. He is tall and fair and uses golden-rimmed spectacles', Manbeer replied.

'And what does Kohli look like?' I asked breathlessly.

'He is quite short and totally bald. He normally does not use spectacles when talking to anyone. If you met him in the evening, he would have changed from his court attire to *kurta-pyjama* and *chappals* he dons in his residential office.'

'Oh my God! It seems the guy you described as Kohli's junior was the tall and fair guy I met in Kohli's house. He was in his court attire except the black coat. He was sporting golden-rimmed spectacles and had black shoes on his feet. No, he had not changed into *kurta-pyjama*s and *chappals* as you said was Kohli's wont. He introduced himself as Kohli. But, how come the chowkidar and the servant never told me that Kohli was not at home?' I gasped.

'Did you ask the servants specifically to take you to Mr Kohli? They are used to Kohli's clients coming and discussing their cases with his junior Trehan, even when he himself is not present. Besides, as Kohli has only one daughter who is in the USA and Mrs Kohli had accompanied him on his trip abroad, the house was quite deserted. Trehan has his family in Chandigarh, hence Kohli had asked him to shift in his guest room for these fifteen days. This way he could look after Kohli's house as well as his clients coming to his house. The servants escorted all Kohli's visitors to Trehan as a routine.'

I was aghast by these revelations. The crux of the matter had to be tackled now. 'Did you receive the money I handed over to him or not?'

'I told you once, and now I am telling you for the last time, I just don't know what money you are talking about! When did you hand over the money to Trehan?' he asked a counter question.

Once again I was caught on the back foot. Neither I nor my lawyer and not even my manager had handed over the money directly to Kohli or this guy Trehan, who had posed as Kohli. And of course, no one had handed over the money to Manbeer Suri personally. I had myself agreed to have the sum handed over through my lawyer to a third lawyer who had claimed to be Kohli's representative. He had made me talk on his mobile phone to this so-called Kohli, to get himself authenticated. There was nothing signed by anybody to acknowledge receipt of the money. The money itself was difficult to be traced back to me as I got the cash arranged through some jugglery by my elder brother's friend, whom I had never met again after that transaction.

I avoided answering Suri's question and shot a fresh question at him, 'Can we get in touch with this imposter Mr Trehan?'

'No. Firstly he is no longer working with Kohli. He left Noida a few days after Kohli returned from USA. He is now practicing law independently at Chandigarh. I do not have his phone number. Secondly, I wonder if any purpose will be served by chasing this wild goose. By the way, what exactly was the amount you said you gave to his friend for delivering to me? And what do you propose doing now?'

I was about to say, 'A cool million rupees', when I realised that Suri was a heart patient. This second shock might be too much for him to bear, I thought. So I just mumbled, 'Forget it. As far as the next course of action is concerned, *Baad mein dekh lenge*.' And then while using this jargon that I had heard from every lawyer who fleeced me, I remembered that Trehan, the neo-millionaire lawyer, had not even bothered to address me as *Jijaji* like so many other lawyers while posing as Kohli. He had coolly vanished through a loophole that seemed to have been created by the operation of the law, solely for the benefit of the likes of him.